**Judy Astley** has been writing novels since 1990, following several years as a dressmaker, illustrator, painter and parent.

*Blowing It* was inspired by her inability to be sensible with money. Being a high-maintenance blonde with a serious shopping habit (frocks, books, plants and music) uses up all potential pension-funds and Judy has unfortunately failed to make any plans for her own fast-approaching dotage except to request that her ashes be scattered in the Designers Guild fabric showroom.

Judy has two grown-up daughters and the world's best-ever grandson and lives with her equally profligate husband in SW London and Cornwall.

www.**booksattransworld**.co.uk

# BLOWING IT

Judy Astley

## BANTAM PRESS

LONDON · TORONTO · SYDNEY · AUCKLAND · JOHANNESBURG

TRANSWORLD PUBLISHERS
61–63 Uxbridge Road, London W5 5SA
a division of The Random House Group Ltd

RANDOM HOUSE AUSTRALIA (PTY) LTD
20 Alfred Street, Milsons Point, Sydney,
New South Wales 2061, Australia

RANDOM HOUSE NEW ZEALAND LTD
18 Poland Road, Glenfield, Auckland 10, New Zealand

RANDOM HOUSE SOUTH AFRICA (PTY) LTD
Isle of Houghton, Corner of Boundary Road & Carse O'Gowrie,
Houghton 2198, South Africa

RANDOM HOUSE PUBLISHERS INDIA PRIVATE LIMITED
301 World Trade Tower, Hotel Intercontinental Grand Complex,
Barakhamba Lane, New Delhi 110 001, India

Published 2006 by Bantam Press
a division of Transworld Publishers

A catalogue record for this book is available from the British Library.
ISBN 9780593056592 (from Jan 07)
ISBN 0593056590

Typeset in 11.5/15.5pt Palatino by
Falcon Oast Graphic Art Ltd

Printed in Great Britain by
Mackays of Chatham plc, Chatham, Kent

3 5 7 9 10 8 6 4 2

Papers used by Transworld Publishers are natural, recyclable products made from
wood grown in sustainable forests. The manufacturing processes conform to the
environmental regulations of the country of origin.

*As always, love and thanks to Jon:*
*still flying with me (14 J and K) and surviving the turbulence.*

# ONE

I am the oldest woman in Top Shop.

If Lottie had happened to be among a handful of customers in one of the smaller high-street branches this observation wouldn't have rated a second thought; but here in the vast and bustling Oxford Circus flagship store, the realization that she was a whole generation away (and in a few cases, two) from every one of hundreds of customers was highly unsettling. Quickly she peered round, scanning across the many rails of bright youthful clothing, seeking another marooned mid-life soul. After almost two hours watching Sorrel trawl every rack and hanger in the place, she could do with another adult woman to exchange sympathy-smiles with; in fact, right now if she saw one she wouldn't trust herself not to fall upon her and hug her. But there wasn't one to be found among the sea of shiny-haired, Bambi-legged, chattering girlhood. Where, when you needed them, were all those hip fashion journalists who smugly claimed they were always in there, snapping up vintage lines and essential vests? Perhaps, Lottie thought in a mild panic, the world-as-we-know-it had ended, leaving other, more sensible women of her age corralled together in Country Casuals where they were considered to belong, whereas she was to be shipwrecked for ever among the teens and twenties, the texters and the gigglers, the shriekers and the twitterers. Hell may yet be an eternity of pink Day-Glo stilettos, shiny, sequinned halter-necks and skinny pre-scuffed jeans cut low enough to show the ogling public exactly who was and who was not a natural blonde.

And it was so exhaustingly loud and crowded, being a half-term Thursday when every cute teenage minx in possession of effective spot-cover and glossy, flicky hair seemed to have descended on the store from many suburban miles around. In twos and threes these beautiful near-women slinked and sashayed between the racks of clothes, self-consciously over-animated while on the slidey-eyed look-out for that dreamed-of tap on the shoulder that could mean a contact-card from a model agency scout. Sorrel said *everyone* knew that the Oxford Circus branch was practically a super-model recruitment centre. According to her, one minute you could be quietly minding your own, deciding between the black lace-edged skirt and the white denim cut-offs, and the next you could be looking at a contract that would wipe your student debt right out.

Wouldn't it be funny, it crossed Lottie's mind, if one of these scouts, bored and dizzied by this glut of youthful perfection, copped a look at *her* and thought, Aha – just what I'm after – a well-upholstered, wild-haired old hippie-type for that *Vogue* retro special? Tee hee, that'd be one in the eye for Sorrel and all the other beanpole, hair-tossing hussies.

Lottie picked up a pale apricot frilled shirt and held it against her front. She'd worn something very like this onstage at the Woodstock festival, all those years ago (though in cheesecloth, so cheap it had shredded on the second wearing), over a fringed suede miniskirt. That was the excellent thing about being with Charisma – singing with a folksy soft-rock band didn't leave you completely wiped out after the gig, though that might have been partly down to her only being eighteen at the time. There'd been plenty of energy left over that night for her and Mac to conceive Ilex in the backstage trailer. Clover, by contrast, had been made three years later in far ritzier surroundings at the George V hotel in Paris. Perhaps that was what had given her this hankering to buy a place in France, to go with her taste for *Elle Decoration* furnishings and detail-perfect clothes. If Clover was ever run over by a bus her underwear would be cooed over by an entire A & E department.

In the mirror the shirt looked very small, cuddled up snug against the baggy bulk of Lottie's loose linen jacket. She wasn't what anyone would describe as podgy, but would her arms fit into those narrow sleeves? Possibly not; no, *definitely* not. It was labelled as size 12 but she doubted

it was designed for a mature adult shape – more for someone whose arms were at their broadest at the elbow. Pretty
though, and she'd try it on if she could face the beautiful,
pin-thin little fox guarding the changing rooms but, feeling
unusually uncertain due to her position as sole senior
customer, she wasn't up to facing a sneer and a smirk and
the humiliation of having to be rescued from the garment
when she got it stuck over her bosom.

She pictured the guard-fox giggling later down her
mobile to a friend. She knew exactly how the conversation
would go:

'And today there was this, like, *woman*? Right, like really,
like *elderly*? And she thought she'd, like, *try stuff on*? Like,
*derrrr*? I like told her, like, I was quite kind, I'm like, are you
*sure*? This stuff's, like, maybe a bit *young*? Why don't you go
down to, like, Jaeger?'

And (like) so on.

'Put that down right now. These aren't for you.' Sorrel
swooped between her mother and the mirror, snatched the
garment from Lottie's hands and crammed it back into
the display rack.

'What's wrong with it? I thought. . .'

Sorrel posed, flicked and pouted (model scout: look
*now*), hands on hips and hissed, 'Mum, you're not here to
think. You're not here to try things on. You're only here
to pay, remember?'

Well, that told her. Lottie remembered there were rules
(Sorrel-imposed rules) for this visit to the teen treasure
house. Number one was Do Not Draw Attention to
Yourself. Sorrel needn't worry. Plumpish middle-aged

mother-figures (even once-famous ones) in shops the world over were invisible until their purchase-laden daughters led them to the till and then, only then, they might be rewarded with a brief but glorious smile of triumph.

'Because this is about *my* gap-year stuff. It's about *me* not *you*.' Sorrel did another bit of furious hair-tossing while Lottie wondered when any single second of time for any seventeen-year-old girl was ever *not* entirely about herself.

'So have you found anything you like?' Lottie asked wearily. Her feet hurt. It had been a mistake to wear heels but it was what you did when you were a Surrey lady, even an ex-hippie one, and went Up To Town. The pounding music, the bright lights, and the hectic citrus shades of the clothes were beginning to upset her senses. A headache threatened. She recalled with fond nostalgia the lush, tender darkness of Biba back in 1968 – her own seventeenth year – and the way that, as you'd walked past the wooden hat stands from which hung clothes in murky muted shades of plum and taupe, swansdown boas and ostrich feathers would waft out and tickle your face. Biba had smelled of secrets and decadence and patchouli. Top Shop smelled of Haribo sweets and hair products.

'I've found loads of stuff.' Sorrel grinned suddenly. 'It's at the cash desk being added up. I just need you to come.'

'And pay. Yes, I know. I hope you didn't go mad, we did say a limit.'

'I know, I know.' Dramatic eye-rolling and don't-start-on-me hand gestures accompanied this. If anyone was casting for a new soap-star brat, they could do a lot worse.

Posh, troublesome totty for *EastEnders*; a feisty *Grange Hill* revival. Sorrel would be perfect for either or both.

'So can we go home now?' Lottie asked, stuffing sheaves of receipts into her handbag. Sorrel gathered up her new possessions but showed worrying swivel-eyed signs of still being on the look-out for a missed bargain.

'Because I'm feeling tired and . . . old,' Lottie admitted, looking longingly towards the exit doors and the dull, normal street beyond. Gap year, she thought enviously. When did that become the essential must-have for school-leavers? Why can't I have one?

'Oh Mum, you're not old!' Sorrel laughed, taking her mother's arm and leading her towards the handbags. 'You're not old at all, you're just . . . *vintage.*'

Mac waited his turn in the queue at the bank and tried to do the necessary sums in his head. Any way up, he kept getting answers that had disturbing minuses in them. He should bank on-line, apparently; it took all the problems out of it. It was what Ilex was always telling him anyway. That way he could, according to Ilex, sort out all his bills and money transfers and his entire financial life would be hassle-free. He'd like to ask Ilex if on-line banking could also make him a useful million quid richer and magically come up with some – any – kind of income to look forward to in his rapidly approaching pension years but he didn't want to see that expression of exasperated disappointment on his son's face, that 'You had plenty of money once, what did you *do* with it?' look. That was the trouble with Ilex's thirty-something generation – they'd become too old too young, which had to be blamed on having been raised in the Thatcher years. Whatever the spendthrift shortcomings of their feckless parents, these strange young/old folk seemed to have a depressing eagerness for saving and investment. That pair of so-sensible grown-up words was completely alien to Mac, whose savings days had begun and ended with two years of the weekly purchase of National Savings stamps at primary school. That was when the state rather than the advertising industry decreed what you did with your pocket money. Back then, on Friday mornings just before milk and playtime, you lined up with the rest of the class (all thirty-nine of them) to hand over six-pence for a stamp with Princess Anne's head on it. Or, if you'd just had a birthday or had swanky show-off parents, you paid a big shiny half a crown for one with Prince Charles on. Eventually these were traded for National Savings Certificates, which you forgot about till some time during your early twenties when you cashed them in to buy a clapped-out Mini. Mac had stacked up row after row of Princess Annes in his little book and could still clearly recall that plump toddler face with its surrounding mad mass of blonde curls. Her Royal Highness had never, in Mac's opinion, quite got the hang of dealing with that hair. Prince Charles had looked altogether more serious (well, he was worth five times as much – where had the junior feminists been when you needed them?); perhaps even then the poor lad had felt oppressed by the burden of future expectations.

'Are you just paying in . . . or . . . ?' A junior staff member was cruising the line of customers. With only one out of a possible six service windows staffed, she looked keen to cull time-wasters from the queue. Mac, mildly confused, considered what she'd said: 'Are you paying in *or* . . . ?' Or what? How about, he thought, 'Or . . . are you intending to stage a colossal armed robbery, which will involve police from three counties and top slot on the early-evening news but are unfortunately too well brought-up to use your sawn-off to shove your way to the front of the queue?'

Or was it completely other as in: 'Are you paying in *awe*? In awe of the uncontrollable debts the bank encourages you to run up on your sundry credit cards? The way the bank gets away with charging £27.50 for a 3p overdraft? In awe of other people who can, so capably, Manage Their Money?'

Another one came to mind – Mac was on a roll now as he shuffled a few steps further up the line: 'Are you paying in *ore* as in good old-fashioned metal ore – did freshly mined gold count as ore?' He'd had a gold ingot once – something to do with tax avoidance, he couldn't remember quite what. He and Lottie had used it to prop open the back door but Clover, who'd been about three at the time, had dragged it out into the garden and dropped it in the lily pond so he'd spent a muddy afternoon fishing it out, had it changed into cash and spent a wodge of it on one of the first-ever Range Rovers. Possibly not one of his best financial moves, but then which of them had been? Like the racehorse, the restaurant, the gallery and (most recently) the herb and salad business, it had seemed a good idea at the time. After all, you couldn't really expect a man who'd spent twenty years fronting a progressive soft-rock band to become an overnight financial whiz, now could you?

Mac's turn at the counter came at last and he handed over an untidy handful of cheques to an adolescent boy who looked as if he was wearing his much-bulkier black-sheep brother's going-to-court suit. Obviously fresh from the sixth form, Mac reckoned. He'd put money on it that the lad was temping for gap-year cash and would be off from Gatwick with a rucksack and a Lonely Planet guidebook before Mac's next final demand arrived. How come the young grabbed themselves months of carefree travel whereas he now had to think twice about a cheap weekend in Valencia? How unfair – as Sorrel would phrase it – was that? Gap year, he thought; if bloody only.

The boy yawned as he shuffled Mac's bills for gas, electricity, American Express, Visa and half a year's council tax.

'Have you considered our on-line banking service, sir?' he asked.

'I have,' Mac assured him solemnly, 'and I decided against it on the grounds of severe risk of identity theft.'

There was a millisecond's hesitation before the youth handed back the stamped counterfoils. The hesitation said only one thing: You sad, broke, balding, badly dressed old git. What kind of tragic, useless loser would want to steal *your* identity?

He had, Mac conceded, got him there.

# TWO

There was a low droning noise from behind the newspaper across the table. Slowly it dawned on Lottie (who was engrossed in the fashion pages and the minimal chances of her ever needing a strapless dress in yellow ruched satin) that Mac was reading something to her and that she was supposed to listen and take a suitable wifely interest. It was really annoying when he did this without first saying something to get her attention. She'd only tune in to the fact that he was talking to her at all when he was halfway through the piece and then he'd sigh in that exasperated way when she asked him to start telling her again.

Lottie, finding it impossible to get her head round how simple rope-and-canvas sandals could carry a price tag of £400, chucked her bit of the newspaper expertly at the recycling box across the kitchen, leaned across the table between the rows of jars (honey, two marmalades, blackberry jam) and rattled the photo of Wayne Rooney on Mac's back page.

'Sorry, Mac, I was concentrating on something. Tell me again.'

He lowered the paper a few inches and grinned across at her. 'It's that column where they do a funny bit each week about words that look the same but aren't at all, "homonyms", are they? I dunno. Anyway, it *says* . . .' And in the short space while he took a breath she sensed those long-ago *Listen With Mother* comfort-words 'Are you sitting comfortably? Then I'll begin.'

' "Pension," ' he read. ' "A pathetically inadequate amount of money, grudgingly handed over by either state or private fund, on which to live out one's declining years in the kind of penny-pinching manner to which no one would wish to become accustomed." '

Lottie pulled a face at this unwelcome reminder as to what the future might not hold in terms of funds. Had her parents' generation thought like that? Everywhere you looked now, there was a piece of finger-wagging government bossiness about savings and investments and Proper Provision. Soon, they would all be told it was their duty as good citizens to die at sixty or be evicted to a north-facing hillside to face chill starvation.

'Or,' Mac continued, ' "*Pension* – a simple yet charming guesthouse in sunny rural France, offering substantial rustic fare and a selection of fine – if robust – local wines." ' He chuckled and turned the page. 'Makes you think, doesn't it?' he said, before moving on instantly to become engrossed in Chelsea's new striker.

'No, no it doesn't,' Lottie said, shuddering slightly. 'I really don't want to think about the "P" word, especially not over breakfast.' More precisely, it was the lack of pension she didn't want to think about. The very thought made her feel mildly faint in exactly the way she used to feel years ago on the train to school when she hadn't bought a ticket, only to see the guard making his way towards her with a look on his face that told her she was about to make his day.

'It's like that parable,' she now found herself murmuring to herself, 'the one about the foolish virgins.'

'Virgins?' Mac looked up. 'What virgins? Where?'

'Pensions,' Lottie continued vaguely. 'Those women in the Bible who didn't keep their lamps trimmed or squandered their talents or something. The squanderers got told off for not being good savers, like we're going to be when we're old.'

'I wouldn't say we squandered our talents,' Mac said. 'We've done OK. We still live on it all. Just.'

There was a silence while they considered their diminishing income and the demanding vastness of the house that income had to support. It had been a massive piece of luck that some of Mac's songs had become such worldwide standards that they'd kept them going this long. But the day would surely come when opening a royalty statement would reveal 'Total: £3.50' at the bottom of the page. Lottie wondered what they'd do then: possibly the choices would be to gamble it on a horse or to buy

Lottery tickets. Growing and selling fancy salad vegetables to the hotel and restaurant trade, as they currently did, but in so half-hearted and desultory a way that it was only half a step up from hobby-farming in what was once a glorious Gertrude Jekyll-designed garden, was never going to earn them more than beer money. In fact, it probably came to less than beer money, really, once Al, the part-time gardener, had been paid.

'I didn't mean that kind of talent,' Lottie told him. 'I meant the money sort. The Old Testament was big on securing the future. Unlike us. All our money's in this house.'

And what a house, a vast Surrey Lutyens gem, far too big for what was now only three of them, and soon to be only two once Sorrel had gone first on her travels and then to university.

'Yeah but . . .' Mac started folding the whole of the sports section into a fat, unwieldy paper aeroplane. For a second she wondered about asking him to save the racing pages, to start checking out form for that £3.50 bet. '. . . what would you rather do now? Stash everything away for a rainy day that we might not live long enough to see? Or should we think about doing something else? In the bank yesterday, I was thinking about kids having gap years and why it was only them. It's our lot would appreciate it more, surely.'

'Mm. I was thinking that way too,' Lottie agreed vaguely, 'but in Top Shop.'

France was perfect in May, she thought, that rustic *pension* would be just the thing. If they simply packed and left Holbrook House right now, they could go on from there, overland towards Italy, down through Greece, Turkey, all points east. It couldn't be a first-class trip though, more a budget break at the moment. Oh you beautiful but falling-down house, she thought as she looked at the peeling paint on the kitchen walls, and the splashy self-portrait of her own naked body that covered up a crack so deep and serious that no one wanted to have to look at it and consider the expense of repairs: why, house, are you such a costly dependant? When Sorrel left for university, would it be so terribly disloyal to this thirty-year home to consider, just maybe, giving someone else a chance to do the right thing by it?

Ilex was always going on about pensions. Lottie sometimes thought he must have been swapped at birth, for how else could she and Mac have raised a son so cautious and sensible? She imagined the hell it must have been for his real parents who'd have been constantly bewildered to find themselves bringing up some kind of junior Ozzie Osbourne. What would these unknown people, a Building Society executive perhaps, paired with a studious librarian, make of their cuckoo? How had they dealt, in his younger years, with his appalling language, his moody clothes and his crash-and-burn music on their quiet Madeira holidays?

A few months before, Ilex had brought to the house with him a collection of brochures about 'Third Age Options', full of deeply unthrilling information about how to maximize investments. Lottie had tried to disillusion him gently, pointing out that she and Mac had long ago learned that in their hands investments tended to settle for minimizing themselves; they wouldn't be making the day of any fancy city brokers unless they had a stonking win during a Las Vegas bargain weekend break. She remembered how he'd smiled so blankly when she'd said all this, as if she'd told him a joke that he didn't want to admit he didn't get. When he and Manda came to lunch this Sunday, Lottie rather hoped he'd bring tulips instead – they would be far more welcome.

There was a rattle and a clunk from the hallway and Lottie went to collect the post from the mat before the dog could steal it.

'Len gets later every day,' Lottie muttered as she carried the small heap of envelopes back to the kitchen. 'I don't feel as if the day can start properly till he's been and now look, it's nearly eleven already and I haven't been down to check the coriander or feed the hens.'

'No rush – nothing's going anywhere. Though I'm really beginning to think we should.' He chuckled. 'Why should kids be the only ones who get to have all the travel adventures? I know we've seen the world, you and me, but that was work.'

It was mostly Holiday Inns, airports, smoke-filled buses and backstage bars too. If they'd played Rome, say, they'd immediately be on the way to Florence and the next gig rather than touring the ancient sites. Even Australia had been an in-and-out job, four days, four cities and on to Tokyo. Lottie looked at him. What was he saying? That he too seriously wondered for the first time about selling up and moving on?

The house seemed to agree – only that morning Lottie had noticed that the fuzzy, greenish patch of mouldy damp on the floor of the downstairs cloakroom had definitely got bigger. It sort of glittered too, like a holy statue weeping mystical tears. It reminded her slightly of a dog holding up an injured paw, asking for it to be fixed, please – and, if you can't do it, please find someone who can. This tiny seed of an idea about getting away could be like idly mentioning you might need an extension to the house – once the thought had been voiced, you realized you simply couldn't contemplate living without the extra space. But oh lordy, the potential for upheaval. Could they really just pack and sneak out when no one was looking?

Mac poured himself another cup of coffee. 'Anything profitable in the mail? A win on the premium bonds? Reader's Digest come up with my name yet?'

Lottie laughed. 'God knows, you deserve it. You must be the only person in the country who fills in every single one of those forms they send you to claim the big prize.'

'That's right. Me and Tom Champagne, we go back a long way.'

'Crazy name.' She shook her head. 'Hope he's a bubbly kind of guy.'

'It would be such a waste if he's a miserable git,' Mac agreed. 'Go on then. Hand over the bad news. Ugh – brown envelopes, bills, bills, more bills. This place, it's like heating a castle. And what's this?' He ripped open a large envelope. 'Some local government bullshit. I just paid the council tax, what more can they want?'

Mac stared in puzzlement at the envelope's contents. He

spread out on the table in front of him the various forms, brochures and information sheets.

'Buses?' Mac said. 'What do I want with . . . ? Bloody 'ell, Lottie, they want me to apply for a sodding *bus pass*! I'm not that old, am I?'

'Ah! Well I suppose you nearly are. You'll be able to join the Twirlies!' she told him.

'What the naffin' 'ell is a "Twirly"?' Mac looked perplexed. 'Sounds like the Brownies or something. Is it a sect? Is it paramilitary?' There was a glimmer of hope in his eye and Lottie fleetingly considered the awfulness of Mac being let loose with any kind of weapon. He'd once taken a powerful air rifle to a flock of pigeons that were devouring the bean plants, a flock so dense no one could possibly miss. And although not a single bird lost so much as a feather, a passing rambler on the far side of the fence had come to the front door showing a pellet hole in his rucksack and raging that if he hadn't bent to look at a grass snake he could have lost an eye.

Lottie considered. 'No and possibly yes. "Twirlies" are those pensioners who line up at 9.25 in the morning to get on a bus and when they try to use their passes, driver says, "Sorry, love, you're too early." Twirly. Get it?'

'Got it,' Mac groaned. 'Nothing paramilitary, then?'

'The uniform for men and women is beige coats, woolly hats. The men are armed with walking sticks and the women with tartan shopping trolleys. Both lethal.'

'You're being ageist. That could be us, one day.' Mac slowly tore up his bus pass application into tiny pieces.

'Never,' Lottie said. 'Our generation didn't fail to die

before it got old just so it could wear beige. At least not me and you. I shall totter to my dotage in Vivienne Westwood and a selection of mad hats, thank you.'

I'd better think about making a start on collecting all that lot now, she thought ruefully – when does dotage start? Or had it crept up already and taken hold without her noticing? There were a lot of things that did that. Her passport had needed renewing the previous year. As she'd filled in the forms she'd had a weird shiver of knowledge that maybe this, or the next, could be the last one she'd have. And then there were the succession of wolfhounds they'd had over the years, even to the extent of being serious breeders and Cruft's entrants at one time. They hadn't got one at the moment; the last one had died in the autumn and was buried, along with four of its ancestors, down in the orchard – but when they did, should they get a puppy and risk it ending up homeless on the grounds of outliving them? Not only was she having these bizarre musings, but she was also furious with herself for them: she was probably wasting carefree time here and should not have to give this so much as a passing thought for another twenty or even thirty years. In fact, if she was given the kind of luxurious TLC the late Queen Mother had had, she could still have another fifty-plus years to live. You just couldn't tell. All she could say was that although she felt as strong and healthy as she had in her thirties, thoughts now shimmied across her mind that wouldn't have got so much as a look-in back then.

Lottie indicated the little heap of ripped paper on the table. 'You should have filled that form in and sent it off,

Mac – it's the ecological way to go. The local green mafia will be very disappointed in you.'

Am I nagging? she wondered. She heard old women like that all the time. They were in the supermarket and the older they got, the bossier, telling their defeated, wizened old husbands that no, they wouldn't like Coco Pops and to get a move on or they'd miss *Countdown*. She didn't want to catch herself turning into that type.

'Bugger the green mafia, I can't start queuing up for buses,' Mac said. 'Suppose someone recognized me? Suppose someone said, "Ooh look, it's that old geezer who used to front Charisma and now look, he's on a free bus pass, just like every other poor and needy oldie." You can just see them, all ha ha ha, and who'd-a-thought-it.'

'Hey, you're not bloody Rod Stewart, you know! No one's recognized you in ages. Perhaps they'd think you'd lost your licence and had to put your Ferrari collection into storage.' Lottie started to clear away the remnants of their very late breakfast.

'And I bet Rod filled in *his* bus pass form,' she told Mac. 'He's your age and looking well up to snuff – he wouldn't let a little thing like a council age-reminder get him down.'

'Ah yes, but he's a Scot. He's not going to miss out on a freebie. So tell me then, where would a bus go that I'd want to get to?'

Lottie thought for a minute. 'India? Didn't you used to be able to go to India from Amsterdam on the Magic Bus? I have a vague memory of ads in *Oz* and the *International Times* for hippie-trail transport.'

Mac laughed. 'I remember that – one of our sound

techies got on a bus in Paris after a bender and ended up in Afghanistan. He thought he was on a coach trip to Versailles. I'm not sure how it would go down here though, getting on the local 170 and asking if they're stopping in Kathmandu.'

Mac picked up the rest of the mail and headed for the kitchen door. 'I'll go and let the hens out on the way to having a look at the coriander. The bloke from The Candle at Both Ends said he needs some later today – he's got a Thai special on this week. The organic-box people are coming to pick up a load of the flat-leaf parsley so I'll sort that as well. And then I'm going to put a few hours in down at the studio. I've got a song on the go in here.' He tapped the side of his head and grinned at her. 'It might do for Robbie.'

If only. Then they'd be talking pensions with a capital 'P' and even Ilex might shut up. Over the years since Charisma had gone their separate ways, several of Mac's songs had been covered by other artists. 'It might do for Robbie', as in Williams, had become a running joke between them whenever Mac felt inspired to take himself off to his studio with a half-formed song in his head.

Lottie loaded the dishwasher and noticed a new line of rust on the side of its door. The machine was probably well overdue for replacement and had done long and loyal service. A bit like me, Lottie thought, then re-considered. No, it's not, she thought. I'm still OK. There was, if she thought about it, a good long list of Still-Haves and Still-Dos. She put an encouraging list together in her head as she wiped down the work-top.

I still have: a full set of healthy teeth/a definite waist/an excellent sex life.

I still don't: leak when I cough/get puffed going upstairs/wish the world would slow down.

I still: buy clothes from Jigsaw, Gap and Joseph/fancy Bob Geldof/wonder what I'll be when I grow up.

That last might not be a good thing, she decided. Surely, once the time with Charisma was over she'd already *been* what she was going to be when she was a grown-up, albeit an occupation that for her had only lasted about five years before family life and Holbrook House took over. You could take toddlers out on the road with you, especially to the summer festivals, but once school-age set in, she and Mac had decided it was time to give Ilex and Clover some home-time. And then there were the things she'd been since: restaurant owner, wolfhound breeder, racehorse supporter, painter, gallery-owner, and now herb-and-salad-crops grower. All of these were things they'd sort of fallen into by accident. Only the children and the house were the constants and with Sorrel about to leave school, what exactly was the point of holding on to a house of this size and this demanding? She felt a small twinge of guilt at the thought of abandoning it, now that it had become needy and she had to remind herself that it wasn't a human, or even a pet. Someone else, someone better equipped, with time and money and energy, would be able to take it on, give it the love and attention it deserved. She wondered if Mac was feeling the same way. Something told her he was.

Lottie scooped up the fragments of Mac's bus pass application from the table and threw them into the bin. Her mother had been keen on bus trips late in her life. The highlight of each fortnight had been her Friday outings to historic houses, gardens, craft fairs, anywhere that could accommodate a mini-bus packed with old ladies in need of a loo, a sit-down, tea and a scone. When she'd died, Lottie had been moved to tears by the collection of small souvenirs her mother had collected on these trips. All the pottery thimbles, scenic coasters, printed tea towels and commemorative mugs tucked away unused in a cupboard were testament to a woman who liked to get out and about a lot and was far too well mannered to visit anywhere without making a grateful contribution to the economy of the venue.

'Your rooster has raced up from the henhouse to crap on your car roof again.' Mac reappeared in the kitchen door-way and indicated the sight of the fat Light Sussex cockerel strutting his stuff on top of Lottie's Audi. 'So do you fancy going there then?' he added, looking oddly shy as if he was still a young boy asking her for a date. He'd looked a lot like that the first time she'd met him, when at sixteen she'd been refused entry (on grounds of looking under eighteen) to The Roundhouse to see Spooky Tooth and he'd managed to get her in, by way of the guest list.

'Do I fancy going where?' Lottie asked, wondering why you couldn't reason with poultry.

'India. On a bus. Or a plane, whatever. Like we were just talking about. It wasn't *just* talk, was it?'

Telepathy like that was what you got, Lottie thought, when you'd lived with someone so long. She held her breath, waiting to see if he really was on the same thought rails as her.

'It's only . . .' he continued, 'I don't want to be harvesting boring bloody leaves for the rest of my days. Perhaps we need to flog this massive great place and go, while we can still get around without needing new hips and knees. *And* I've been reading this great book about world events not to be missed. There's a camel fair, at Pushkar, up in Rajasthan, sometime in November. It's a sort of mixture of Glastonbury and the Appleton horse fair but with camels. Very colourful, very noisy. Smelly too, probably. '

Lottie pushed the door of the dishwasher shut with her foot and heard something fall off inside the machine. It was a loud clunk and sounded terminal. When, *if,* the time came for clearing out to be done, and she felt a choking rush of both terror and excitement at the thought, this gadget would be first into the skip.

'Sounds great! And in theory, I'm right with you. But there'd be a huge amount to think about, wouldn't there? I don't want to put any kind of a downer on things, but what about Sorrel? This has always been her home. We'll have to sit her down and talk to her about it properly, give her some idea where we might be thinking of living when we get back. Wherever it is, unless we stay in the village she'll be leaving all her friends.'

'But she'll be leaving them anyway – and they'll be leaving her when they all go off to university. She's only got a few more weeks in school, and she'll keep the friends who really matter. They do far more getting together on the internet than they do in real life. She'll be OK, one darkened room with a computer in it is much the same as another. For one thing she can always go and stay with Clover. She's got plenty of room over in Richmond.'

Lottie looked at Mac warily. He seemed more determined with every sentence. He was persuading her now, fielding each and every possible problem with growing enthusiasm. She'd seen him like this before, many a time. The first had been when he'd come home one night from Kempton Park races, half-cut and half-owner (with best friend George, late – in every sense, sadly – guitarist from Charisma) of a two-year-old thoroughbred called Lacy Lil. Lil had been hailed, by Mac and George, as the great post-Charisma way forward.

'She'll keep us occupied, off the streets, out of trouble.' George had draped his drunk, stoned self lovingly round his furious wife Kate and tried to persuade her and Lottie that horseflesh really was a cracking investment.

'She'll run at Ascot. We'll get a box and you girls can do the fancy hat thing,' Mac had joined in, carried away by Tequila slammers and wild ambition. '*Owners*' box,' he'd said, fist up in a victory punch. 'One up from all that Royal Enclosure bollocks. And you two can lead her in when she wins. I can see it now.' Kate and Lottie had accepted defeat and hoped for the best.

Possibly as sweet equine revenge for being a drunk's five-minute novelty, Lacy Lil had not even remotely fulfilled her new owners' eager expectations. In spite of being placed with a first-class trainer she simply didn't understand this concept of the 'way forward' in a race at all, not unless she had another horse to follow and preferably several. George and Mac bought themselves all the kit – the Barbours, the sheepskin jackets, the top-of-the-range binoculars, shooting sticks and hip flasks – and followed their protégée from race to race but eventually the trainer gave up on her, complaining she was taking up valuable yard space and making him a laughing stock. Kate had insisted they did their best for her and Lil had been retired at some expense to a sanctuary in Gloucestershire. You couldn't put teenagers like Sorrel out to grass though, Lottie thought as she filled a bucket of soapy water to clean the rooster's mess off the car roof. You couldn't re-home them like cats.

'Maybe if we sold the house we could set Sorrel up with a flat in the village if she really didn't want to leave the area,' she suggested. 'There's a lovely little place going in the high street, just along from Susie's gallery. I saw someone from Digby, James and Humphreys putting a For Sale sign up.'

Mac laughed. 'OK, maybe when we've made some sort of decisions we'll put that to her – if she's not interested then we'll know how much she really wants to stay where her friends are. But I know what she'll say. It'll be a big, fat "no". If she gets the idea there's a flat on offer, Sorrel will hold out for Chelsea Harbour.'

Lottie went out to scrub the Audi's roof. The rooster eyed her from the arch in the yew hedge. The Pushkar Camel Fair, she thought. She'd read up on it. It surely had to be more fun than Ladies' Day in a heavy drizzle. Apart from the smell: camels were horribly pungent things. And didn't they spit? She hadn't seen a lot of spitting at a smart race meeting – at least, not among the horses.

# THREE

Clover, blonde, thirty-three and as scrummy as a mummy could get, was having an attack of the doubts, her biggest enemy. This Sunday had started badly from the moment she'd skimmed through the Property Abroad pages of the Home section from *The Sunday Times*. Clover longed for and planned for a dream holiday home in the sun. Somewhere she and Sean and their fast-growing daughters could spend long, sultry summers together before their pair of lovely, sunny-natured little girls vanished into the dreadful whirlpool of hostile teen-dom, begging and scheming to be anywhere that their parents weren't. It would also be somewhere for friends and family (even Sorrel, so long as she didn't spend all day having noisy sex with that hormone-charged boyfriend Gaz) to visit. She could see them all now, eating artichokes from a rustic market with *pissaladière* and village-baked bread, beneath a shady jasmine-scented pergola while the children shrieked and splashed happily in the pool. Sean would have to take weeks at a time away from work and relax properly rather than collapsing in an exhausted heap on the draughty terrace of their annual rented house in Rock. It was such a depressing feature of that Cornwall fortnight – the sight of so many tense holiday fathers, pacing the road outside the Mariners Bar, talking urgent share prices and legal waffle into their mobile phones while trying to marshal small children across the road carrying wetsuits and centre-boards and dodging the 4x4s whizzing along to the car park. Awful. Exactly like the school run, only in Boden-wear and Birkenstocks rather than Joseph and L.K. Bennett.

Clover had long ago set her heart on France and had it all mapped out in her head, right down to the lush taupe rough-plastered bathroom walls combined with sleek Starck 3 fittings. Sale time at Fired Earth had her hanging about in the Fulham Road shop, tempted to invest in a few dozen square metres of bargain terracotta for future floor-ing. And yet . . . recently the property pages had been featuring more and more adorable places in Italy, Portugal and Greece until she'd felt her dreams slip and alter. Today they were featuring Spain. It seemed you could still pick up an absolutely darling *finca* for practically next to nothing.

It was now just possible Clover had selected the wrong language for Elsa to learn. She'd started her at the *Bébé France* classes the previous autumn because Mary-Jane at

Toddle-Tots had gushed on and on about how wonderful it was, how fast they picked it up and how cute her Jakey had been the summer before, happily approaching the *patron* in the Provençal *boulangerie* and asking, with complete confidence and no hesitation at all (according to Mary-Jane), for a *pain au chocolat*. Well he would, wouldn't he? Clover had bitten back the thought before it escaped out loud, the child spent every blissful summer holiday moment at Mary-Jane's to-die-for pink-shuttered villa near Avignon. You'd think he'd be bloody well fluent. But with France not now necessarily her sure-fire choice, Clover was having second thoughts. Also Elsa would be learning French when she joined Sophia at St Hilary's next year. She could, now, be sorting the basics of Spanish or Italian or possibly even Greek instead. Was it too late to change? Would Elsa become hopelessly confused or could four year olds absorb any number of vaguely similar European languages? It was a bit late to do much about Sophia. At seven she was now well grounded in schoolgirl French. If necessary they could find her an after-school tutor for whatever else she needed. Now, sitting in the kitchen of her Richmond Edwardian four-storey semi and sighing over photos of a happy ex-pat family lolling on hammocks in a shady Mallorcan courtyard tendrilled with vines, she wondered if becoming trilingual might yet be a realistic goal for Elsa, obviously bright as she was.

Choices, choices, she sighed. Where to buy if not France? Everyone in Spain smiled, everyone in Italy hugged, everyone in France ... she couldn't think what the French did except shrug and say '*merde*' a lot and hate the British.

That wouldn't be good, would it? Being loathed and resented in your chosen community? And there would have to *be* a community, beyond the high, pink, vine-clad walls of her lovely garden. The idea of being totally remote, even marooned among glorious fields of sunflowers and lavender, did not appeal at all. No. Clover wanted her girls to be able to frolic in the *plaza / piazza / place* of a steep medieval village, happily accepted among a laughing band of local infants. They would become brown and scuffed and tousle-haired and . . . bilingual. Such a head-start in life.

It was important to share concerns like this with Sean. And Sunday morning (even this one, where they were soon to race around getting ready to go to the big parental lunch) was the only time to pin him down about the children. He worked so hard, was rarely home before eight during the week and often away overnight in some miserable provincial hotel, poor darling. (She firmly refused to question the 'poor darling' aspect of it; that stupid fling he'd had, that had been a long time ago now. And it was only a one-off, a silly mistake. She really didn't think about it any more. And very soon she really would stop checking through his Visa bills and cellphone call list.)

It was possible Sean might not come up with a useful opinion while he was reading the Motoring section of the paper but at least she must try. And there he was, lying on the cream leather Barcelona daybed, wearing a hotel bathrobe purloined from the Lone Star, Barbados, tanned bare ankles crossed and toes (rather unpleasantly hairy ones, in Clover's opinion) twitching slightly as if he was aware of distant music. She went and perched on the end of the daybed, careful to avoid those unattractive feet.

'Sean? Darling? Could we talk about Elsa please?'

'Hmm?' He lowered the paper slightly, but did not quite take his eyes off it, clearly reluctant to miss the last delectable detail about a Maserati so deliciously upgraded that even Jeremy Clarkson had drooled.

'Elsa?' he asked, sounding puzzled.

Clover gave him a tight little smile. 'Your daughter. The younger one,' she teased.

'What's she done? She's all right, isn't she?'

'Fine. You'd know if she wasn't, darling. It's just, I wanted to ask you about languages. Her French.'

Sean snorted. 'Her *French*? What about it? Has she had a crap report already? Bleedin' 'ell, these swanky schools! The kid can barely get her fluffy little head round English yet! What do they want?'

'No, no, listen!' He just *didn't* listen, that was the big problem. Deep down she suspected it was because his children were girls. He seemed to think they'd more or less bring themselves up, hardly needing any input from him at all apart, obviously, from loads and loads of cash. What was it he'd said when she'd been doing the frantic rounds of schools? Oh yes, 'So long as they're cute they'll do fine. Don't want the girliness taught out of them, do we?' Clover hadn't liked the way he'd ruffled her hair as he said it, as if she was merely some kind of pretty-pretty lamebrain. She did *have* a degree; though it would have felt churlish to remind Sean of this, seeing as he didn't.

'Toddle-Tots don't do reports,' she told him. 'At least,

not till the term ends and then only nice, positive things. No, it's the *Bébé France* classes. I'm wondering if we should have started her on Spanish instead. She'll be doing French soon enough when she goes to St Hilary's.'

'I suppose Spanish would be handy if she marries a foot-baller . . .' Sean mused, picking up his paper again.

'Or if she *is* a footballer,' Clover countered. Well, you had to fight your corner sometimes.

'No daughter of mine's playing footer.' He laughed. 'She'd get muscles like a docker.'

Clover said nothing. They were straying from the point and, actually, she privately agreed about the muscles. A woman should have shapely calves, but not legs that looked as if they'd been stuffed with rugby balls. Her own were slender and smooth, toned but not unattractively sinewy. She'd bear that in mind when Sophia started junior tennis. Unless she showed a serious possibility of being Wimbledon material she would not be encouraged to overdo it beyond the level of competently social.

'It really depends where we buy the new place.' Clover wanted to chew her nails as she always did when there was a dilemma to be dealt with. She sat firmly on her hands. Her Jessica manicure was only a day old.

'Ah. That house in the sun you're always planning for . . .' He treated her to a swift smile then picked up the paper again, adding casually, 'We might have to put that on hold for a bit, darlin'.' Sean returned to his car fantasies, oblivious to the fact that he had just punched a massive hole through Clover's personal dream-world.

She hesitated for a stunned moment, turning his simple,

careless sentence over in her mind in case it could be changed into something encouraging. It couldn't. One hand wriggled free from under her thigh and her index fingernail went straight to her mouth; bugger the varnish and £60 of expert shaping.

'What do you mean?' she whispered eventually. 'On hold for how long? I thought we'd very nearly decided . . .'

An impatient and not encouraging sigh came from behind the paper. He was supposed to reassure her now. He was supposed to give a bright, light laugh and say something along the lines of: 'Oh it's nothing, it's just that I'd organized a little Maldives break for the two of us.'

That might have compensated, a little.

'If you must know, though there's no reason why you really need to,' he said at last, folding the newspaper and slapping it rather emphatically onto the table beside him, 'if you really want to know, there's a bit of a work down-turn at the moment. It's a bit tricky flogging mega-bucks hospitality packages to companies that are tightening the corporate belt – and right now more of them are having to do that than we like to see. Doesn't look good, you see, sweetie. A big business providing lavish jollies for the punters can look too much like it's squandering the share-holders' assets.'

'Oh. Yes I do see. But it's just a blip, isn't it? Things will get better?' she prompted, giving him another chance to patch up her plans.

'Course they will, princess. They always do, don't they?' He grinned at her and then stretched. 'And anyway, if you're so dead set on a place in the sun, maybe you could ask your folks for a sub. They should at least be good for a deposit, wouldn't you say? Nice little nest-egg for their darling daughter? You should get your dad on his own when we go there today. After lunch. Put it to him when he's had a few.'

Her *parents*? Clover sat back on her hands, wondering if this suggestion of Sean's was really so completely off the cuff or whether he'd been thinking about it for a while. She wouldn't put it past him. And was it really a work down-turn as he'd put it? Or had he found something else, something/someone expensive to lavish the credit cards on? You couldn't, according to her favourite newspaper, run a mistress on next to nothing these days. Women weren't so desperate as to be grateful for being someone's second string. Being a bit on the side might be convenient for the ultra-busy (or married) who didn't want the hassle of a proper relationship, but it seemed it required costly compensation in terms of luxury spa treatments and desirable jewellery.

'I don't know, Sean. No, really, I wouldn't ask them. I mean, they already gave us lots of money when we got married, so we could buy this place. I'm not even sure they've got any left these days.' If the run-down state of the kitchen at Holbrook House was anything to go by, her parents were practically stony. The bathrooms could do with more than a bit of paint too. Ripping out and starting again would be more like it. If they'd only let her get her hands on it, she could make it look wonderful, attic to cellar. Just because she'd given up working at Home Comforts when Sophia was born, it didn't mean she hadn't kept her eye in, interior-design wise.

Sean laughed. 'What, Mac and Lottie? Are you kidding? Don't tell me those royalties don't still wallop in twice a year! I bet you at any given hour of the day there's some radio station or other in the world playing old Charisma tracks – and it all adds up. And anyway why *not* ask them? It'll all be coming your way one day, won't it? Yours and Sorrel's and Ilex's? What's a hundred K or so on account to an old rock star? Better for them to see you enjoy it now, surely, than know you'll be taxed to buggery when they pop their clogs.'

He stretched again and yawned and the robe fell open revealing a broad expanse of tanned chest (thankfully *not* hairy – so what was the thing with the toes? Was he growing fur from the feet up now he'd hit forty?). It crossed her mind that only a few years ago she wouldn't have been able to resist reaching across and stroking that gleaming skin. Now she just wanted to tell him to hurry up and go and have his shower: they were due at her parents' before two. When did that happen? How come all that anywhere-anytime lust had become condensed into occasional fast under-the-duvet duty-couplings in the dark while you hoped you'd keep quiet enough not to wake the children and you wished he'd remembered to take his watch off? Sure, she still fancied him, but where was the romance in it all, these hectic family-driven days? No wonder, Clover thought as she went to drag the girls away from their allotted half-hour on the dreaded PlayStation, no wonder she obsessed about soft furnishings and paint charts. A woman at her early-thirties peak needed somewhere to focus her passion.

*

It would have to be another whole year now. One last chance for Ilex to get his act together and just bloody propose. Why couldn't men read minds the way women did? You could talk at them all you liked about the relationship and where it was heading and they'd just look at you with blank incomprehension as if they were underwater and couldn't hear. Manda had check-in passengers like that at work. Every day there'd be at least one who didn't understand the concept of a valid passport for travelling abroad. It was how she'd met Ilex. Someone in the group he was travelling with had booked his ski-trip ticket for him and had him down as Alex instead of Ilex. Of course, she couldn't let him travel without a ticket that matched the name in his passport – it was against the rules. But he'd had trouble understanding the problem, just as they all did. She needed Ilex to be a bit smarter than that or she'd be single and sixty before he got the message. On that day at the airport when they'd first met, she'd been going off duty and had offered him and his baggage a lift back to London but, after some awkward moments sitting in the car outside his flat, she'd had to be the one who suggested they went for a drink somewhere. Talk about slow on the uptake.

Manda rolled over in bed, looked at the date on the clock radio and sighed the sigh of the deeply disappointed. May 12th. Her wedding day. Except that it wasn't going to be this year. Even yesterday, even ridiculously far too late, with only hours to go, she'd still clutched the dream tight to herself like something too precious to set free. Ilex hadn't a clue of course. This was Manda's big, sticky, cream-bun of a secret. It would take a good year to organize the kind of wedding she had in mind so he'd better hurry up and propose. She wanted the full works – the fabulous dress, the village church, the reception at Mac and Lottie's gorgeous, scrummy house. If she could persuade them to get a grip on that fabulous garden the place would make such a wonderful setting (those vegetables in the long borders would have to go, obviously. What they needed were romantic, cloudy drifts of soft-shaded blooms). There was plenty of room for a marquee on the side lawn and for glorious photos in front of the porch and on the sunken terrace if they could get the little old fountain-thing functioning. And Mac and Lottie would be so glad to do it all for her, she was absolutely certain. Knowing she had no parents alive, no mother to help her with the shopping and choosing (she could almost feel the tears pricking), no father to harrumph jokingly over the expense, they'd surely gladly take on making the day the most specially special for her and their only son. Money, after all, wasn't important to old hippies. Especially to those who had it.

Her sister Caro had suggested she do the proposing bit herself: 'Just ask him!' she'd urged, laughing, as if it was the easiest, most obvious, thing in the world. It was all right for Caro, all happy and secure with her stolid accountant husband and her sweet twin babies. And she was right of course, really, she *could* ask Ilex, of course she could. Manda knew that. But she wasn't going to: it wasn't part of the plan – plus she'd always wonder, forever more, whether he'd ever actually have got round to it if she hadn't asked him first. There wasn't to be any suggestion that she'd pushed him into it. And after five years together a lot of people could wonder about that when they suddenly booked that *Times* engagement announcement.

What was supposed to happen was that, very soon, preferably during the next week (Wednesday night would be good), he had to take her out to dinner and, across champagne and a luscious dessert, all he had to do was simply take her hand – the one not holding the spoon, obviously – and ask her if she'd consider doing him the honour of becoming his wife. Perfectly simple – nothing to it. He was not to do any silly tricks with the ring (emeralds were lovely and would look superb with her hazel eyes) such as hiding it in the champagne glass; she knew a woman who'd swallowed a diamond solitaire that way. The nearly fiancé had insisted she get it back and there'd been a couple of days' tense wait for sluggish digestion to kick in. Apparently she hadn't felt the same about either the ring or the man after that (well, who would?) and they'd broken up soon after. No, Ilex could just take her out, the morning after she'd said yes and while they were still all after-glow from a tip-top bed-celebration, to choose something instead. That would be much better, not to mention very speedy, for in Tiffany's the ring she wanted was in the left-hand display cabinet, nestling in white silk, third row down. It was all she could do to stop herself going in on her way home from work and bagging it with a deposit.

And now, on Manda's non-wedding day, they were to go

to Ilex's parents in the smoothest depths of Surrey for Sunday lunch and face his sister Clover and her so-perfect pair of peachy-skinned, fair-haired daughters. Manda would look at them and see how they'd grown from the last time and wonder if they'd soon be too old to play with any little cousins that she might produce for them. At this rate, Sophia would be old enough to babysit by the time she and Ilex started their own family. She *hated* seeing Clover. Nice woman and all that, but she'd got Manda's life.

Manda climbed out of bed and looked in the mirror, running her fingers through her hair as she did every morning to see if any tiny hint of grey had crept in overnight. It might – she was very nearly thirty-four – and it was time to be vigilant about these things. She wrapped her shell-pink satin robe round her and thought about getting ready for the day and what she'd wear. The shower had been running for ages. Ilex would use up all the hot water. She'd seen him take a magazine in there with him, which was ridiculous – it would get all soggy and he knew how much she liked the Sunday colour supplements.

'Ilex? Are you going to be all day in there?' She wandered out into the corridor and shouted through the closed door. Did that sound like nagging? She could have phrased it better. That might be something else she should start being vigilant about.

'Won't be long!' he called back after rather a long pause.

Manda went back into the bedroom and gave her hair a vigorous brushing. It was still long and glossy and silky and an even shade of milk-chocolate brown, like the ears on a Siamese cat. And her body beneath the satin wrap was smooth and unlined and slender, just the way Ilex liked it. Manda smiled at her reflection and made a decision: this *would* be the year of the wedding. No question. One way or another she'd be looking at the end of next 12 May as the new Mrs MacIntyre.

On the far side of the bathroom door, and mindful that Manda had super-charged hearing, Ilex stealthily shifted aside the heavy marble shelf that covered the workings of the loo cistern. Into the tiny gap behind the tank he stowed out of sight the latest edition of his favourite reading matter, a slim speciality magazine by the name of *Fuzz*, featuring strong, burly girls and boys in (though mostly half out of) the police uniforms of many countries. He was fully aware that as time wasting went, this was about as crassly adolescent as you could get, possibly a notch down from lying in bed in the dark, freeze-framing the crotch-flashes from Sugarbabes DVDs. Grown men, he was sure, had long left behind this kind of thing and moved on to pretending they bought men's magazines with slick-skinned barely dressed totty on the cover purely for the articles on designer luggage and must-have sunglasses.

She was a bit special, the American Fed in the 'On the Beat' centre-spread: a big chunky girl, with a bull-dyke haircut and an unashamedly lived-in body that had never agonized over low-fat options on a menu. If those thunder-thighs pinned you to the bed, you'd stay pinned. Just the way Ilex liked it.

# FOUR

The clematis had collapsed again. Lottie could see it flapping limply against the kitchen window as if it knew there was little hope of her racing out to rescue it. This was the fourth time this spring it had done it and given a stout ladder and better secateurs than the ones that lay rusting in the kitchen drawer, she would have ruthlessly chopped the whole lot down to ground level, pouring on a dose of something lethal and possibly illegal just to make sure. But as these wicked plant-murdering thoughts crossed her mind, she knew that even such desperate measures wouldn't kill the bugger, for it was a strong and resolute thing and survived her worst efforts at obliteration with sly perseverance. It was also one of the few survivors from the garden's original Gertrude Jekyll design and even Lottie could only admire the stealthy guile with which it

managed to get the better of her horticultural incompetence and keep inching determinedly in the
direction of its prey – the crumbling undersides of the
fragile roof tiles.

When had this war started? she wondered. This series of
skirmishes between her home's fabric and its occupants?
When did the house become bored with its simple role as
safe and solid refuge and begin showing signs of troublesome rebellion? With only three of them now living in it
(and Sorrel so often in that mysterious teenage place called
'out'), the house was far too big. More than one person had
commented that next year when Sorrel had gone to
university, she and Mac would rattle around in it as if they
were a couple of loose, forgotten balls on a wonky pinball
machine.

The problem was that Holbrook House was becoming as
cravenly high maintenance as an ageing movie star.
According to the estate agent when they'd bought it thirty
years before, this was 'Classic Lutyens in the Surrey
Vernacular'. Mac and Lottie hadn't had a clue what he was
talking about, seeing only the family-raising potential in
the solid H-shaped building, the large, light rooms along
with acres of beautiful flower garden, leading down to an
orchard, meadow and woodland. But it didn't come cheap,
keeping in good repair sharp-angled, low-hipped gables,
tall, fancy-patterned brick chimneys and over-sized multi-
paned windows that were heavily chequered with lead. If
a downpipe fractured you couldn't just run down to B&Q
for a bit of plastic replacement. You had to look things up
in the heritage book, plead with the miserable sod who

guarded the local architectural salvage yard as if every inch of ironwork was solid gold and then pay well over the odds for a very slow craftsman who would remind you that his was a dying trade and charge by the millisecond.

And then there was the garden . . . It was all very well for Ms Jekyll to lay it out as a charming series of delightful rooms, amusingly linked by pergolas, mellow brick walls and with a gently trickling rill running from parterre to orchard – back in 1901 *she* would have employed an entire team of skilled gardeners to keep it all perfect. At first, mindful of the responsibility of taking on one of Gertrude's precious gardens, Lottie had employed a full-time man for the job. The rot had started, quite literally, the minute he'd retired and Al, a former Charisma roadie, had decided he could take care of it, no problem, two or three days a week. He was still there, doggedly putting in the hours in return for fairly minimal cash-in-hand pay and free eggs from Lottie's chickens. Looking back, she and Mac had simply been far too young to take on premises as demanding as this. A childhood spent making mudpies, growing mustard and cress and squeezing snapdragons in the vicarage garden of Lottie's early years hadn't been anywhere near enough practice for dealing with flower-planting on this scale. Slugs and snails ate the delphiniums. Swathes of lupins vanished thanks to greedy fat bugs. Black, green or possibly purple fly chewed holes in the hostas and Lottie was amazed to discover that roses as well as cars could be afflicted with rust. Al was terrific for loyalty and no alarmingly obsessed Charisma fan would get to the front door past his smoking-lair between the gates and the house, but he had limits, horticulture-wise. He wasn't keen on subtleties of colour, preferring plants that gave you your money's-worth in eye-watering brightness rather than Gertrude's choice from nature's more gentle palette. He'd sneaked in displays of lobster-pink begonias and scarlet geraniums. He favoured lollipop marigolds and hanging baskets of vibrant fuchsias and he loved sitting for hours smoking roll-ups on Mac's fancy mower. Gradually the rill stopped trickling and silted up with blanket weed. Between the magnificent York stones of the sunken terrace grew a stubborn crop of dandelions and moss. The yew hedges, which Al longed to obliterate entirely in the interests of extending the lawn (and time spent mowing), became as overgrown, shaggy and untameable as Mac's hair *circa* 1973. But the paddock now housed three polytunnels full of herbs that supplied several restaurants across the county, the orchard flourished somehow and was home to an ever-growing collection of mongrel hens and the long herbaceous border in front of the warm mellow wall was now (just about) successfully stocked with Lottie and Mac's latest venture – organic home-grown vegetables, proof, according to a sceptical Sorrel, of the seductive powers of Friday-night TV gardening programmes. What those programmes failed to put across was the mind-numbing dullness of daily contact with . . . vegetables. If you planted them, then could simply come back a month or so later and marvel at how they'd grown – the way you did with a rarely seen small child – then that would be fine. But obviously you couldn't do that. You had to watch them creep to maturity, a day at a time, as you tended and watered them. It was almost literally like watching paint dry. They should, Lottie sometimes thought, have gone in for huge competition blooms. Agapanthus would have been a good choice – huge bluey-mauve heads of flowers, like the ones that grew wild all over the sandy dunes of Tresco in the Isles of Scilly.

Lottie, geeing herself up for preparing a full-scale family Sunday lunch, glared at the flapping clematis and dared it to fall down in a heap. While it clung stubbornly to life it at least served one useful function: it obscured the crumbling brickwork. The cost of repointing that lot using a hundred-year-old mortar-recipe didn't even bear thinking about.

If, as Lottie suspected, Sorrel had still got Gaz holed up in her room with her from the night before, and if, as teenagers always did, they'd troop downstairs claiming near starvation as soon as the scent of cooked food wafted up the stairs to tempt them out, that would make a total of ten for lunch and they all came with their various catering requirements. When did they get so picky? Lottie was sure she hadn't raised her children to turn up their noses at potatoes (Clover), all kinds of bean (Sorrel) or anything that looked as if it might have an aubergine hidden in it (Ilex). You'd think that now they were adults (even Sorrel) they'd have left that sort of faddiness behind long ago. And that was only hers. Clover's husband Sean could only eat fish if it had no trace of skin, bone, eye, fin or tail and absolutely no sauce or other covering in case that was hiding the other five. Possibly only Captain Birds Eye prepared seafood the way he liked it. Ilex's long-term girl-friend Manda shuddered at the very idea of anything connected with chickens – especially eggs.

'It's where they come *out* from,' she'd once whispered to Lottie, as if she had, at past thirty, only recently discovered the shells weren't, after all, individually hand-crafted from super-fine organic pastry in a stylish – though pleasingly rustic – Conran-esque kitchen. Gaz, bless him, would eat a knitted tea-cosy if you poured enough gravy on it, and thank you for it.

Lottie was tempted to lie on the squashy pink kitchen sofa browsing idly through the Sunday papers until they had all arrived and then simply hand them the sheaf of pizza emporia flyers off the dresser and let them phone for a delivery. Instead, here she was taking out her clematis-wrath by stabbing a sharp blade into two legs of lamb and inserting slivers of garlic and rosemary into the cuts. This, she thought as the knife pierced the flesh, must be close to what it physically feels like to murder a human. There would presumably be that same initial light resistance, then the 'give' into soft yielding tissue till the knife stopped short against solid bone. Horrible. She hurriedly washed the knife under the tap as if scrubbing the evidence. Where did such awful thoughts come from? They happened frighteningly often, these days. Only a week or so ago, bored while waiting for the delayed tube at Oxford Circus with Sorrel, she'd looked along the platform to pick out the person she'd be most likely to select to push under a train, for no other reason that it passed the time. Surely a sane person would have read the cinema posters or peeked over someone's shoulder at the *Evening Standard* headlines?

She stuck the cleaned knife back on the rack, covered the prepared legs of lamb with a tea towel and moved them further along the worktop in case she was overcome with an urge to go crazy, savaging them till they were shredded and inedible. Never mind the delicate tastes of her children and their various partners, she wasn't sure if even she could eat them now. Calming herself, she decided she would roast a huge dish of potatoes – sweet ones that brought to mind sweaty Caribbean markets, as well as sensible English King Edwards, freshly dug up early that morning. Clover could surely compensate with other vegetables. Plus there were to be Delia's cauliflower and leeks with cheese sauce (so calm, Delia, you couldn't imagine her considering the casual slaughter of innocent strangers, or even a clematis), and, as the courgette plants in the greenhouse were well ahead, she'd pan-fry some of those with tomatoes, garlic and lemon juice. Not an aubergine, bean, egg, chicken or fish in sight. Unless . . . an elfin streak of temptation flittered across her mind. Manda surely wouldn't ask, wouldn't even think to question, how the pastry on the rhubarb and apple pie came to look so glossy, would she? How much would a little bit of egg-yolk glaze hurt? It wasn't as if the girl was actually allergic to the things, just strangely squeamish about them. Lottie took the uncooked pie out of the fridge and put it on the worktop, then took an egg from the box by the window and checked the felt-tip date she'd written on it. What would it matter, a lovely bit of free-range, organic home-laid bantam egg? But fearful of karma – for one day this egg-phobic Manda could well wield power as the mother of Ilex's children – she put the egg back. There was nothing wrong with a matt finish on a pie. In the interests of being kind it could go without a glossy burnish: she wasn't bloody Nigella Lawson.

They really didn't care. Sorrel couldn't believe her parents sometimes. Didn't they want her to get brilliant A levels and make it into her first-choice uni? How was she supposed to get the grades for Exeter, burdened with parents who kept such slack, undisciplined habits? Did they even care she'd got Gaz in for an overnight? Suppose there was a fire and she was rescued unconscious and they didn't know he was in there to send the fire fighters in?

She lay beside Gaz in her bed staring at the sloping attic ceiling on which the greying stain from a long-ago burst pipe seemed somehow bigger than last time she'd given it a proper look. It was roughly the shape of the Queen's profile on a stamp. She'd get Gaz to go up a ladder and paint a face and a crown on it. And maybe draw round it, see if it changed and really was getting bigger. Someone had to keep an eye on these things. That pair of irresponsible old hippies wasn't likely to. That was the trouble with being the afterthought child: they'd worn out all their parenting skills (such as they were – she had an opinion on that too) with Clover and Ilex and sort of imagined Sorrel would somehow bring herself up. She hadn't done too bad a job so far, Sorrel considered, but now and then any seventeen year old could use a bit of a telling-off, a bit of No You Can't and Because I Say So, like her friends at school got. Her mum hadn't even asked her if she was on the pill. Suppose she got an embolism and collapsed and they couldn't answer questions at the hospital about any medication she was on. She might die and end up with 'Parents couldn't be arsed' as cause of death on the certificate.

Sorrel prodded Gaz in the ribs. He was a real gold-medal sleeper. And not only that, he specialized in waking up really quick and wanting sex, like instantly. Not attractive in a boy, she and Millie at school had concluded. You wanted someone who'd give you some conversation and a bit of a lead-up. He could at least clean his teeth. She prodded him again, harder, then leaped out of bed and across to the door before he could pounce. He could stay shag-less this morning, she decided. She had better (well, other) things to do. If her folks weren't going to get on to her about her exams and the state of her room and what was she doing having boys in all night at her age then she'd have to take responsibility and deal with things herself. There was the big trip to plan. She'd got the clothes and the guidebooks and the websites, it was just a matter of sorting the itinerary. And, if he was really serious about coming along as well, sorting Gaz.

# FIVE

Manda wasn't the only one with a wedding on her mind. Lottie found that memories of her own and Mac's came to her as they all ate lunch together (and surprisingly delicious the lamb had turned out to be, considering the vicious stabbing it had been treated to. It must have had a tenderizing effect). It was the paired-off arrangement of her children at the table that made her think of it: Manda within hand-patting distance of Ilex, Clover across from Sean and the stringy, pallid Gaz smirking unsubtle sexual complicity down the table at Sorrel. The long-ago wedding day had been a perfect one: as sunny as any loved-up teenage bride could want – at least weather-wise. Her mother had worn a huge mushroom of a hat in a fate-tempting shade of unlucky green – defiantly eager to hex this marriage in the hope that her daughter would eventually come to her senses and settle with a solid civil servant. The Revd Cherry had bravely overlooked the way Lottie's scarlet and purple Ossie Clarke dress bulged like a full-sail spinnaker over the lump that was very soon to be Ilex. He'd managed to welcome in the many parishioners who'd turned up uninvited to the service 'to wish them well', so they said, but really to see their bossy vicar get his comeuppance by having to marry off his pregnant daughter to a hairy, dissolute rock musician. He'd even chivvied press photographers off the graves outside the church without entirely losing his temper. He must truly have been in a mood of profound relief, Lottie recalled, for back then wayward girls were such a dire responsibility for a parent. What to do with them? How to deal with a girl who refused point blank to turn out just like her mother? And yet now, what seemed only a few brief years later, here was Lottie, assembling her own family round the scratched old elm table and being pleased that the lamb was the right shade of pink. For several seconds she had a flash of utter unreality, half-wondering who all these people were who seemed to have originated via herself and Mac. Where had they come from? Because in her head she was still an eighteen year old all geed up about life's possibilities and couldn't be anywhere near old enough to have produced a grown-up family, plus partners and children. And what unlikely people they'd turned out to be, with their proper occupations (Ilex with a slick Chelsea office suite and two assistants) and ordered family lives (Clover colour-coded her bedlinen). Lottie's parents would have been thrilled, right through to the next generation with this pair of almost unnaturally pink and tidy grand-daughters. Impossible ever to imagine Sophia being busted for smoking dope at school or Elsa throwing paint round her bedroom (across furniture, carpet and all) in the manner of Jackson Pollock, as Lottie had. Would these little girls ever take off on a Friday night, not to the pub as planned but hitching lifts in lorries to Scotland on a whim to see a band? And what staggeringly well-mannered children they were, Lottie thought as she watched the girls sitting prim and straight in their matching polka-dot Mini Boden dresses and tidily eating the lunch she'd prepared. Surely they weren't stunned to silence because for once they were eating in Holbrook House's rarely used dining room instead of in the haphazard muddle of the day-to-day kitchen? It was certainly a quirkily imposing room – a mixture of dark wood panelling, blood-coloured paint-work and many unfathomable splashy abstract paintings (left over from Lottie's short-lived phase as an artist), none of which should give a qualm to a pair of lively under-tens. How come they didn't shout or squabble or slop their food about or knock over their drinks? They did not wield their knives and forks awkwardly like medieval daggers; they didn't whinge about not liking garlic and they never forgot to say please and thank-you at the appropriate times. Much as she loved them, Sophia and Elsa reminded her of Midwich Cuckoos – small perfect aliens planted in a com-munity to unnerve the residents. They certainly unnerved Lottie. Clover (who as a seven year old herself had eaten all her meals under the table, convinced she was really a poodle puppy) must have painstakingly drilled Table

Manners into these two from the day the breast-feeding stopped. Lottie caught Manda studying the children from across the table as if taking in exactly what a four and seven year old should be like. They're not all like this, Lottie wanted to tell her; this isn't even close. Go hang out in any shopping mall, look over the fence of your nearest primary school, see the tantrums and the rampaging and the off-the-scale energy. Not that Manda would. When (if) Manda had children they, just like these two, would be hurtled between Tumble Tots and Monkey Music and Kodali violin and be fed on Baby Organix and the wholesome, child-friendly recipes of Annabel Karmel. And Lottie would sadly acknowledge that when she and Mac volunteered to take them on their customary muddy annual adventure with their tepee to Glastonbury, Manda would be ready with well-rehearsed reasons as to why not, just as Clover always was.

'Manda, more potatoes?' Lottie, feeling as if she was playing the role of Granny Perfect, offered the extra ones to her putative daughter-in-law before she asked anyone else. If Manda thought this counted as a comment that she needed fattening up, well, it wasn't a million miles from the truth. Manda's body hovered between pin-thin and skeletal. Also it seemed logical to start the offers of seconds with the one who looked the hungriest as opposed to what her own mother had done, which was to begin with the biggest and greediest male – her own husband. The Revd John Cherry had never said no either, especially not on a Sunday when the preparation of this ritual lunch was a frantic business crammed in by Mary Cherry between

Family Communion and Evensong. Why no one had ever considered moving the full-scale roast beef extravaganza to Monday or Saturday and serving up a simple soup and salad on Sunday was beyond Lottie. She'd suggested it once, on a day when her mother had yet again raced out of church, pushing past the vicar's usual gaggle of fond old ladies lined up to congratulate him on his sermon, to baste the joint and shove the Yorkshire puddings into the temperamental Aga.

'Don't be ridiculous! It's *Sunday* lunch.' Mary had looked at Lottie in amazement as if her daughter had questioned why Christmas had to be in December. '*Sunday* lunch – that's the point!'

'No more for me, thanks. I've had *loads*!' Manda held up a long skinny hand and fended off the dish of potatoes as if terrified by such proximity to carbohydrates.

'No you haven't.' Sorrel pointed her knife at Manda's plate. 'You've had two tiny ones. And you can't be on a diet, so maybe you're—'

'Sorrel! Pass the potatoes down to Sophia, will you?' Lottie interrupted hurriedly.

'I was only going to say . . .'

'Yes, well, please don't.'

'Candida.' Sorrel grinned at her mother and at Manda. 'I was only going to say you might be avoiding potatoes because you'd got a yeast infection. It's called *Candida albicans*. I looked it up.'

There was a short silence while everyone worked out how much of an embarrassment factor this carried. About 98 per cent, was Lottie's guess, recalling gynaecological plain speaking from some *Guardian* article or other. Still, at least Sorrel hadn't said 'pregnant'. Manda would be aware enough of her biological clock without people like Sorrel carelessly setting it chiming. At past thirty Manda must have lots of friends who were producing babies. The poor girl was probably thoroughly sick of being invited along to baby showers, turning up each time clutching a beautifully wrapped gift and having everyone say, 'Hey, maybe your turn next, Mands!'

'You thought I was going to say "pregnant", didn't you, Mum?' Sorrel declared triumphantly. Lottie groaned.

'Potatoes are nothing to do with yeast infections,' Manda said calmly. 'I'd actually be completely fine with potatoes if I had candida. But I haven't. Thank you for your concern though, Sorrel.'

'Isn't candida something to do with thrush?' Clover asked Manda, who looked so startled Lottie wondered if eyeballs really could drop right out.

'Yes, but you can get it right through your digestive system as well as up your fanny,' Sorrel explained breezily. 'It's not *just* sexually transmitted, you know.'

'I definitely haven't got anything like *that*,' Manda blurted. 'I'm very well. Peak condition, in fact.'

She smiled nervously around the table, at all the faces that now gazed at her, as if waiting to hear her deny each of a long list of unpleasant and deeply personal symptoms and possibly proffer a signed-off appointment card from her local genito-urinary clinic.

'Thrush! *Perlease*, I'm still eating!' Sean shuddered, his loaded fork poised halfway to his mouth.

'She still didn't answer the pregnant bit,' Sophia hissed loudly across the table to Sorrel. 'Not *actually*. Are you having a baby, Manda?' The child stared, bright-eyed and waiting. As, by now, were they all. Poor Manda was brick-scarlet. Lottie looked at Ilex – the one person who possibly should have been expected to come to her rescue. He was beyond helping, deep in murmured conversation with Gaz. She caught the words 'offside' and 'penalty'.

Manda hid her face inside the twin curtains of her flat brown hair and stared down at her empty plate, trusting the personal speculation would soon move on to someone else. She considered saying that yes, actually, she did think she might be pregnant. Maybe this way Ilex, if he actually could be arsed to listen, would be kick-started into commitment mode, but then that would very nearly be as bad as having to ask him to marry her. She didn't want her magical special day to come about under any hint of pressure, though how much longer she could leave it before giving in and pushing him right into it she really didn't know. As they'd arrived at the house she'd had a good sneaky look at the front porch, checking it for wedding photo potential. Close to perfect, was how it appeared to her, although it needed a lot of tidying up. It would take more than that idle part-timer Al to get the garden sorted. They should get Green Piece in and give it a total makeover. Weeds pushed through the gravel in clumps, roof tiles needed replacing and the rampant passion flower scrambling up the walls could use a serious trim. Some tubs and hanging baskets of trailing white fuchsias and surfinias would help to soften the look. If all else failed, she could get the nursery to send round fully grown white-flowered climbers in pots. And roses. Of course there must be roses, for a wedding.

'No, of course I'm not pregnant, Sophia,' Manda said, sounding close to defeat.

'Is that because you and Ilex haven't been doing *mating*?' Sophia persisted, her voice so clear and loud that even Gaz and Ilex looked up.

'What's mating?' Elsa chipped in.

'Bloody good fun, that's what it is.' Sean chortled.

'Sean! *Pas devant les enfants.*' Clover leaned across the table and hit her husband's arm sharply.

'That means you can't say things in front of the children. Jakey's mum's *always* saying it,' Sophia explained to her little sister. Lottie marvelled at the child's worldly wisdom.

'Still doing the French classes, are you, Sophia?' she asked.

'*Oui.*' Sophia nodded.

'*Je pearl fronzee,*' Elsa chipped in.

'Fantastic,' Lottie told her. 'What brilliant girls you are.'

Poor kids, did Clover ever give them time to lie on the lawn and watch the clouds drifting over?

Sean interrupted. 'Is no one having these potatoes? Cause if they're going begging . . .' He didn't wait for an answer but leaned across towards Sophia and scooped up a crisp roast potato in his fingers.

'Dad*dee*! I was saving that one!' Sophia leaped from her seat and ran out of the room, sobbing dramatically. Oh good, Lottie thought, feeling immensely cheered. The child shows signs of being pretty normal after all.

'Sorry, princess!' Sean called after his daughter. 'Think of it as leaving you more room for pudding! So, Mac, how's the mighty herb project coming along? Cornered the market in minority mints yet?'

Mac groaned. 'Don't bloody ask. You won't believe how fast a polytunnel full of parsley can drop dead if you water it in a heatwave.'

'So why did you?'

'Good question,' Lottie said. 'The hose was on a timer and something must have tripped. Just about every leaf was sun-scorched and useless. Restaurants can't use anything less than perfect so we were stuck with a glut, only good for compost.'

'Tastes the same though.' Mac shrugged. 'I made the most amazing green mayonnaise with it.'

'Brown, you mean,' Ilex interrupted. 'Wouldn't it be, with scorched leaves?' His parents' incompetence at matters of simple business practice never ceased to stagger him. How many failed ventures had they ploughed their enthusiasm and loads of cash into during his lifetime? He hardly dared add them up. There was probably a club for people like them – hundreds of ex-musicians with a string of doomed hobby-careers. They could all get together and chat about their trout farms and nightclubs and pheasant shoots and where did it all go wrong? If Mac and Lottie had only re-trained as something sensible when the music faded away instead of relying on short-lived enthusiasms and the comfort of twice-yearly royalties, they could be winding themselves down towards a nice quiet retirement, all nest-eggs hatching nicely. Instead, it looked like all funds had flown the coop long ago. And was this really the first time he'd noticed how run-down the house was looking? *Tired* was the word that came to mind, bordering on the exhausted and clapped-out. The curtains in this rarely used room – once glorious rich gold devoré velvet – were saggy and dulled. The Moroccan kelims would have proved a sound investment if they'd been preserved safely hanging on the walls rather than on the floors where they'd become scuffed and threadbare from a lifetime's worth of sharp-clawed (and often incontinent) cats and dogs. It needed a sharp injection of serious funds, and fast, before real rot set in and the whole thing fell down.

'The green mayo was all right,' Mac protested. 'I chucked in a couple of drops of food colouring from a bottle at the back of the larder. Could have packaged the stuff up, given it a fancy label and flogged it, no trouble. In fact, it gave me an idea.'

Ilex looked hard at his father, trying to work out whether he was joking or not. You could never tell with Mac. When he and Lottie had attempted to run a restaurant they'd had quite a lot of trouble understanding the concept of Health and Safety. Mac had had a huge row with the visiting inspectors over the wolfhound-of-the-time dozing in its basket in the corner of the restaurant kitchen, pointing out to the outraged clipboard-toting official that it was either that or being on the wrong side of yet another set of authorities for leaving the poor creature slowly stewing to a certain death outside in the hot car.

'What kind of idea, Dad?' There was a certain amount of

dread in Clover's voice. 'Please don't say it's another restaurant?'

'God no! I'd never do that again. You have to be nice to people *all the time*!' He laughed. 'Though I suppose I could sit back, keep out of the way and not try to be hands-on . . .'

'What, and just, like, count the money? Sounds cool.' Sorrel nodded.

'Nah – there wouldn't be any money. Never is, not in food. The more rules and regulations, the less cash. And chefs are such prima donnas. I've had enough of those to last two lifetimes.' Mac reached across for the wine and poured some into Clover's glass and then his own. 'No, I just thought, what about doing a range of herbal sorbets? You could package them up all arty-tarty and flog them off in upmarket delis. Got to be a winner because they'd be frozen – they'd keep. That way I wouldn't get stuck with a glut and be at the mercy of those bloody up-their-own-egos chefs.'

'You know, Mac, that's not such a bad one.' Lottie also refilled her glass and offered the wine to Sean who, mindful he'd be driving his car-full of family, looked at it longingly before passing it on to Sorrel. 'We could have a competition for the package design – get some of the students down at the art college to do it – much cheaper than hiring some rip-off company.'

'Mum, slow down! That's just so typical!' Clover interrupted, laughing. 'There you go, straight to the fun bit before you've even given a thought to marketing and demand and a business plan! Can't you and Dad *ever* think things through first?'

Lottie looked with amazement at her agitated daughter. 'Think *what* through? Hey, lighten up, will you, Clover! It's just an idea. We're only at the playing-with-it stage!'

'Mum, you're *always* at the "playing-with-it" stage,' Ilex said, leaning across the table and tenderly patting his mother's wrist. He had to back up his sister here. If someone didn't slow them down to a sensible pace right now, Mac and Lottie would soon be in full possession of a run-down food-processing plant and a warehouse full of unsold tarragon ice-cream rapidly heading for its Destroy-By date.

'Ooh, you know sometimes I can't believe you and Clover are really our children!' Lottie got up and started collecting plates. 'You're so ... *straight*! Where's your imagination? Your vision? Where's your sense of rebellion and your natural-born anarchy?'

'Anarchy doesn't get the bills paid, Mum,' Ilex pointed out primly.

'Or the children into a good school,' Clover joined in.

'Which is *your* rebellion – pathetic as it is,' Sorrel pointed out to her sister. 'Mum and Dad are old hippies who somehow got away with never having proper jobs so obviously your idea of rebelling was to go the other way.' She looked carefully at her older brother and sister and added, 'Of course you can rebel too far. I mean, Ilex, for Chrissake, you're an *estate agent*. Like, how deadly is *that*?'

'I am *not* an estate agent! I'm a property management consultant!'

'Same difference,' Sorrel snorted, pushing her chair away. She collected up the remaining plates and followed

Lottie to the kitchen, calling as she went, 'Whatever name you give it, Ilex, you're still a no-life nine-to-five office slave who's scared to leave home without a tie!'

'And I suppose you think a few months back-packing is going to make you an authority on the romance of a wanderer's life?'

Sorrel came back into the room and treated her brother to a pitying smile. 'Well, at least I'm *going* somewhere. You and Manda never do any travelling.'

'We go away. We went to Italy last September, and then to Bruges to the Christmas market. Or doesn't that count?'

'Yes, but it's not *travelling*. It's just a holiday. You knew exactly where you'd be from day one to when you came home and where you'd stay and everything. *Travelling* is when you really get the feel for how people live in the places you go to, not just hanging out in some tourist complex. It's an adventure, the possibilities of the unknown!'

'Sounds like being on tour with Charisma.' Mac chuckled. Lottie came back in, carrying the rhubarb and apple pie. 'Remember Cairo, Lotts?'

'Oh I remember Cairo,' she agreed, preparing to slice the pie. Was Clover on a diet this week? Probably. 'Rats, dysentery, the wrong airport and two deported roadies. We should go there again. What do you think?'

'Hmm. Put it on the list,' Mac murmured to her.

'Happy memories, then, if you'd go again.' Sean laughed. 'Sounds like my idea of hell.'

'Yes but we . . .'

'. . . were young.' Ilex finished for his father. 'And rich, by then. It's not like you really had to worry.'

'I wouldn't worry now,' Mac said, shrugging. 'Rich or not. I mean, now I'm older I don't much care what goes wrong on a trip. I know the worst that can happen is going to be the airline over-booking or a strike somewhere or crap food. If you sit tight with something to read, it usually works out. It's you lot in the middle that get in a flap, expecting everything to run hitch-free all the time. You fall to bits and look for someone to sue if something goes a bit pear-shaped. You want to be "kept informed". For God's sake *why*? What's the rush all the time?'

'There could be bombs or the plane could crash,' Gaz pointed out, helpfully.

'Oh cheers, Gaz, thanks. Just when we're planning a round-the-worlder.' Sorrel prodded him hard in the ribs. 'It's all right for Dad, he's not gonna be doing that, is he?'

'I don't see why not,' Lottie said. 'Actually, we were sort of vaguely thinking maybe we should have a gap year too. Why do teenagers think it's something invented just for them? God knows, we deserve one after raising you lot. Thirty years of child care is about the same as the longest life sentence.'

'Was it that bad?' Clover looked hurt. 'You must have liked it at the time, or after me and Ilex there wouldn't be Sorrel.'

'No, darling, of course it wasn't. I was joking. It's just been a long time since we didn't have anyone to think about but ourselves. Obviously with Sorrel being so much younger it was like having two goes at it.'

How frighteningly easy it was to shake Clover's security, Lottie thought. Where had that fragility come from? She hoped it wasn't Clover's babyhood, when she and Ilex had spent several months being ferried round the USA and Europe in tour buses. Which was worse? It was that or leaving them at home in the care of a nanny. You didn't do that, back then. You let them dance in rock-festival fields and wear daisies in their hair and have their faces painted like fairies. They paddled in warm oceans, thrived on a multi-national diet and slept under soft, antique patch-work as the bus rolled on to the next city. Possibly, in these over-careful days, all that would qualify for a care order.

'Now Sorrel's about to leave school and go travelling,' Lottie continued, 'what's to stop Mac and me packing up and travelling too? Apart from holidays, it's a long time since we've seen the world. Maybe we'd like to have another look before it's too late. See what's changed.'

The pie was now all sliced. Big bits, little bits, they could choose, help themselves. It didn't look particularly thrilling, very matt, very wholemeal, very worthy. She should have gone with the egg – let the thing sparkle. She could have decorated it, been artistic with pastry leaves and swirls of icing sugar. She pushed the pie-plate towards Clover, who took a tiny sliver but waved the cream on past in the direction of Manda.

Sorrel laughed. 'Yeah, but you can't have a gap year, Mum, I mean, not you and Dad.'

'Actually, why can't we?' Mac asked her. 'Wouldn't you rather we went off travelling than stayed here trying to market frozen coriander? Nice pie, Lottie. You on a diet again, Clover?'

'You wouldn't want to do that,' Ilex said. 'You'd hate it, hanging out in cheap hostels with scuzzy adolescents. Mum would worry they weren't phoning home enough and Dad would keep asking if they'd downloaded any illegal Charisma on to their i-pods.'

Manda wasn't eating any of the pie, Lottie noted. She could have dolloped a dozen egg yolks on it if she'd wanted to. Maybe the poor girl was worried – surely what Sorrel had said hadn't upset her? Teenagers were always like that, deliberately chucking in something to shock. It was their function in a family. She could see Manda darting little looks at Ilex as if there was something on her mind that she wanted him to read. He wouldn't, of course. He'd always been the type of boy (man, now, she reminded herself, and for a long time too) who needed everything spelled out for him. When his first girlfriend had tried in a kind way to dump him by suggesting they take a bit of time apart for seeing other people, he'd been phoning her after a month, utterly confident of getting straight back to full-scale romance thinking she'd be ready for him again now, having used the free time innocently going to movies with friends and catching up with homework.

'Ah yes, but you see, Ilex,' Mac was now explaining, 'we wouldn't *be* staying in cheap dives with "scuzzy adolescents" as you put it. We'd do it the five-star way, me and Lottie. Flash-packers, not back-packers, that'll be us.'

'Mmm, sounds good when you put it like that!' Lottie agreed.

'Cost you, that,' Sean warned. 'Doesn't come cheap.'

Mac frowned. 'Who said anything about cheap? When do I do cheap?'

'But how . . .' Ilex held his breath; perhaps he wasn't going to have to worry about the old folks after all. A pension maturing, that must be it. Well, thank goodness – they'd been more prudent than he'd imagined. Not going to be the big old-age burden after all.

Mac grinned. 'What's the point of sitting on a load of cash if you don't use it?'

Clover and Sean exchanged glances. 'None at all, Dad,' she smiled, 'if you've got it, spend it.' How reassuring that would be. Perhaps the little place in France (Spain? Portugal?) was a possibility after all.

'Yeah, well, we've got it,' Mac said, looking around the room. 'Right here – this place must be worth truckloads. Should take us round the world at the front of the plane, wouldn't you say, Lottie?'

'Well, I hadn't actually thought how much it would come to, exactly . . . but . . .' She too looked around at the sagging curtains, the ornate plaster on the cobwebby ceilings that could do with an expert painter and the floors that in places creaked so ominously. Tatty but tasty, that was their home. 'Yes, it should take us round the world several times over, I'd say!'

They were all looking at her as if she'd lost her last remaining senses. But if there were any pennies to drop in the collective junior branch MacIntyre brains, they were taking their time getting under way. It was – and who'd have thought it? – Gaz who finally got the words out.

'What, you'd, like, flog your house, *this house*? And, like, blow all the cash? Wow, awesome!' he said, reaching across Clover to spear the last big slice of pie.

'But you can't do that!' Clover blurted out. 'You couldn't sell this house! It's ... it's *home*! It's the whole family ... centre!'

Lottie and Mac smiled at each other; the surrounding expressions of horror were wonderful to behold, the tease was irresistible. 'Sure we could! It's our new, great idea.' Mac shrugged. 'Why not?'

# SIX

It was, for a weekday, a pretty good way to be woken up. Ilex watched the top of Manda's glossy brown head snaking its way back up the bed and smiled happily.

'Mmm. It doesn't get much better than this,' he told her, feeling a delicious post-coital languor creeping on.

Manda, who rather thought it did, gave his shoulder a swift kiss and climbed out of bed to go and run the shower. She wasn't due at work till midday, which gave her plenty of time to go to the gym, have a swim and a workout and maybe join in with the advanced yoga class. All that lot would give her energy, get the *chi* flowing and help her to feel positive, something that she badly needed. Where now, if not at Holbrook House, were she and Ilex going to have their wedding party? What were his parents thinking of, so casually coming up with the idea of selling the place?

It was their family's home, for heaven's sake, not some superfluous gadget you could offload on eBay. And Clover, who sometimes seemed so babyish as to be barely out of her pram, must be spitting blood at the very idea of Mummy and Daddy getting rid of the house. She probably still kept her soft toy collection there, all cutely lined up on her little pink bed.

Manda knew perfectly well that there were any number of grand venues to choose from for a wedding these days. Kew Gardens was a good one – she'd been to a lovely one there. And there were various hotels and historic houses. Compared with a simple village church and Holbrook House, though, everything else would seem too impersonal. Plus it was hard enough to drag Ilex to an unfamiliar restaurant, let alone expect him to spend the happiest day of his (and her) life at some starchy, swags-and-chintz place he didn't know inside out. Her friends, when they were being kind, called him 'traditional'. But when they got a bit pissed and kindness went out of the window, the word 'anal' occasionally surfaced.

'Ilex, darling? Wake up.' Manda, back from the shower, shook him gently to wake him from the doze he'd fallen into. He looked shiny, she thought; in need of a wipe-down like a bar-top late at night. She turned her attention to her underwear drawer, selected a pink and black Elle Macpherson bra and matching knickers with side-tying bows. She paced around a bit and took her time putting these on, her body prettily posed for her audience as she dressed. Ilex, infuriatingly, wasn't watching. He stretched and yawned and gazed up at the ceiling. She was wasting her time and should have done this half an hour ago: now he was sated he was focused on the day ahead.

'Ilex – this thing about Mac and Lottie selling up. Do you think they really will?' She stood in front of the long mirror and tweaked at her bra cup. Ilex sat up, blinking sleep from his eyes.

'They'd be mad to right now – prices in that bracket aren't doing too well. Which means that yes, they'll probably have it on the market by the end of the week.' He laughed. 'I mean, they're my folks, aren't they? Never knowingly gone for the smart money option!' He considered for a moment. 'But . . . if they could hold on for another year, we could be talking another half million at least. I despair of them. I mean, what are they going to do for a pension when they've blown it all? By the time they've got the travel thing out of their systems and bought a place when they get back, there'll be sod-all left for them to live on.' He sighed. 'And by music business standards, they're pretty much clean living. They could go on to well over a hundred. Imagine financing that at whatever-you-need a year by then. Who's going to fork out for the care home?'

'Yes, but it's not *just* about the money, is it?' Manda ventured gently, knowing perfectly well that in Ilex's case, it certainly was. Worth a try though, so she persevered. Her sister Caro had said, 'Nothing will happen unless you make it happen.' She just needed a bit more practice. 'It's so much more than a heap of cash to you all, surely, a house like that; it's somewhere you've always called home. You're all so lucky. Caro and I didn't have a proper kind of a home after Mum died. Nowhere we could go back to for Christmas and family celebrations.' She emphasized her point with a deep sigh.

Ilex looked blank. 'Isn't this home?' He looked round their bedroom, puzzled. 'When I'm out and I say "I'm going home", this is where I think of.'

This was good, Manda conceded, but in this particular case, today, it was good *and* bad.

'But think of Sorrel. She's got only Holbrook House, the home she's always had. Where's she supposed to live? *And* I don't think Clover feels the same as you either,' she ventured. 'I think when Clover thinks of "home" she thinks of where her mum and dad live.'

'Oh, well, Clover; she was always the little girl. It's high time she grew up.'

Ilex climbed out of bed and strode into the bathroom. He didn't shut the door and Manda could hear him peeing loudly. Why did men do that? It was so unattractive. He'd be completely repulsed if she did it. 'A man likes a bit of mystery' had been a favourite adage of her mother when trying (too late) to persuade her adolescent daughters that virginity wasn't something to offload lightly. Manda felt tears welling up. What would her mum think of her daughter now, reduced to sliding down a bed at 7 a.m. to give a man a blow-job in the hope he'd be brain-addled enough to ask her to marry him? There wasn't a lot of mystery there.

Ilex emerged from the bathroom. 'I was thinking,' he said, scratching his head as if helping the process along, 'maybe I should have a word with Clover about this house-sale thing. And Sorrel too. Maybe between us we could persuade them to hold off for a bit, think it through. Just till the market perks up again. And till they've made firmer plans. I mean, they haven't a clue yet where they're heading, have they? No point going to the expense of advertising the place if they're going to change their minds.'

Manda felt enormously cheered. She put her arms round him and kissed him softly. 'Now that's a brilliant idea!' she murmured into his ear as she snuggled against his bare chest. 'I do love you, Ilex!'

There, Mum. She sent the thought up to her mother among the angels. See? Job done.

Clover had tried telling herself several times that she was a Big Girl Now who had long since left the cosy world of Mummy and Daddy and she would normally be the first to admit that it was pretty pathetic for a woman in her early thirties to feel so upset about her parents making plans to change their lives. But these weren't normal times (Was Sean about to be made redundant? Or was he whooping it up at vast expense with some easily impressed slapper? Should she give up her subscription to *Sunshine Property* and forget the Dordogne and blissful sunny peace?) and they certainly weren't normal parents. When other people's mums and dads got to a certain age they took up golf or they bought into nice chintzy time-share apartments in safe places like Malta or Torquay. They went on cruises where they were lectured to about Cretan myths or Roman relics and they went to see ancient relatives in

New Zealand before it was too late. You weren't going to get a pair of old rockers like Lottie and Mac to join in with any of that (and to be honest, it crossed her mind she was probably thinking of people a good twenty years older than they were). Clover liked life to be settled; she relished the comfort of the familiar, and having her parents continuing at Holbrook House represented safety and solidity to her. If she really wanted to analyse it (and she didn't much like to, for fear of what she'd find) she'd have to admit that the place still represented somewhere to run back to, a refuge when she needed it. And boy, had she needed it, a mere six weeks after Elsa was born. There'd been Sean, working away from home at a rugby awards event up north, celebrating second-time fatherhood by shafting a waitress across a table-full of trophies. His assistant had walked in on them and immediately phoned Clover as she 'thought she ought to be told'. Clover, engrossed at the time in breast-feeding and Sophia's emerging sibling rivalry, wasn't so sure. Some things you can really do without knowing at a time like that – she had quite enough on her plate, thank you. Once you were told, you had to deal with it.

There'd been several sessions of counselling after that, for Clover had been feeling very shaky and unsure of herself. Sean unhelpfully diagnosed post-natal depression, presumably to deflect from the more obvious post-being-cheated-on sort. One day she'd taken Elsa out in the car to buy some nappies at Sainsbury's and instead of coming back just that one mile home, had driven in a complete daze down to Holbrook House, silently gone up to her old room and climbed into her childhood bed, snuggling up to her baby as if she was a comforting teddy. Mad, Sean had called her, completely certifiable. He'd been furious (which might have had something to do with having had to cancel his golf to stay at home with Sophia) and had told her to grow up, get herself sorted. It had only, he'd said, been a stupid, one-off shag – it wasn't going to happen again and there was no need for all this palaver. Apparently it was a well-known man thing, so he claimed (so that was all right then – perfectly normal). Nature, in her skewed wisdom, gave men an irresistible desire to go out and spread the seed around immediately after a birth, while the females of the species could see the living proof of the males' fertility. It was something to do with the survival of the species giving them a primitive urge to impregnate as many women as possible. All this made Clover wonder if she was supposed to be grateful it was only one waitress he'd had, not the entire team, all lined up in their black skirts and little white aprons. If it *was* only one. He was away over night so often, she couldn't possibly know what he did. She didn't want to let herself board that particular train of thought. It was too hard to stop.

The counsellor she had seen hadn't been much use and had also assumed Clover was suffering crazed delusions brought on by post-natal depression and he had only really taken notice when she'd talked about her early childhood. Nodding and occasionally grunting, the blank-faced therapist had almost chewed the end off his pencil as Clover conjured up her earliest memories: the time she and Ilex were taken round the capitals of Europe in the

Charisma tour bus with a selection of beardy old musicians, their sandalled, mantra-chanting women, and the gloriously untamed children of the other band members. Sean had said the therapist was probably stashing all the info away as a case-study for a future self-help bestseller and wasn't at all interested in Clover's part in her own childhood but it had left Clover wondering if she'd had her fragile baby-roots shaken by random child-care and the nightly stage-side view of her parents entertaining crowds of thousands instead of tucking her into her cot with nursery rhymes and a Fisher-Price mobile. It had surely left her childishly needy. When she'd worked at Home Comforts, assembling sample boards of paint colours and furnishing fabrics for customers, she'd too often tried to insist that a classic Victorian sitting room really needed candy pink. Now, here she was outside the gates of St Hilary's, blurting out to her best school-gate friend Mary-Jane that her parents were thinking of selling up and planning a year-long world-trip, and wondering who to blame for her failure to turn into a properly formed grown-up. Hastily, she tried a bit of back-pedalling, looking to make herself feel better.

'Of course I'm sure they didn't mean any of it. It was probably just my crazy parents' idea of a wind-up. It would be typical of them to come out with it for effect. They've probably forgotten all about it by now.'

She smiled and shrugged and opened the door of her VW Touareg in an attempt to put off an approaching traffic warden. Did they have to hover so close to the school at dropping-off time? It wasn't as if anyone was going to be more than a minute or two and it was only a single yellow line, nothing serious. She sighed and chewed at a nail – and why not? After Sunday they were all thoroughly ruined. Late last night she'd had to take off all the shattered varnish and file away the chewed edges. She'd have popped into Hand Job on the high street for repairs but Sean had now made her feel wary about spending casual cash, in case the redundancy thing really was true. She wasn't sure whether she hoped it was, and had to face a downgrade in outgoings (and she could handle that) or that it wasn't, and she had to go through all the angst of being convinced he was stashing money offshore as a lead-up to a cheap divorce or spending money on a mistress.

Alongside Clover, watching the girls going into school, Mary-Jane's face was only mildly sympathetic. She waved distractedly across the playground in the direction of her daughter Polly, who, trailed by Clover's adoring Sophia, was plodding with dramatic misery at a snail's pace towards her classroom but was absolutely *not* to be allowed to get away with yet another day off for a sore throat.

'So . . . it was just a spur-of-the-moment idea, maybe.' Mary-Jane looked thoughtful and then said, 'But are you sure they haven't been planning a trip for ages? I mean, selling a house they've lived in for over thirty years to fund a serious amount of world travel is a pretty crazy idea to come up with, just on a whim. Imagine how much stuff they'll have to clear out – how brave is that!'

Unaware she was making things worse and that this wasn't the role Clover had planned for her, Mary-Jane continued, 'Perhaps that was the whole idea behind the big lunch – to get you all together to tell you they were cashing in the family chips. Good on them – my parents never went further than the Lake District. They moved into a bungalow the year I went to university in preparation for old age and the time when they couldn't climb stairs. They weren't even out of their forties!'

The Lake District. Wouldn't that suit Mac and Lottie? Why weren't they the sort who took up gentle hill-walking if they wanted a challenge? This wasn't even remotely reassuring. Clover had only told Mary-Jane because she thought she could count on her saying the right thing, something along the lines of, 'Oh how sad, your parents selling up the family home. End of an era.' A hug would have been nice. Except that obviously it *wasn't* sad – well, not the kind of sad you could expect anyone who wasn't a family member (and who already had her own to-die-for dream-home in France) to understand.

'No, really I don't think so. It came out a bit too spontaneously for that, as a sort of follow-up to something else. And besides, planning isn't my parents' strong point,' Clover told her. This was true: the existence of Sorrel was surely proof of that. Sorrel was a brilliant little sister – at a safe distance – but what on earth had they been thinking of, producing another baby when their first two were practically finished with school?

'I mean, on the one hand why shouldn't they go travelling while they've still got their health and strength? Fine, go for it. Take a holiday. But just getting rid of the family home, *our* home, our *base*, well, that's a shock to the system, really kind of final and drastic. They could have run the idea past us a bit more gently. They didn't give us any consideration at all, as if the place was just, like *nothing*, like any old anonymous semi. Holbrook House is so incredibly special, full of all our memories and still quite a lot of our stuff. I felt as if they thought it didn't count for anything, that they could casually chuck it all away.' She felt ridiculously close to tears. '*And . . .*' she added, summoning up a bit of fury, 'Sorrel still lives there! When she goes off travelling, where's she going to come back *to*?'

The terrifying word 'You?' hovered unsaid between the two women. Imagine, Clover thought, Sean's reaction to the news that they were to give house-room to a moody teenager and all her chaotic possessions. She daren't so much as put that possibility into words, not even to Mary-Jane.

A dawn chorus trilled out from Mary-Jane's soft, buttery and so envy-provoking Mulberry bag and she delved in to find her phone. She checked the caller ID and switched off, slinging the phone impatiently back in her bag. 'It's Polly, no surprise,' she said. 'Bugger. I wish Lance had never given her that stupid little phone. What does a seven year old need one for?'

Clover rather thought it was for what Polly was almost certainly doing now – calling to insist that, in spite of what every harassed early-morning mother promised, she didn't feel at all better just because she'd gone into school. But yes, why *had* she got a phone with her in school at her age? Her little brain would fry and, worse, every child in her class would be demanding one, starting with Sophia.

'Quick, let's get out of here before Mrs Thing comes out of the class and sees I'm still within catching distance. I can really do without Poll around me today – I've got *loads* to do.' And Mary-Jane was round the front of Clover's car and in through the Touareg's passenger door before Clover had a chance to go through the polite motions of offering her a lift. Clover looked back across the playground as she started the engine in case Polly was actually there, standing on the main-door steps, in pain and weeping. How awful it would be for the poor child to see her own mother being driven away at bank-robber speed rather than rushing back in to scoop her up and take her back home for a day's sympathetic cherishing.

'You don't mind dropping me off back at mine, do you, sweetie?' Mary-Jane settled back in her seat. 'We've got a new nanny coming for an interview. I've got a little job starting in a few weeks – chauffeuring Wimbledon tennis players around. It's for three and a bit weeks, including training. So, cross fingers, this new girl absolutely needs to be The One.'

'You said that last time!' Clover laughed. Mary-Jane's nanny-disasters were well known: the cheery one from Newcastle had been arrested for shoplifting (how useful Jakey's fancy three-wheel stroller had turned out to be, equipped like a Barbour jacket with enough pockets to hide half the John Lewis cosmetics counters), the posh Cotswold one had had sex with the Fed-Ex delivery man in Mary-Jane's bed and at least two idle souls had quit after a mere week, finding that the care of two small children in a terminally untidy household was simply too much hassle.

'I don't know why you don't have a nanny too, Clover. It would free up so much of your time.'

What *did* Mary-Jane do with all this time? Clover wondered. It certainly wasn't housework and she didn't have a regular job to go to or even a dog to walk. She was quite scruffy too, albeit in an attractive, jeans-and-quirky-tops sort of way. It was one of the things Clover liked about her. A lot of the other mummies seemed so positively hell-bent on achieving personal yumminess that you'd think their skin would be exfoliated to bone level. Clover slicked ruinously costly Crème de la Mer across her face and indulged a passion for having her nails done but didn't spend hours having hot-stone massages or hay-wraps or Restylane treatments. She kept her blonde hair at convenient shoulder-length so it could be tied back or piled up or scuzzed about for maximum sexiness if Sean needed reminding that she was the one he was supposed to fancy but it didn't take much hairdressing effort beyond the usual four-weekly trim. Mary-Jane's hair was spiky, as if she had had a bad fright. Clover had heard she cut it herself. So it certainly wasn't pampering that took up all her time. Perhaps Mary-Jane climbed back into bed and read trashy novels till it was time to collect Jakey from pre-school. How lovely to do that, Clover thought, imagining the guilty bliss of a daytime duvet. How wonderful to have so little conscience. Clover was amazed Mary-Jane had found herself a job at all – even for just a few weeks. She didn't seem to need the money. No one with children at St Hilary's *seemed* to need money. This job's appeal couldn't have anything to do with sharing closed-in car-space with staggeringly fit champion sportsmen, could it? Surely not. Or was school-hours sex the time-consuming little hobby of Mary-Jane's that Clover didn't know about?

'I don't really need a nanny,' Clover said. 'Not since Elsa's been at Toddle-Tots. What would the poor girl do all morning? What does yours do?'

'Children's laundry, their lunch, shopping, you'd think of something. And then in the afternoon she takes Jakey to his various activities, cooks their supper. I can usually get them to do my ironing as well, when they've got a moment. I find it terribly hard to manage without one,' Mary-Jane said, yawning. 'I really hope today's candidate is worth missing my Pilates session for.'

Clover had actually considered employing someone so that she could find herself a part-time job. Perhaps Home Comforts would take her on for a few mornings a week. It would be so lovely to get back to handling and choosing fabrics again, not to mention the staff discount on anything she might need for when that little house in the sun became reality. But Sean had been adamant – not to mention crudely basic – about not having someone living in. 'We'd never get any shagging time,' he'd complained. 'We'd be sure to get one with ears like a bat. I don't want some dolly grinning at me in a knowing way over breakfast.'

Clover could have suggested getting one who lived out, but in fact she wouldn't have minded someone within listening distance. It might force Sean to be a bit less vocal in bed. She sometimes wondered if he'd been a cowboy in an earlier life, the way he whooped and hollered during sex. It could be so off-putting. Never mind a nanny, in a year or so it would be Sophia giving him the knowing looks and Clover a permanent blush of shame. Her own qualms about employing a nanny were that there'd be someone around all the time seeing what she did all day, which was actually, perhaps like Mary-Jane, far too little. Daniella came in and did the cleaning twice a week, and did it so thoroughly, silently and competently that Clover's domestic input was whittled down to being merely concerned with chauffeuring the girls to gym club, ballet, Penguin swimmers, violin, extra maths, Monkey Music and *Bébé France*. She obviously dealt with food (and even that was mostly ordered on-line and delivered, thanks to Ocado) and there were the ever-growing heaps of clothes the girls seemed to need. It wasn't so much a nanny they needed as a wardrobe mistress. Not that they could probably afford one now anyway, not since Sean had thrown in that terrifying spanner about work taking a downturn. She prayed they'd at least be all right for the school fees: how mortifying it would be to have to give a term's notice and then slap on a brave face every day at the school gate. Whatever protests you made about a sudden political commitment to state education, all the mummy-radar would home in on exactly what your financial score was.

Clover dropped Mary-Jane off at her house and watched her de-code the lock on the high wrought-iron security gate, then pick her way along her untidy, lavender-strewn garden path, side-stepping three cats, a jumble of small bicycles and several overflowing bags of hedge-clippings. The casual domestic chaos reminded Clover of home – not of the bright, ordered house where she lived with Sean and their daughters but of Holbrook House and her muddy, happy childhood. It hurt, this sad, bitter feeling that her whole life's comfort-base could be about to vanish for ever. She'd trusted it would always be there – not for anything specific but . . . just in case. It wasn't a grown-up feeling; it wasn't worthy and it wasn't generous but it hurt. She bit her lip and carefully executed a tidy three-point turn. What was it that life coach (last year's must-do-better attempt, Sean's idea) had told her? Always concentrate on the results you wanted, think only of that successful solution to any problem. She needed to snap herself out of this mood. Carefully she visualized herself a few minutes from now, pulling up in her own driveway, opening the shiny pink front door and stepping onto the seagrass carpet in the hallway. Out loud she told herself, 'Now I'm going *home*. I'm going to my *own home*.' It almost worked: she focused on the new Brora cashmere catalogue she'd left on the console table in the hall and on the silver-framed photos of her daughters that would smile up at her, remind her who loved her most in the world. That's better, these were her people, the ones she'd made. *Her* family. *Her* home.

She would make a cake. This calm, pale, silent house would fill with the snug scent of baking and chocolate to comfort and steady her. And later she'd choose something lovely from the Brora catalogue as she ate a soft, sticky slice. Cashmere and cake, was there ever such a perfectly soothing combination?

# SEVEN

So. It seemed she and Mac weren't the only ones with plans to sell up. As Lottie went through the gates to the road on her way to visit Susie at the gallery in the village, possibly with a view to offloading some surplus paintings from the house, she could see a new For Sale sign across the road outside the old Major's house on the green. So where's he off to, at his time of life? Lottie wondered. He must be at least eighty-five, probably older. She hoped it was a move he'd chosen, rather than one forced on him by age and infirmity. She liked to imagine he was going back to Sri Lanka, to recapture the sparkling times of his youth where he'd enjoyed a glamorous colonial social life of racy cocktails and silky ladies. If where he was heading was a care home, well, there were plenty in the area to choose from. Recently, driving from London, Lottie thought that if

someone blindfolded her and took her for a six-hour winding drive in a dark lorry, she'd have no problem at all
recognizing Surrey when at last allowed to look out of the
window. Surely no other county in England was so over-
provided with garden centres, nursing homes and – for
some mad reason – boarding kennels and catteries. The
area must attract people from miles around in search of
every kind of pedigree kitten from Abyssinian to Siamese,
and a place to park their dogs for the holidays.

Now she and Mac were planning to leave the place,
Lottie felt as if she was looking at her surroundings for
close to the last time. Alongside the Major's house, a row
of gloomy leylandii (another Surrey speciality) had
sprouted new growth, surely taking it way beyond bear-
able heights. Not that she'd complain. That had been the
Major's hobby. He had taken years to come to terms with
the appalling scandal of having Mac living in the village,
considering all popular music people to be of the same
shockingly deep depravity. He'd done a lot of muttering
about standards and what-were-things-coming-to and he
probably wasn't alone in his thinking either, for at one time
during the 70s, a rock musician was a Surrey must-have. Just
about every village had one in residence, like a mascot. Their
function was to be fodder for dinner-party gossip by driving
expensive cars into swimming pools, landing helicopters on
the village greens and seducing pink-faced Pony Club
daughters fresh out of boarding-school. It was a terrible local
let-down when they behaved well and took up golf or
merely pottered around quietly minding their own business
and becoming a fixture on the pub quiz team as Mac did.

'Your COCK woke me at FOUR!' The furious voice of the Major jolted Lottie out of her thoughts. The stocky, bull-headed man stormed out at an impressive pace from behind the leylandii and stood in his gateway as Lottie approached. He must have been watching for her. Maybe he had some sort of tracking device that triggered when-ever the electronic gates of Holbrook House opened. Lottie tried not to laugh – he reminded her of an elderly version of Grant Mitchell from *EastEnders*, about to order her – with menaces – out of the Queen Vic.

'Sorry, Major, but I can't do much about it. Crowing at dawn is what they do.'

'Get rid of the bugger, that's what you can do! Eat him!'

'Well, he's very old. He'd be a bit tough.' She tried a reasonable approach. 'He's kept in a dark hen-house at night – that's the best I can do, I'm afraid. It's just nature.'

'Nature! This is Surrey, not the wilds of bloody Dartmoor! We don't want "nature" and the racket it makes shoved in our faces!' the Major ranted, getting into a familiar stride. What had it been last time? Lottie tried to remember. Ah yes, Gaz's car, pimped up with a go-faster exhaust of ear-splitting volume and roaring away from the house at 2 a.m. There, she'd admit, the Major had had a point. And before that it had been Adrian from Treescapes, up an oak by the gates with a chain-saw, taking out a rotten and potentially lethal branch. The Major had sent the con-servation people round about that, citing planning laws and talking about wilful destruction, only to find all permissions had been properly granted.

'Nothing but trouble . . .' the Major now muttered.

'Hey, look, it's not for long,' Lottie soothed. How surprisingly easy it was to be kind to the moody old man, now that they were leaving.

'What do you mean, not for long? Don't tell me you're actually going to kill the bloody thing, just when I'm off to Eastbourne for the peace and quiet!' The Major's long nose almost quivered with curiosity. He looked pleased at the prospect of rooster-slaughter.

'Kill the chicken? No. Well . . . I hadn't actually thought about the hens yet. I suppose they'll have to have a new home somewhere.' Lottie mentally added the livestock to her list of things to be dealt with. It was becoming a very long one.

'No, it's us – we're thinking about selling up, moving on.' She'd said it now. Lottie realized, the second the words were out, that the news would be all round the village by the afternoon. The place might be bigger on fancy gift shops, antiques and delicatessens than on corner-shop gossip-exchanges but when it came to house sales, every resident pricked up their ears, agog as to what could be price-tagged at that magic million-plus and what couldn't. Telling the old man was more than passing on a bit of information – it was a commitment of the no-going-back sort.

'Ah! So where are you going? And when?' he asked. He seemed quite pleased about that too. She'd made his day.

Lottie laughed. 'To the first question I'll have to admit I don't quite know. Everywhere and anywhere we fancy, I think. We thought we'd see what's going on in the world. And to the second, I suppose we'll go as soon as someone wants to buy the house.'

'Hmm . . .' The Major shuffled his feet and looked doubt-ful. 'I hope you'll be, you know, careful about . . . Well, I mean, I just hope the buyer . . .'

Lottie waited patiently for him to choose his words, wondering how he was going to get across what he actually meant (which was: make sure you sell it to the Right Sort) without actually being thoroughly offensive. Perhaps she'd suggest a high-profile footballer had shown an interest, just to stir up the village into collective excitement.

'Of course . . . um . . . we'll, er . . . you'll be missed and all that,' he mumbled. Lottie looked at him closely, wondering if she'd heard him right. He looked ancient suddenly, rheumy of eye and his face randomly sprouted with whiskers, a sign of failing eyesight and having no one to prompt his grooming efforts. He went on, gruffly, 'I know we haven't exactly seen eye to eye about everything. You young people—'

'Not young any more,' Lottie pointed out gently. 'Not that young for a while now.' She and Mac would go on their travels and when they came back the ancient Major might be back in the village, but this time alongside his wife under the yew in the churchyard.

'I'll miss you, Major,' she suddenly said, giving him a swift kiss on the cheek. 'You haven't been such a bad neighbour. After all,' she laughed, wondering what he'd make of her word choice, '*your* cock never woke me before dawn.'

'Yo, Sorrel! I hear you're flying off to Oz in September. Everything's, like, *soooo* sweet for you li'l rich girls, innit?

You don't have to slave for months in some crap job saving up the air fare like the rest of us.' Carly did a bit of her trademark queen-bee blonde hair-tossing as she looked round her circle of loyal allies and was rewarded with a collective snigger of support.

'*Some* of us have to pay rent at home as well as save up for travelling.' Carly's second-in-command Rosie got in quick with her back-up contribution and Sorrel, who had been crossing the canteen with Millie on her way to the lunch counter, stopped to see if the rest of this alpha-girl group had anything to add. They were, as at every lunchtime, gathered like a leggy coven round their prime window-side table on which the only evidence of food was three low-fat yoghurt cartons and the arch-minger Stacey's empty family-size Doritos bag (possibly not the easiest lunch choice for someone who'd deliberately sicked up every school meal since Year Eight. Perhaps she liked a challenge). Sorrel's thinking was that she might as well get this bitching session over with in one go. These things dragged on otherwise and she could be fielding spiky little digs for the next few weeks till the A levels were over. Not what you needed a few minutes before you had to come up with your best-ever reasoning as to why, exactly, Othello thought it a great idea to murder his wife. Gaz must have been shooting his mouth off again, telling them about her plans to go away straight after the summer. If it was him, they'd know everything by now, from the universal sink plug on her packing list to all the stuff she'd bought in Top Shop, right down to colour and size.

'I can't go off travelling at all – I've got to bank what I

earn to pay my own way through uni *and* get a job when I get there.'

Sorrel looked with derision at the girl who'd just spoken. 'Polly, you need to take Kwells just to get the train from Guildford to Waterloo. No way would you choose to travel the world. Or have you got a new hobby, collecting sick-bags?'

'Nice one, Sorrel.' Millie laughed.

'OK, anyone else got anything to say?' Sorrel asked calmly. 'Anyone with a terminally ill mother to support, a house they've got to rescue from repossession? Couple of orphan cousins to raise?'

'We were only saying, like, you're *sooo* lucky, Sorrel, that's all.' Carly put on her best hurt and misunderstood face, the one she'd perfected over the school years for the benefit of teachers who might dare to accuse her of talking too much in class, of putting less than her best effort in to homework, or of reeking of cigarettes after every break time. 'So are you flying first class, then?' Carly added.

'Well of course I am. And there'll be a guard of honour and a limo waiting for me at Sydney airport. What d'you think?' Sorrel snapped.

Why did they do this? Why hadn't they grown out of it after seven bloody years in this place? It had always been that same little cluster of stupid, bitching girls. Sorrel wasn't the only one they picked on – though it had reached a peak after Christmas when she'd passed her driving test and got her car. Maybe she should have held out for an old-style rusty Mini but that was devoted dads for you, they just wanted you to be the safest, even if it meant she got crap from the school divas for driving something so offensively new. You also got it from this lot if you were too poor, too fat, too clever, too blonde, too sexy. Obviously not if you were too dumb though, or they would have to start on each other. How had they scraped together enough GCSEs to get on to the A-level courses when they clearly had IQs smaller than their bra sizes in inches?

'C'mon, Sorrel, I'm starving. They'll run out of chips if we're not quick.'

Millie pulled on her friend's arm and Carly grinned, triumphant. 'Yeah, go on, Sorrel, go and stuff your face. Charge it to your platinum Amex.' Carly's entourage laughed long and loud with their pout-painted mouths wide open showing flawless teeth and greying knots of half-chewed gum.

'Bunch of slags,' Millie muttered as the two girls walked away. 'They're so not funny. They're just jealous – no change there.'

'I know,' Sorrel said, feeling miserable. 'But why are they so pathetic? Why do they think I'm loaded? My family just so *isn't*. They should see our house – it's falling to bits around us.' She felt in need of comfort and chose both pasta and chips to go with a token bit of salad and sod Jamie Oliver.

'Yeah, but to be fair, it is mega-big and kind of historic and grand. Plus you're one of those girls who looks annoyingly fantastic without making any real effort *and* you drive that black Mini *and* you're going out with Gaz. Carly wanted Gaz. Still does – you saw her at Tasha's eighteenth, practically oozing herself over him.'

Sorrel giggled. 'I think I'll tell her she can have him, and then, when she has – because he's not going to say no to her, is he, not when it's on a plate and she's in that denim micro-skirt? – I'll get her on her own and come over all girl-to-girl and tell her he's left us both with a nasty little infectious problem that needs clearing up.'

'Excellent! I've still got some of those flyers they gave us after that sexual health reminder-lecture last year. You can give her the phone number.'

'Better yet, I'll make an appointment for her and offer to drive her there – make sure she goes!'

Millie thought for a moment. 'Yeah, but then you won't have Gaz any more. Wouldn't you miss him? And who'll you go travelling with? I can't go – I don't want a gap year. Med school is long enough as it is without taking time out as well.'

Sorrel sighed. 'I'm not that sure if he's really serious about going. He likes the idea but he's not what you'd call organized. And he's broke – everything he gets he spends on computer games and stupid pimping-up toys for his car. But anyway,' and she laughed, 'I could always tag along with my folks. They're selling the house and spending the dosh going round the world. And, hey, Carly would love this – they really *are* talking about going first class!'

'Mad! Mad but brilliant! Are they serious? Where will you all live after the trips are done?'

'Who knows? Up a tree or something.' Sorrel arranged her chips in sunflower petal formation round the edge of her plate. 'They're always serious – at first. They were serious about the restaurant; then Mum was serious about the gallery in the village – the one she sold to Susie Granger – and serious when she gave up on that and did painting for a couple of years till the house filled up with horrible sticky canvases that we've mostly still got because nobody wanted to buy them. Now they're both serious about their herbs and their vegetables and being self-sufficient if you don't count having to buy in the meat and the fish. Plus stuff in tins and pasta.'

'And loo rolls and washing powder and tea-bags and wine and just about everything else?'

'Yeah – my parents' idea of self-sufficiency is a bit lacking. Or was. I guess they're over that phase now. Still, I'm just glad they didn't decide that keeping a couple of pigs would be a great idea. They'd probably have let them into the house in winter and have them sleeping in front of the fire. You're right about mad though. It's highly possible that I'll come back from travelling and not have anywhere to live. I just hope they leave their new address with Clover.'

'Chips *and* pasta, Sorrel? Tut tut!' Carly commented snidely as she swaggered past, leading her team out of the canteen.

'Chips, chips, straight to your hips,' two of Carly's minions chorused as they passed.

'God – who'd think they were eighteen and not eight?' Millie said.

'What, Carly and friends or my parents?' Sorrel spluttered. 'Because sometimes, Mills, when it comes to my family, I do wonder.'

\*

Mac's studio was the one bit of Holbrook House that was truly up to twenty-first-century standards. Separate from the house and alongside the back terrace, it had once been a barn then was later converted to a five-car garage until Mac had concluded that he wasn't the type to collect cars, especially the kind that needed indoor pampering. What was the point of having a Cadillac under a tarpaulin? Or a Ferrari that simply begged some envious waster to run a key along its body-work every time you parked it in a street? Toys like that drew attention. Mac had had plenty of that onstage – you didn't want people gawping at you twenty-four/seven. Even at Charisma's peak, he preferred, when not actually performing, to be Joe Normal. The garage had been rebuilt and fitted out as every rock musician's must-have accessory: a fully equipped recording studio. Most of his original kit had been sold off several years before. The days of needing a full-scale mixing desk and ninety-six track recorder together with a selection of wardrobe-sized synthesizers were long gone and he could produce all the sounds he wanted using a simple Macintosh computer, a Yamaha Clavinova, his beaten-up Steinway grand and a couple of old favourite guitars. All the same, the studio room still smelled authentically businesslike – a mixture of new wood, warmed-up electronics and the faint, ingrained scent of old coffee and cigarettes. If he closed his eyes he could easily conjure up a memory of studio two at Olympic and Eric Clapton playing table football in the studio kitchen. In here he kept the gold discs, the framed *Billboard* listing from the time the band topped both the US singles and album charts, his

Ivor Novello songwriting awards and various other bits of Charisma memorabilia that Lottie considered far too naff to have in the house.

'I'm not having that lot in the downstairs loo like some kind of shrine to the glory days,' she'd declared when Mac had had the builders in to update the studio and he had jokingly suggested, after being impressed by a visit to the Long Room in the Lord's pavilion, having a trophy cabinet built. And so Mac's past successes were displayed on the studio shelves, reminding him uncomfortably that such a lot of time (and an awful lot of money) had vanished since he'd last achieved anything of note – either musical or otherwise. He was pretty glad now about Lottie's loo-ban. He could quite easily face the evidence of how decidedly the best part of his career was over in the once or twice a week he ventured into the studio: being reminded every time he went for a pee would be just too much.

Mac would not, if he was honest, be able to claim these days that he could still put down 'songwriter' under the heading 'Occupation', even though his work still turned up on the world's radio playlists often enough to provide a good (if alarmingly dwindling) income. He'd still have put it on his passport, if it had been required, for old times' sake and for the small, rare ego-stroke of having immigration officials ask him if he'd written anything famous. He had never admitted to it for car insurance, as he knew from bitter experience that it would draw only a sharp intake of breath from the other end of the phone and either an eye-watering quote or a swift refusal on grounds of unacceptable risk. He'd always wondered exactly what it was about musicians that gave them such a reputation among insurers. It didn't seem to matter whether you played a disciplined double bass in a symphony orchestra or were Keith Richards – apparently anyone who strung a few notes together for a living was tarred with the same wayward brush. Was it a simple matter of a collective reputation for drink, drugs and women? Did that mean that highest-level sportsmen could insure, say, a top-of-the-range Mercedes for about thirty quid simply because they tended to have early nights and a whole-food, temperate diet?

Such ramblings of thought occupied Mac as he strummed his old Martin guitar in the hanging egg-chair in the studio. It wasn't a bad song, this new thing he was working on. He'd become very fond of it and out of the half dozen he'd demo'd in the past few months this was definitely the most promising. It was possibly heading towards being one of his best ever, or could be once it had had a bit more of a work-up. It was still at the early stage where it could go either way. He'd got the melody down with a basic backing track and had written some canny lyrics but it could all come to nothing if he couldn't place it with someone capable of taking it to the dizzy heights.

Mac flicked a few switches and played back what he'd done so far, leaning back in his chair, eyes closed. Not for Robbie at all now he listened again, but certainly one of those cute girl bands could do it justice, if he could find one with a bit of an edge.

Mac yawned and stretched and clicked the computer on to the Charisma website and the link to the guestbook and recent comments. He didn't much want to read fans' e-mails. Frankly, there shouldn't be any – what sort of people clung to the memory of a long-past band? Sometimes you just didn't want to know there were all these sorry loners out there thinking they might find the meaning of life or that the reason they couldn't get a shag was there in your old lyrics. He imagined these not-so-young men (never the not-so-young women; it seemed they moved on far more successfully from their musical pasts and were out there having a real life), holed up in stuffy bedrooms that smelled of socks and french fries. He saw them Googling as if their lives depended on it, imagining a teeny fleck of stardust would descend on them if they got an e-mail through to their ageing hero who might, if their query had been entertainingly enough phrased, send a personal reply. Mac rarely did – it was a mistake he'd made in the eager early internet days when he'd felt bound by politeness not to ignore questions that seemed innocently enough asked. That way lay the stalkers and loons who questioned whether a comma accidentally inserted into a new print-out of lyrics was 'significant'. These were the kind of crazies who'd come round and torch your car out of pique over an unanswered e-mail.

'Is it true that "Target Practice" is being re-released?' he read from Johnno – one of the regulars. That was the fourth time that question had come up recently. They seemed to think there might be some connection with a Keanu Reeves movie. He didn't know where they'd got that one from. No one had told him, though he was due for a meeting with Doug, the band's former manager, in a couple of weeks. Why didn't these people have better things to do?

Feeling unaccountably grumpy, Mac closed down the computers, locked up the studio and went off towards the long border. There were tomatoes to feed, lettuces to thin out . . . a journey to plan. He looked back at the H-shaped house from the far side of the terrace. There were rooms on the top floor he hadn't been in for at least a couple of years. Each wing on its own could accommodate an entire family at a push. Part of the first-floor area was equipped with a perfect, barely used Smallbone kitchen *circa* 1987 from when Clover had gone through her late-teen phase of wanting a separate (though bills-paid) life. Sorrel hadn't wanted it – she liked her snug, messy lair way up under the east gable. Whatever were he and Lottie doing now, rattling around in a seven-bedroom, five-bathroom house? When Sorrel had gone on her travels, and then presumably to university, the two of them might just as well move into the studio and let the rest of the place fall into the landscape. Or be a fabulous family home for some-one else. It felt right, this idea of selling and moving on. Time to go, he thought, testing out whether this made him feel sorrowful. It didn't. In fact, he could feel his spirits instantly lift at the very idea. *Wonder if Lottie will think of phoning estate agents?* he thought, tramping on towards the vegetables.

'They'll be biting your hand off. You'll have agents queuing down past the primary school once they know your house is up for sale.'

It was reassuring to have friends like Susie, a person

who always saw only the upside of life. Lottie, enjoying a lunchtime glass of white wine in the stockroom at the back of Susie's gallery, was very much in need of this kind of reassurance.

'It's not the agents I want queueing – it's buyers. I think they'll take one look inside the front door and run a mile. I know I would. There's so much *stuff*.'

'Rubbish! It's only a matter of . . .'

Susie hesitated and Lottie leaped in, laughing. 'See – even you have your doubts! I know what it takes to get the punters interested; I've watched all those property pro-grammes where some know-all breezes in and says, "Hey look, this place will be fine if you simply get absolutely every surplus item out and paint it all cream and caramel." Holbrook just is not a cream-and-caramel kind of house. And what are they going to make of the black walls in the sitting room?'

Susie was a woman who, decor-wise, could spend an hour on the exact arrangement of one single perfect dahlia and a pebble. That she would allow more than one paint-ing at a time on the walls of her gallery was ever a surprise to her friends. When Lottie had owned it, the place had been an absolute crash of colours – the more vibrant the better. Artists soon came to know that if they wanted her to sell their work, there was no point in turning up with a selection of gloomy, doomy offerings. No wonder it hadn't done too well in her hands – she hadn't exactly catered for all tastes. Susie, on the other hand, was doing brilliantly. She understood the terms subtle, minimal and pared-down – perfect for Surrey. She certainly understood cream and caramel – it was a standard she lived by and dressed by – and was not a person who would fully comprehend the vast task Lottie faced. If a fire broke out in Susie's house she would be ready to climb out of her bedroom window with a small bag of essential cosmetics and a capsule wardrobe by the time the firemen had got their ladder up.

'I was going to say,' Susie went on, 'that it's probably just a simple matter of hiring people to do a thorough tidy-up. Surely it wouldn't take much more than that? What about that wonderful cleaner you've got?'

'Ah well, Mrs Howard has her routine,' Lottie told her. 'She's brilliant with the vacuum cleaner and floor polish but would definitely think helping to sort thirty years of accumulated possessions a responsibility too far. And she'd be right really – I mean only Mac and I and the family can decide what to keep and what to chuck. We'll have to get a skip. Possibly two. Do they come in fleets?'

Susie looked as if she didn't quite understand, but then she was a woman whose holiday photos actually made it into albums rather than being bundled into a drawer for the kind of sorting out that comes under 'one day, when there's time'. Lottie bit her lip. That was just the photos she'd thought of. You had to multiply that by the children's entire school art-work output, the cupboards full of old fabric from the time she'd thought (wrongly) faux-vintage silk dresses were going to be the next fashion must-have and a room crammed full of books that were quite possibly being eaten away by some kind of paper moth.

She took a large, comforting gulp of wine as Susie continued brightly, 'And once everything's sorted, well, then you could have a look at what you really need and what you don't and carry on from there.'

Lottie sighed, feeling the burden of the word 'sorted'. Easy to say, another thing to achieve. It would take months. And by then, the momentum would all be lost. Mac would have settled into winter mode, curling up like a cat in the warm studio in the afternoons with a guitar and a seed catalogue and possibly a vague plan for yet another career-change. No – that wasn't going to happen.

Lottie swigged down the last of her wine and stood up. 'Right. Nothing's going to happen unless it happens – I'm going down to Digby, James and Humphreys to talk house sales. It's time to take out that half page in *Country Life*.'

# EIGHT

Ilex didn't mind hanging out in the pub at lunchtime with Simon from the office but the incredibly slow pace at which he liked to amble along on the way back did irritate him. Perhaps it was because Simon was a bit on the short side, smaller steps and all that, though it couldn't be the whole reason. Manda was about the same height but perfectly capable of getting along at a cracking pace even if she was wearing serious heels.

'Listen, I do have to get back pretty quickly today.' Ilex tried to gee him up. 'I've got those Pilgrim Prospect guys coming to see me about putting their new riverside block on the market.' He looked at his watch and wondered how rude it would be to gallop on ahead, leaving Simon to wander along gazing into shop windows at his own re-flection and fiddling with his upswept executive hairstyle.

'Oh yeah – marketing advice. The stuff we're supposed to be good at.' Simon laughed with little sincerity. 'Got some new ideas lined up?'

Ilex shrugged. 'Nothing new. It's all been done to death, all those developments with show-off gyms and parking for the must-have second Porsche. There's no original angle left that I can come up with if the advertising bods can't. If I hear one more twat in a Paul Smith suit and over-gelled hair banging on about "buying into the lifestyle" I'm going to have to deck him.'

Simon slowed even more and flicked a look at himself in Starbucks' window. If ever there was a guy who would nominate himself as the Ideal Date, this was surely your man, Ilex thought. Did he spend hours in front of his bath-room mirror, telling himself how adorable he was? Still, Ilex considered him an easy enough office companion. He didn't complain or smell or upset the women. He could talk football but was not obsessed. And he was good at his job, though not so good that he was going to overtake Ilex for any promotion that might be going. So he was all right really, Ilex conceded, trying once more to force up the walking pace.

'They're aiming at the wrong market, that's where they're falling down,' he said. 'They're still on that thing of going for the young city types, as if they're the loaded ones.'

'Well, aren't they?'

'Not any more, not the new lot. Life's too expensive for them now. This new wave are all stuck with student debts, expensive social lives and a taste for lots of hot, boozy holidays. It's the older market they should be going for, would be my opinion, if anyone would listen. Our parents' generation.'

Ilex was convinced this was true and was absolutely certain he could offload an entire block of glass and concrete double-height duplexes onto the newly retired baby-boomer generation if a developer would just give him total charge of the advertising budget. With that, plus a couple of paragraphs of editorial in the weekend property supplements, he'd be willing to bet serious money he'd have sold signs stuck to every window in the Pilgrim development within a week. And there you'd have it, a block full of ageing ravers, cultivating connoisseur cannabis in garden-centre gro-bags on the wrap-around terrace and annoying the crap out of passers-by, playing Free, Led Zeppelin and Jimi Hendrix at top volume.

Simon was looking doubtful. 'Yeah, but how do you pitch the market? For a start, you'd have to do the photo-shoot all different. Strip out the pink suede sofas and shagging rugs and bring in the floral chintz.' He laughed. 'And they'd want net curtains!'

Ilex gave him a pitying look. 'Do you really think people who were young in the sixties are really net-curtain types? Can you see Mick Jagger with net curtains? Even I know better than that.'

It was depressing, the stereotyping that went on. Older people had big, expensive properties to trade in. (Look at his own parents and their half-arsed travel plans, which reminded him – they hadn't called him yet for advice about the sale. If they were going to ask anyone about sorting it, surely it should be him?) It was older ones whose families had grown and flown who were ripe for persuasion to downsize that old five-bed villa in the outer suburbs, move further into town where the getting about was easier and cheaper and have change of a six-figure sum, no problem. But it wasn't sexy enough for the big boys wondering what to do with their surplus, unsold buildings. Oh no. Whenever the term 'grey pound' came up everyone under forty simply shut down their brains. Pink pound, yes, that always pressed the right cash-register buttons. That was good, with its associations of skincare for boys, hip designs and lots of child-free spending power. Grey pound was bad – think inadequate pensions, incontinence pads, stairlifts and the smell of boiled cabbage. Wrong, wrong, wrong. Perhaps he was in the wrong job. Maybe his parents had the right idea and he and Manda should just chuck it all in and take off round the world too.

'Well, good luck – if you can think of a way of getting those Pilgrim places off their hands, you'll be in line for a whopping bonus,' Simon said. 'Listen, why don't you go on ahead? I've got dry-cleaning to pick up.' Simon came to a stop outside Scrubs, checked his hair yet again in the reflecting doorframe and went inside.

Why didn't he bloody say earlier? Ilex thought grumpily. He crossed the road quickly, narrowly missing being run down by a motorcycle courier who swerved over-dramatically and gave him the finger.

'And you, mate,' he muttered, at the same time catching sight of something immediately cheering, further along the pavement, just outside the Tesco Metro store.

The uniformed female police officer had parked her patrol car on a double yellow in front of a Volvo estate, which she now peered into for clues as to the sort of driver who would so carelessly leave it here, disrupting the smooth flow of traffic. She was bending forward just a bit, her over-generous, blue-trousered rump displayed to perfection. Swap trousers for a tiny, tight skirt and she'd be a ringer for page sixty in this month's *Fuzz*. Ilex, all thoughts of his meeting blanked from his mind, paused and watched, holding his breath as if the slightest sign that he was there would scare her off. For him, this rated up there on the thrill-scale with David Attenborough suddenly spotting lion cubs playing in a bush clearing. He almost wished it were still the thing to do to have shoes with laces so he'd have an excuse to stop and retie them and indulge in a really good stare. Instead, he loitered awkwardly outside Boots alongside a window display of Safe Tanning Essentials. He was just about close enough to see a nice bit of visible panty line as the policewoman's polyester trousers stretched against her flesh. So, not for her a cheese-wire thong under those heavy-duty keks. Good. He'd be willing to bet she was also wearing a sturdy sports bra, all the better for comfortable running when a suspect made a bolt for it. He crept a bit closer, past Boots' doorway and to the second window (Travel-Size hair products – three-for-two). Now he could clearly see she'd got all the accessories – the handcuffs, the chunky stick, the rather too big radio, even the gloves were there, supple black leather dangling from a back pocket even though the day was a warm one. She was obviously a stickler for details. He'd love to see all that lot kind of dismantled, lined up on the chaise longue at the end of his bed. Apart from the hat: as the Tom Jones song went, she could keep her hat on.

'Wotchoo lookin' at?' A bulky teenage girl appeared in front of him, startling him out of his reverie and blocking his view. Her face was strangely large, like a great white balloon, and her hair pulled back so very tightly into a ponytail that her thin, pencilled eyebrows arched crazily. Her wire-thin gold earrings were big enough to be a doll's hula hoop. She stood firm as if she'd been anchored – feet stolidly apart, bare legs pink and mottled from a well-hard no-tights winter of very short skirts.

'You lookin' at me, innit?' She wasn't a quiet girl. Passing heads were turning.

Ilex, who hadn't so much as noticed her till she appeared in his view, stepped back, feeling shaken. 'No, no I'm not looking at you . . . I was . . . um . . .'

'Ere, you! Police-person! Over here – this bloke's bin eyeing me up! Fuckin' *pervert*! He's a paedo, miss, I know him. I've seen him hanging round.'

Well of course she had, he only worked round the corner. Ilex wasn't sure whether to say this or not. Would it make things worse? Passers-by were slowing to watch, as they always did when police were around, taking an interest. He was starting to feel like a road accident. He wished she'd keep her voice down – at this rate he'd end up lynched, hanging from the illuminated Boots sign as a deterrent to all foul-minded men.

The owner of the Volvo (a sleek scrummy-mummy type) raced out of Tesco clutching a four-pint bottle of milk and began plea-bargaining with the police officer. The mummy was half the width but a good four inches taller, all skinny jeans and killer heels and a broad smile of insincere apology that reminded Ilex of Clover when she knew she was going to get away with something. The teenage girl was still there, shouting obscenities at him, and the policewoman looked across, torn between lecturing the pretty mother and dealing with something potentially more serious.

'OK, love, stay right there. And you, sir,' she called. She dismissed the Volvo owner, approached Ilex and out came the radio and the notebook. Ilex felt his blood pressure rising. How difficult was this going to be? And what exactly was it he was supposed to be defending himself against? It certainly wasn't the girl he'd been staring at.

'He was lookin' at me. I seen him. I was in there getting my Bodyforms and he was staring at me in the shop window and when I moved he moved and he was watchin' me, like, really hard?'

The girl's words tumbled out fast and angry and her eyelids flashed up and down so hard that thick flecks of mascara now peppered her moony cheeks.

'I didn't actually—'

'Hold on a moment, sir, I'll come to you in a minute,' the officer interrupted, holding up a hand to stop him. Ilex risked a closer look at her. She wore some make-up, not Manda-quantities for sure but he could see she'd gone to a bit of trouble with some eye shadow and blusher. Short tufts of dark red hair, lightly streaked with bronze, peeked out from under her hat. The hand she held up had no rings, her fingernails were square-cut, short and clean. Ilex felt an increase in excited stirrings and tried shifting his weight about awkwardly in a futile attempt to setting things down. Suppose she noticed? Suppose she thought it was this idiotic girl giving him a stiffy? The front trouser department would surely be the first place to seek out evidence of intent when faced with a potential stalker.

'So you're accusing this man of what, exactly?' the officer asked with professional politeness. 'Is it the same thing you accused that elderly gentleman of last Thursday? And the boy with the guide dog a couple of weeks ago?'

The girl narrowed her eyes and jabbed a blunt finger at Ilex. 'He was lookin'! I don't like people *lookin'*!'

Ilex felt mildly guilty. Of course he *had* been looking – but at the police officer, not at the girl. Would the woman feel as furious as this if she knew? It was highly possible. He felt conscious that he must look as guilty as a schoolboy exam-cheat.

'OK, Charlene, thank you, but you go on your way now and leave me to deal with this.'

The girl hesitated. 'What, like, you're going to arrest him? Don't you need me to—'

'No, really, it's all right, Charlene, I know where you live if I need you again. You can go now and just . . . well, stay safe, OK?'

Charlene pouted and shifted her feet. 'All right, but I know he was *lookin'*. People are always lookin'.' And, giving Ilex a glare that could have slain a vampire, she stalked off, still muttering.

'Thanks. I wasn't looking at her, you know,' Ilex said, cringing at how feeble that must have sounded.

'I know that. Charlene's a silly thing, always coming out with the same line. I think she only does it so we'll give her a lift home. If she doesn't want people to look, she could try wearing a few more clothes – I thought the bare-midriff thing was supposed to be very last year.'

'That's what my girlfriend says too.' Ilex almost bit his tongue off. Buggeration. Why, in the name of Pingu, did he have to bring Manda into this? Was he imagining it or did this officer look disappointed?

'Um ... I'd better get back to work,' Ilex muttered, miserably feeling all excitement drain away. He was late for the meeting now. Not the best start if he wanted to impress the Pilgrim wallahs.

'Oh not yet,' his captor said brightly. 'Young Charlene is still there, across the road, waiting to see me doing my duty by her, so if you don't mind, I'd like you to get into the patrol car.'

Ilex allowed himself to be led away, trying to look suitably penitent but feeling utter joy. He slid into the passenger seat and fastened his seatbelt, watching the broad, taut thighs beside him and the hand that was dealing so firmly with the gearstick.

'Where to?' she asked, smiling at him. 'Do you live round here or just work?'

'Um ... work. On the right, down there, across the square. Property company.'

'Like the job?' Expertly, she pulled away into the traffic. If he asked her nicely, told her he was running late, Ilex thought, would she put the blue light and sirens on for him?

'Not really, it's nothing special.' He felt like a small boy, being questioned by a distant relative. It wasn't a bad feeling – comfortable, mildly sexy. He was sure he could smell the uniform's fabric, a mixture of polyester, acrylic and washing powder. A hint of dry-cleaning fluid, possibly, or was that the scent of Kevlar body armour?

'What would be your idea of the dream job then?'

Ilex thought for a minute, feeling as if he was Helping Police with Enquiries. Ideally she'd have him in a bare, darkened room, across a small cheap table and a cup of lukewarm instant coffee. There'd be a bored constable, shifting his feet over by the door. She would sit opposite him, crossing her legs, getting comfortable, leaning forward . . .

'Perfect job? I'm not sure. When I was growing up I kind of wanted to do something . . . safe, I suppose. So I did.'

'*Safe?*' She laughed. 'Didn't you ever want to be Chelsea's star striker or a rock star or something?'

Ilex felt his bubble of fantasy deflate. Rock star. How to explain that one in the family was more than enough. Was she likely to be the sort who'd understand about the downside? Of looking forward so much to your dad coming home from three months touring in the States, and then having to creep round the house for the first two weeks because he's sleeping most of the day? Or how about the bit where you had a friend round after school and they told you their auntie wanted a signed photos of your dad because she'd always had a bit of a thing for him?

'No, not really,' he said. 'I wasn't much cop at either games or music.' It sounded very lame. He didn't ask what her fantasy job was – she was obviously already doing it.

Only a minute or so later Wendy Murphy, as he now knew her to be, pulled up outside his office building. 'There you go. Stay out of trouble, as they say!' she said brightly.

'Oh . . . er, I don't suppose . . .' What to say now that he'd so stupidly mentioned Manda? No, go for it. 'I don't suppose you'd fancy meeting up for a drink later? Just so I can say thanks?' he blustered, feeling his hands go clammy. She'd be sure to say no. She must meet dozens like him every day. Chancers, nutters, weirdos – how did she tell one sort from another?

'Yes, OK. I'd really like that! What time?'

'About six? I should be finished then . . . I could meet you . . .'

'No, it's fine, I'll pick you up here. I'll be the one in the silly car!'

And it was as easy as that.

Oh Lord, Ilex thought, what have I done?


'See that one, over there with the Prada boots? You know, Caris Potter's mother?' Mary-Jane squinted across the playground. Clover, her mind on what Sean was likely (or not) to get up to, working away overnight yet again, didn't immediately connect and found herself staring instead at the Hugh-Grant-lookalike father of the St Hilary's great hope for a St Paul's scholarship. She blushed, half-smiled and concentrated on working out what Mary-Jane was on about. That was the trouble with keeping too many thoughts going in her head. She really had to learn to work her way through them methodically like one of the lists she was always writing, instead of jumbling everything altogether so haphazardly. Her head was like a big casserole dish into which she stirred the Sean question, upcoming sale of her parents' house, ideas for this summer's family holiday (if they could actually afford one, that is – Rock might be beyond the price range this year. They'd probably end up camping – nightmare) as well as the shopping list for Sophia's vegetable project this week. The children had all been allocated something to bring and Sophia had been chosen to bring in beans: as many types as she could find, which she said was unfair because Tallulah Thomas only had to come up with a cauliflower and Polly was on beetroot. Clover didn't mind at all – she took it rather proudly, as a compliment that she was rated a top mother who could be relied on to come up with the full range of whatever she'd been asked. She'd have been mortified if Sophia had come home saying she was down for a turnip.

'. . . had her teeth completely done. New veneers, a couple of crowns, full-on whitening. She used to look like a dog. No, literally, a *dog*. Fangs like a German shepherd.' Mary-Jane was on a roll, alternately yacking close into Clover's ear while brazenly staring across at her quarry. Clover tried hard to look fascinated. It was difficult to keep up with Mary-Jane – she seemed to have a kind of

*Heat* magazine-type take on every playground mother's on-off looks. Last time it had been Spot the Botox while waiting for the coach to come back from Wednesday netball. Clover quite liked the idea of Botox and had it in mind for five years ahead. By then she wouldn't have to care about being the focus of the mums' mafia speculation – they'd all have had it too, and more.

'So guess how much?' Mary-Jane prodded Clover in the ribs. 'Bearing in mind the attention to detail, down to making the bottom ends of the teeth a big darker, and adding in a little false crack to one of the front ones, for a natural look. Go on, guess!'

'No idea, really.' Clover shrugged, wondering if she was looking at the right mother. She'd found what she was pretty sure were the Prada boots (bit over the top, surely, for mid May, though with those legs they looked great with that little denim skirt), but the woman wasn't baring her expensively imperfect teeth, not even in a smile. You couldn't go up to people, especially ones you had to share school space with for the next several years, and ask them to open their mouths for inspection.

'Couple of thousand?' she suggested.

'*Eleven* and a *half* thousand! That's all!' Mary-Jane shrieked.

'*All?* God, that's mad!' It was crazy, no question. Clover could add a swimming pool to the house in the sun for that. If she ever got the house in the sun. She was back on France again this week, if Sean and finances ever allowed for it. Or maybe she should just do what her parents were doing, sell up the Richmond house and take off, dragging her daughters round the world like universal wanderers. There were people who'd say that would be the best education, rather than being deskbound doing worksheets and test papers in this outer-London exam hothouse. Clover was very confused. All she wished, right now, was that she and Sean had the kind of all-time certain-of-each-other relationship that her parents had. Was it too late now? Had something between them been messed up for ever when he'd cheated on her that time after Elsa was born or should we all be allowed one mistake before the slate is indelibly sullied? She wouldn't run that one past Mary-Jane. It would be all round the school by Thursday week if she did.

'The new nanny's a dream. We're thrilled.' Mary-Jane was still in chat-mode. 'She says she doesn't mind how many she has in the house, because the more you've got the more they entertain each other. I'll take advantage of that while she's still young and keen. I was wondering if you'd like her to pick up Sophia and Elsa on Thursday and they can come for tea with Jakey and Poll? What do you think? It's not a ballet or gym day, is it? Or is it violin? Extra maths?'

'No, no it's not. It's . . . for once, not anything. That'd be great, thanks! And it means I can go down to my folks for the afternoon. They've got the first estate agent coming round to have a look at the house, see what kind of money they're looking at. I wouldn't mind being there.'

'Oh you should definitely be there,' Mary-Anne agreed, 'Make sure they're not getting ripped off. And you of course, too. I mean, it's your inheritance they're cashing in, isn't it? It's not just theirs?' Mary-Jane laughed. 'You want to get in there, girl, stake your claim!'

She sounded like Sean, Clover thought. Why did they think it was all about money?

Clover's phoned trilled and she quickly checked the caller ID: Sean.

'Where are you, darling? Collecting Sophia?' Sean sounded his usual, no-problem self.

'Yeah – I'm outside the school right now,' she replied. 'Sophia's just coming out, with Polly as usual. Are you definitely not back tonight? Are you sure you can't make it home?'

He was in Manchester, sorting a problem with the banqueting company that had been booked for a bi-centenary event for an ancient wool guild.

'Sorry, darlin',' Sean said. 'I'd love to but it's a problem that needs a hands-on approach. There are still people who'd rather see a face than a fax. Now if we had a nanny . . . you could come up here for a couple of days, join me. Think about it.'

His voice went seductive, quieter. She could imagine him in an office, keeping his voice down to talk intimately to her. '. . . swish hotel, a spa, just you and me and a bottle of Cristal and no little girls barging in wanting another glass of water. Like I said, think about it. In fact, you don't need to: why not come anyway? Come now – get your mum to drive up and stay overnight with the girls, why not?'

Sean's obvious eagerness made Clover immediately tingly with longing, tempered by embarrassment that every passing school parent, clucking on their way to their cars about lunch eaten, sports triumphs scored and maths marks gained, was looking at her and knowing she was indulging in adult talk in child-hours. She put a hand to her hot face, flustered by Sean's spontaneous suggestion and the promise of a night of hot, child-free sex.

'Sean, I'd love to, you know I would, but I can't just drop everything . . .'

Sean chuckled. 'It's not everything I want you to drop. Just your best silk knickers. Come on, Clover,' he coaxed her, 'for me? Just a forty-minute shuttle flight away? You could be here by seven. I'll chill the fizz, ready for you.'

Clover dithered. 'Well . . . no, be sensible, Sean, really. Elsa's got ballet and it's Sophia's night for violin practice . . .'

'OK.' He sighed. 'I know which bit of No means No. Don't say I didn't ask though, darlin', will you?' And he was gone.

What was that supposed to mean? Clover gave Sophia a hello hug, took her lunchbox from her and led her safely across the road and into the Touareg. It sounded like a threat. Very much like, 'If you don't want me, I'll find someone who does.' Or was she imagining things?

Quickly, she climbed into the car then took out her mobile again, calling Sean back. Perhaps she could race off and be with him, just for a mad, lust-filled night. She should, in fact. Wasn't she forever reading about the dire consequences of letting a marriage slide into a slough of stale routine? If they were ever to break up, she mustn't let it be through her negligence.

His phone was now switched off. Bugger. She started the car and considered the options. She could keep ringing, or she could simply catch a plane and go and bank on him having switched it back on by the time she got there. Except she didn't actually know (how careless was this?) which hotel he was staying in. It could be that she landed at the airport and his phone was still off and she'd end up spending a miserable night alone in some dismal runway hotel. Or she could do the sensible thing and stay at home, taking care of her daughters as she'd originally planned. After all, it was mid-week. How irresponsible and selfish would running out on them be? And if she went this time, was she supposed to race off round the country every time he was feeling a bit lonely, randy, generally loose-endish? Bordering on tears, for she now so much wanted to go, she stabbed at the phone again; still nothing.

'Clover?' Mary-Jane startled her, rapping on the car window. Clover wound it down.

'I just wondered,' Mary-Jane said, 'as it's such a lovely day, Polly and I were thinking, why don't I do us all a barbecue in my garden later? I've got to take Jakey to Tumble Tots but any time after that. The kids have got the water-slide set up. What do you think?' Polly was bouncing up and down beside her mum, grinning and excited.

'Well . . . I was thinking of . . .' What to say? The truth? She was crazily desperate to get to Manchester for a night of the rare kind of uninhibited passion that you don't often get *post*-babies? She longed to dally with her husband in a vast bath full of bubbles and scented oils, drinking champagne?

'Oh Mum, please let's! I want to go to Polly's! *Please!*'

And that was the thing when you had children; you had to put them first, didn't you? If there was a manual that came with childbirth, that would be the first instruction, right there on page one.

'OK, we'll do that,' Clover agreed. 'I've got a chocolate cake I can bring for pud, with strawberries and ice-cream.'

Sean was a grown-up; he could wait. The children couldn't. There'd be another time.

She hoped.

# NINE

'I think room by room is going to be the best way,' Lottie said, as she, Susie and Clover settled round the kitchen table with coffee and cake to fortify themselves for the daunting task ahead. The agent was booked in for Thursday for a preliminary lookaround and a guess at a valuation, and although there was obviously no chance of having even a single room completely clear and perfect by then, Lottie at least wanted to be able to assure him that she was ready for the challenge.

'I really need to get an idea of what can be thrown away before I start on getting the place ready for buyers to look at properly. Maybe I should have put the agent off till it's ready for viewing. He might take off a hundred thousand on grounds of clutter overload.'

'No, no – they know what they're looking for. They can

see beyond the . . . er . . . evidence of long-term residence. But what you really need is that *Life Laundry* woman,' Susie suggested. 'She'd be far more ruthless than we will. You'd be down to a bed, a sofa and a photo album by the time she'd finished with you. She might let you keep your wedding dress, preserved in framed Perspex!'

'Oh no, you couldn't get her in!' Clover shuddered. 'She lines up everything you possess outside the house and makes you get rid of absolutely all of it, even if you cry and plead. It would be too awful to see the house stripped bare like that.'

She knew it was an exaggeration, but these two had to be discouraged. Susie was so far into minimalism that she only ever wore one colour at a time, accessorized by a single stunning jewellery piece. Today she was in cocoa brown with a bracelet that was a hunk of plain beaten gold, a good five inches wide. If she took over and got into Lottie's head, Lottie would be exuberantly setting fire to the equivalent of a warehouse-load of possessions. Clover was there to make sure Lottie didn't get swayed into thinking that the results of living in a place for thirty-something years added up to no more than a heap of expendable junk.

Lottie and Susie exchanged glances; this was getting them nowhere. Clover, who Lottie had thought she could count on for advice about how best to present the house to potential buyers, had been brought in to be helpful, not to scupper the whole enterprise. She was the one with the interior design experience, after all. Since she'd arrived she'd done nothing but sigh a lot and look sorrowful.

'This is a lovely cake, Clover,' Susie ventured, using the

kind of careful voice that goes down well when encouraging small, reluctant children who hang back at birthday parties. 'You must have used espresso coffee in it. Am I right?'

Clover brightened. 'I did! I'm so glad you can tell! Hardly anyone can. When it says "coffee" in a recipe, most people just mix up a bit of Nescafé. I like it with more bite.'

'It's absolutely gorgeous,' Lottie agreed. 'Your cakes always are. I don't know where you got the baking gene from, because it certainly wasn't me. Can I keep some for Mac and Al? They're down by the paddock, doing something weird to the marrows with paintbrushes. I think they said it's artificial insemination, but that doesn't sound right.'

'Yes, of course, Mum – keep it all! I wasn't going to take it home again with me. There's plenty more in my cupboard for the girls.'

Lottie didn't doubt it. Clover was a prodigious cake-maker. A comfort-baker, she'd have to say. Well, you'd need comfort, being married to Sean. Not a man you could call reliable or entirely trustworthy. Lottie tried but mostly failed to forget that he'd cheated on her daughter when she, newly post-natal, was at her most vulnerable and had the cheek to brush it off as 'just a stupid blip'. He was always sliding out of the door and revving up the BMW for a fast getaway. And did he ever take time off work? Clover only seemed to see him on the occasional evening and Sunday. If he left to live with someone else, she'd barely notice the difference. Perhaps he already had. Lottie couldn't stop herself wondering, now it had crossed her

mind, if he actually had another home and family somewhere else, the way some cats (and apparently some men)
did. No wonder Clover said he was always tired. But presumably the other woman didn't go in for a lot of cake –
otherwise he'd be an awful lot fatter as well.

'Look – how about starting at the top and working our
way down with a big notebook?' Susie suggested. 'Do you
actually use all the top-floor rooms, Lottie?'

'Sorrel has her hovel up there,' Lottie said. 'I think we'd
better leave that for her to sort out.'

'Oh Mum, she'll never do that!' Clover laughed. 'I bet
she puts a lock on the door and won't let anyone in.'

'Well, she'll just *have* to let them in,' Lottie pointed out.
'How can buyers be expected to make an offer if they can't
see the whole place? They might think we're hiding a
massive outbreak of death watch beetle or a mad old
family retainer or something!'

Clover sipped her coffee and said nothing. There didn't
seem any point. Her parents had obviously made up their
minds and were going full steam ahead with the house
sale. They did this, this kind of spontaneous stuff, and too
often the consequences hadn't been pretty. When she was
fifteen they went off to Heal's to buy a sofa but came back
as the new and hyper-excited owners of the Flaming Cow
restaurant in Fulham. That must have been about the time
they made Sorrel as well, probably that very night as a
celebration. A few weeks or months on from now, when
they'd sold this house and realized they'd got nowhere to
live, they were really going to regret it. This house was the
big, beating heart of the whole family. If they'd just talk to

her – the two of them, not with this know-nothing Susie woman hanging about – if they'd just slow down a bit and give it a bit more time, maybe they'd come round to the idea of investing in a lovely little place out in the Dordogne, perhaps quite a big place where all the family could meet up for holidays and celebrations. That way, they'd have somewhere to go when they got all wander-lusty and yet still keep this as a family base.

'What about Christmas?' Clover, inspired, suddenly blurted out. 'Where will we all go for Christmas? We always come here, all of us. Sophia and Elsa really love it. They so look forward to the huge tree in the hall and the fires being lit and all the candlelight and shadows. It's so perfect, it's almost classic *Victorian*.'

'Which is older than the house is.' Susie sounded crisp. 'And do you actually mean you'd miss the freezing cold, the scabies and the massive child mortality of those times? Are you sure?' Susie went on, her perfect eyebrows arched. Clover scowled at her. OK, she knew she might sound a tad immature to an outsider, but really, what did it have to do with Susie? What did she, a woman whose Christmas venue of choice was a Maldives spa where the only decor-ations were petals in the bathwater, know about their family traditions and the comforts of a snug, safe home?

'We could come over to you in Richmond!' Lottie suggested brightly. 'You make your house look completely wonderful. I always think it's a bit of a waste when on the big day itself you all leave it and trail over here. And you've got enough room for everyone.'

'But—'

'Clover, stop this right now. Please,' Lottie snapped. She had had enough, 'Next Christmas Mac and I probably won't even *be* here. OK? I know it sounds brutal but you're past thirty, not three.'

'So where will you be, then?' Clover sounded defeated.

'Junkanoo!' Lottie got up and started swaying around, waving her arms rhythmically, the little mirrors on her purple skirt catching the light and sending miniature rainbows dancing across the table. 'It's a festival in Nassau – parades and costumes and music and all that and it starts in the early hours of Boxing Day so I'm afraid we're not likely to be dragging in the yule log this time round! I don't get it, Clover – why can't you just be happy for us? You moved out from here a long, long time ago!'

'Shall I go up and make a start in the attic?' Susie suggested. 'Leave you to sort out your demons on your own?' She stood up, opening her taupe leather bag and pulling out her notebook (cream suede-backed and rather covetable, Clover noted) and her silver ballpoint pen.

'No. I'll come. If you're chucking things out, I want to see what's going. I want my rocking horse. And I'm bagging Ilex's train set for him.' Clover followed Susie to the hall staircase, squashing an urge to shove her over on the wide oak boards that Mrs Howard had so thoroughly polished to a glassy finish that morning. She was going to need back-up, she could see that. She would have to get together with Ilex and Sorrel, out of range of Mac and Lottie, and plan some sort of strategy. If they really were determined to sell the house and take off round the globe, they were going to have to do it with proper organization and safety in mind. They were not, whatever they thought, gap-year students at the peak of health, strength and vivacity.

'Dear Trinny and Susannah . . .' Sorrel, taking advantage of being alone in the school computer room, didn't know quite what to say next. How best to convey, in an e-mail, that she was on her knees here, in classic begging position? She should probably have asked for this years ago, starting after the time her mum had come to the primary school nativity play in one of those bright Peruvian gathered skirts with rows of braid all round it and a matching knitted Inca hat with the ear flaps. All the other mums had looked like lawyers in little black suits, every one of them the ultimate example of perfectly groomed high main-tenance. Lottie had looked as if she was dressed for a folk festival. And then there'd been the episode of the ancient Afghan coat. A few years ago, when fake versions of them had been in fashion, Lottie had gone up to the attic and, after a good afternoon rooting through various boxes, had triumphantly retrieved her original one, bought in Kensington Market, 1972. She'd scorned the new ones, say-ing they didn't have the right smell. Too bloody right, that was. Once whiffed, never forgotten. That time it had been the carol concert. Sorrel, from the church choir stalls, had gone sweatily sticky with mortification, as she watched the congregation members closest to her parents starting to mutter to each other, wafting the air, holding tissues to their noses and shuffling as far away as the crowded pews would allow. Lottie and Mac, of course, had been totally oblivious, no doubt all blissfully loved-up in a memory-lane sort of way, maybe recalling Times Gone By where that hideous, stinking coat had figured. Euw ... Sorrel thought – wishing this hadn't crossed her mind – maybe they'd used it as a rug, for outdoor— No-no-no! She mustn't think like that. Too, too gross to contemplate.

'Wotcha doing?' Gaz crept up behind her and fluffed up her hair. Sorrel, reacting automatically, leaned forward with her hand over the screen.

'Gaz! Don't *do* that! Did no one ever tell you it's rude to read people's private stuff?'

Gaz pulled out a chair beside her and pushed his leg against hers. She wriggled away, cross and embarrassed, quickly changing the screen back to her Hotmail inbox.

'Hey, settle, why don't you?' he said. 'I only came to say hi. I thought you might be looking up stuff for the trip. I am still coming with you, aren't I?'

'Are you? I don't know. Only if you get it together. Have you had your shots yet? For Thailand and Vietnam if we're going there on the way back? You need yellow fever and typhoid and hepatitis and—'

'Whoa ... wait – what happened to Australia?' Gaz looked pale. 'And have *you* had all those? Already?'

Sorrel relented. 'Well, no not yet, but I will be. Some of them you have to have a few weeks before you go. I've had other things to think about anyway.'

'Like what? Like revision and stuff?' He ran a hand up her bare leg and under her skirt. The hand felt, as it always did, warm, firm and eager. That was the good and bad thing about Gaz – he was really good at the sex stuff and more or less always up for it. When you were feeling stressed and nervy, he knew all the right moves. He could be a bit quick, but then so could she – they didn't go in for blaming each other when one of them was way ahead. It could just as easily be the other way round another time. Whichever, it worked for them.

'No, not revision. Just small things, like where, exactly, is the place I call "home" going to be, once my folks have sold up and vanished? They haven't thought about *me* at all. I'm, like, way down the list. Probably after packing the mosquito repellent and re-homing the chickens.' Sorrel felt a bit tearful, which wasn't at all what she'd come into the computer room for. She was supposed to be persuading Trinny and Susannah to sort out what her parents intended to wear for the Leavers' Family Lunch. They were sure to say she was a horrible girl for asking. Stupidly suburban and selfish. She flicked away a tear.

'Whassup, babe? Why are you so stressed? You can always come and live with me, over at mine.' Gaz put his arms round her and pulled her close. He smelled of Dove deodorant. She'd wondered where hers had vanished to, the last time he'd stayed over. Now she knew.

Sorrel laughed. 'At yours? Let me see, do we live in your room with your swotty brother or go in with your sister's baby? Or what about your gran's room? Don't let's miss her out! I think not, Gaz; one more person in your place and the walls will burst. But thanks for the offer.'

'Just a thought.' He shrugged. 'Hey, we could get our own place! What do you think? When we get back?' He pulled in closer to her. 'We could be together, like properly, you know?'

Sorrel smiled but said nothing. She'd been with Gaz for over a year now. Lottie had been younger than her when she'd met Mac. By the time she was Sorrel's age she'd had Ilex and was actually married, a full-on wife, albeit a rock-chick teenage one. Sorrel had asked her about that, wondering why she'd gone through with actually marry-ing, so very young. Sorrel had expected her to say, 'Because you had to, back then' or 'To make Ilex legitimate' or some-thing, but no. Instead she'd come out with the simplest, most honest one of all: 'Because I loved Mac.' How harsh and cynical Sorrel had felt. She hadn't thought of that one.

She liked Gaz a lot. He could be stupid and lazy and slack about being on time and keeping enough petrol in his car but he was funny and sweet and he loved her. But she didn't love him. And there must be something of her mother in her because, when it came to thinking about who she lived with, *properly* lived with in the sharing-it-all sense, the way Manda and Ilex were, rather than the just-friends-sharing-a-flat one, she definitely wasn't planning to shack up with someone she *didn't* one hundred per cent love. So that would have to be a no. She nuzzled closer to him, hoping he wouldn't really be expecting a serious instant answer.

'Gym showers?' Gaz, misunderstanding, pushed a wisp of her hair aside and murmured in her ear, all soft, damp breath and sexy warmth.

Sorrel giggled. 'What *now*? I've got a Pinter class in half an hour!'

Gaz pulled her to her feet. 'That's plenty of time, for you!' he said, leading her to the door.

'But someone might come . . .'

'Who's gonna come? Apart from us?' He laughed. 'You know it's always safe in there. No one's used them since the day they were built. You can tell by the rust. Come on, let's go.' Tugging her along the corridor with him, Gaz picked up speed, dodging clumps of younger kids mooching in slow groups out of the lunch hall.

Sorrel gave in and raced alongside him, clutching his hand. A fast blast of dirty, half-clothed sex would set her up for an afternoon of Pinter revision and for having queen-bee Carly and her back-up crew making snide remarks every time she contributed to the discussion.

Sorrel had put her hands over her ears and sung 'Way too much information' to the tune of 'We Are the Champions' when her mother had told Sorrel (and the rest of a drunken lunch table of old-hippie friends) that she'd been conceived in the pantry of the Flaming Cow restaurant while the builders renovated the dining room only a few feet beyond the door. Would she now be surprised that her daughter was about to have speedy, breathless, teenage sex against the grubby tiled wall of a potentially rather public shower cubicle? Or would she simply put it down to genes?

Oh God. Oh God-oh-God-oh-God. Ilex put his hands over his ears, closed his eyes and just about managed to stop himself from laying his miserable head down on his desk. What a mistake he'd made. What a fucking catastrophic idiot he'd made of himself. Wendy! Wendy Bloody

Murphy! Aaaagh! He could barely think of her name without groaning. Whatever had he been thinking of? Well actually, he could answer that. He'd been thinking of having some extra-mural hot, furtive sex with a firm and sturdy policewoman, fumbling under her uniform like an eager terrier going for a rabbit. And what had he got? Well no uniform for a start.

What was it she'd said, that first day when she'd dropped him at the office door? Oh yes, 'I'll be the one in the funny car!'

Well, obviously, he'd imagined it would be the cop wagon. Anyone would think that. But no. Any idiot wouldn't: they'd realize that off-duty cops didn't wander around in their uniforms simply for the fun look of it. Their out-of-hours life wasn't a bloody fancy dress party. No, of course they didn't get to take the car home. It wasn't a toy. So there she was, all disappointing in come-and-get-it mufti (black skirt, one of those leather link belts, tight pink top-and-cleavage job), sitting in a drop-head old-style pink Beetle with scarlet and orange cats painted all over it. No surprises, she'd referred to the dreadful vehicle as her 'Pink Panther'. She had a nodding cat on the dashboard, a dangling air freshener in the shape of a cat's head and a Garfield collection lined up and grinning on the back seat. Could it get worse? Oh yes.

'You look a bit shocked!' she'd said as he climbed in, keeping his head down and looking over his shoulder as he prayed no one from the office caught sight of him. He'd tried a nervous laugh and she'd given him the look: a bit fierce, disconcertingly challenging, and said, 'OK, so it's a surprise. But what did you expect? You're not one of those men who hoped to have me in the police car in full-on uniform, now are you?'

A joker would say, telling it to this point, 'Oh how we laughed!' And he'd done his best. Oh, he'd really done his best, laughing till he thought he might throw up.

It was only a couple of drinks. She'd been on orange juice, down at the pub by Hammersmith Bridge, and when he'd said that no, he didn't think he'd better go back to hers, not this time, things to do, etc, she'd whipped out her diary and got him booked in for the next day, lunchtime.

'I don't want to rush things,' she'd claimed as she dragged from him his mobile number, office number and the exact position, window-wise, of his desk. He'd hate to be up against her in a professional sense. She could drag a GBH confession out of an Archbishop. And so 'rushing things' would be what, exactly? Having full-on sex with him right there and then against the wall, under the bridge, before his first pint had settled? She was a very touchy-feely sort, all little flickerings with her fingers on his arm, squeezing past him far more closely than she needed to. Hardly what you'd call subtle in her intentions. Now if she'd been in the full-scale navy blue . . .

So now here he was, three dates in and a victim of his own stupid fantasies. Wendy was so keen, it was terrifying. She must have taken lessons from the police dog-handlers in Not Letting Go. She kept saying she 'Just Knew' they were meant to be together. She called him Lexy and had given him a photo of herself, in a frame decorated with kittens, for his desk.

She was outside now. He could see her from the window, parked up opposite the building in her horrid little car, tweaking at her spiky hair in the rear-view mirror. The lipstick would be out in a minute, and then when he tried to sneak out and simply go home for an evening of peaceful telly, curled up with Manda (aah . . . lovely, uncomplicated, beautiful Manda – why did he ever look at anyone else?), she'd pounce and make him go to the pub with her, ask him yet again to go back to hers and maybe this time tell him she'd moved the flatmate out so they could make a proper home together. At what point could he, he wondered, get enough nerve up to tell her she was barking, both in the 'mad' and the up-the-wrong-tree senses?

The phone rang. He hardly dared answer it. If it wasn't for the Pilgrim riverside apartment thing still going on, he'd divert the calls to Simon and let him deal with everything. Very gingerly, as if half expecting electric shocks, Ilex picked up the phone.

'Ilex? Clover. Listen, I think we should get together, don't you? About Mum and Dad and the house?'

Ilex said nothing, feeling almost tearful with relief.

'Ilex? Are you there? Don't you think we should talk about it, just you and me and Sorrel? See if we can get them to slow down and think things through a bit?'

'Mmm. Maybe. What are they actually doing?' Ilex felt a bit out of the loop here. Any spare brain-space seemed to have been taken over by the Wendy dilemma. He hadn't given Holbrook House or his parents much thought at all over the past days.

'They're selling it, Ilex, that's what, selling the *family home*. And you know that perfectly well. Don't you think it's even a *bit* important?'

He blinked and glanced out of the window again. Wendy wasn't in the car now – where'd she gone? Oh please, don't let her be in the lift on the way up. She broke across boundaries every day. Soon, she'd be moving into the cleaner's cupboard, along by the stairs, probably accompanied by a small cat, complete with litter tray and sundry other feline accessories. It would probably have kittens, and Wendy would hint that she too would love to have babies. His.

'Yeah, yeah I know what they're doing. Well, I don't. I mean I know what they *said*,' he told his sister.

'Haven't they talked to you about it? You'd think they would, you being in the property business and all that.'

Yes, Ilex considered, you'd think they would. That was pretty insulting, possibly, that they didn't think their own son worth consulting about whether it was a good time to sell, who to sell *with*, all that.

'No, I haven't spoken to them since Dad called to say he was wondering about the chances of getting away in time for the *La Tomatina* fiesta in Spain.'

'God, what's that?'

'A tomato fight, basically, so he said. People chuck them at each other for about four hours on some particular tomato-harvest day. Millions of them, apparently. Mad.'

'And Dad wants to go and do *that*?' Clover paused. '*Why?*'

'He's making a list of the world's big festivals and traditions and they're planning on doing the rounds, joining in.'

Clover hesitated again. 'Worse than I thought. We really need to talk about this, Ilex – how are you fixed for Friday night? Can you come over to us in Richmond, and Manda too? I've got Sorrel coming as well – she and Gaz are staying over. What do you think?'

Think? He thought anything that got him out of being Wendy's hunting target for a few hours would be hugely welcome. He wouldn't even have to tell her a lie. He would simply tell her it was family stuff and trust that even she could work out he wasn't yet so completely bagsied as a life-partner that she could expect to tag along.

'Manda and I'll be there,' he told Clover. 'Can't wait.'

If only she knew how true that was.

# TEN

Of course, as it turned out, Mac had to be away from home for the first estate agent's look-see at Holbrook House. He would be well into a session of remembrance of past rock festivals at the Wolseley restaurant with his music publisher while Lottie was bigging up the finer points of Holbrook's flagstone-floored kitchen.

Lottie was a lot less than delighted at the prospect of showing it off on her own, being sure that defending its dingier corners from almost-certain professional sneering was going to need the two of them. Even though she and Mrs Howard whizzed round, cleaning, polishing and swooping as many superfluous items as possible into cupboards and drawers, tidying and generally sparkling up the place, she couldn't help wishing the house would simply join in, smarten itself up and make an effort. Even on the outside there were things that let it down: everything that was good about the garden – the lupins, the self-seeded annuals, the poppies – was flourishing, but the weeds and the grass were more than keeping pace. Al should really have a team in to help him give the grounds a blitz. It might be worth running that past him, though she didn't think he'd be too thrilled at the interference. He was a man who liked to work at his own ambling pace. Frankly, they didn't pay him the kind of rate that justified extra-effort. While she was outside pulling surplus weeds from the terrace she crossed her fingers the blue tits wouldn't show up the state of the weatherboarding on the end gables by flying in and out of their nests in the many holes.

'It should be a doddle – just emphasize the good points,' Mac told her breezily as he left for his meeting. 'It's a brilliant house. They'll love it: and remember, the only thing the agents care about is the commission.'

And they probably would love it. Or at least see it in terms of a satisfying lot of desirable noughts on the price. From a decent distance, Holbrook House was a stunning arts and crafts masterpiece. Even inside, it would be hard not to be impressed by the large, square, light rooms. And perhaps it was, after all, an advantage having a kitchen that you could so definitely classify under the heading of 'unfitted' – according to *World of Interiors* that was right on the money as the current smart thing. All the same, Lottie considered that the house was very like a fabulously ornate dress that had wonderful appeal when seen on the hanger, but that once you tried it on you realized the hem was wonky and the zip kept getting stuck. She would have to do what she could, along with back-up from Clover, plenty of good humour and the hope that Charlie the cockerel wouldn't wander in and crap on the hall floor.

Mac, meanwhile, had the excuse of an urgent meeting with Doug at Charisma's management office in Soho. It was an appointment that apparently required an entire day if it was also to accommodate the lunch at the Wolseley, a lot of good claret and enough music business insider gossip to send him home feeling that a chair was still kept for him at the table of rock music's dysfunctional family.

And to be fair, he did have a genuine reason for his absence. It seemed the Charisma website gossip had been pretty much accurate.

'There's a possible cover version of "Target Practice" on the cards,' he'd told Lottie. 'Movie rumours; they're talking Keanu Reeves, possibly Angelina Jolie.' He was careful not to sound excited by the prospect – the moment you started thinking about what might happen, the faster the mists of possibility wafted away again.

Lottie could hardly object to such a heady mix, although versions of it had surfaced a few times before only to vanish the way of distant dreams. Whether anything came of this one or not, in terms of whether to stay at home or go to the meeting, it was game, set and match, no question. Who, in their right minds and in sight of the need for a pension fund, would – for no more personal effort than a signature on a contract – swap the possibility of a song they'd written years previously being used to play out the end-titles of a film that was odds-on for a dozen Oscar nominations? At the very least it meant a hefty fee plus performance royalties for years to come from every country in the reasonably civilized world. Only a demented fool would say, 'No thanks, I haven't got time to talk terms, rights and royalties. I've got to point out the finer aspects of our antiquated electrics to a smooth-talking bloke from Digby, James and Humphreys.'

The initial walking-round-the-house bit was now over, fairly painlessly as the sleek young estate agent ('Harry-delighted-to-meet-you') had a fine and tactful line in saying 'Mmm' in a way that didn't sound too damning and in reasonably positive nodding, entirely in the direction of a stubbornly uncommunicative Clover who had stamped about with a face like fury. Now that they'd reached the tea-in-the-kitchen stage and Lottie no longer had to concern herself with dreading an outburst of horror on Harry's first impression of Sorrel's burglary-ransack of a room, she had a moment to wonder why Clover had volunteered to come all the way down from Richmond at all (and by train too – her car being in for a service) if what she'd intended to do was be appallingly rude and un-helpful. She thought she'd got over that one after the morning with Susie. For once, when it would have been most welcome, she hadn't even brought one of her cakes – certainly to underline her protest that this whole house-sale thing was a vast mistake. Lottie, embarrassed, considered it a dire shame her daughter was too old to be sent out to sit on the stairs until her sulk was over.

Clover, across the heaps of travel books that covered the kitchen table, now stared sullenly down at the back page of that day's *Guardian* on which she'd doodled a child-like

square house, thick squiggles of smoke billowing dangerously from its chimney. What, exactly, Lottie considered,
had been the point of Harry-delighted-to-meet-you trying
so hard to get Clover on-side? Perhaps he fancied her.
Perhaps he had a genuine passion for moodily pouting
blondes who could barely be bothered to say hello. If so, he
wasn't making much progress, though Lottie couldn't fault
his efforts. So far, in the hour he'd been looking round the
house with the two women, all his remarks on the house's
many good selling points had been addressed to Clover, as
if she had personally been responsible for the quality of the
oak floorboards or the intricacies of the carved panelling
on the stairwell. Lottie had once or twice been close to
reminding him that Holbrook House wasn't actually
Clover's to sell and that Lottie was the one who needed to
be cajoled, smiled at and persuaded of Digby, James and
Humphreys' success at flogging choice Surrey properties.
But she felt rather sorry for him. What must the poor man
have thought of Clover, trailing round after him and Lottie
in a silent fury while they went from room to room, discussing en suites and favourable vistas? Clover's only
contribution to the afternoon had been a savage pillow-
straightening after Harry had sat for a moment on Sorrel's
bed to make a note about the strange dark stain on the
ceiling.

But then, Lottie conceded, if he'd flannelled her like that
('*Lovely* newel post, *silky* quality, don't you think?',
addressed to Clover as he stroked the knobbly carved
wood in a manner queasily close to suggestive), she'd take
against him too. It wasn't really his fault: Lottie just wasn't

keen on his *type*. She didn't trust people who felt they had to smarm themselves up to look professional. He had over-whitened teeth. He carried a distinctly cosmetic aroma and had clearly spent about the same amount as Clover on having his highlights done. His dark grey suit had a sky-blue and white polka-dot lining that the firm's senior partners would probably think was pretty racy and bordering on the Jonathan Ross. She imagined him at night, peeling off his house-sales persona along with his clothes. Perhaps what he really liked was to sprawl on the sofa in a wife-beater vest, slobbed out with boxed pizza, belching into cans of lager to a background of heavy metal. Unlikely.

'Of course we shall be describing the house as "important".' Harry tapped another note (presumably also 'important') into his Blackberry and smiled hopefully across the table at Clover, who continued to ignore him.

'Important,' Lottie now repeated, stifling giggles at the term. 'Is that an example of estate-agent speak? It seems an odd word for a house. Wouldn't "comfortable, lived-in, secure, airy, light", simple terms like that, be rather more descriptive, less abstract?'

Or in this case, she thought to herself, dampish, dated, decaying, if anyone was looking for the truth. Either way, whoever would feel encouraged to buy a house based on it being described as 'important'?

'No, believe me, we'd definitely class this as "important", Mrs MacIntyre.' Harry leaned forward a little, looking serious, and Lottie felt a moment of alarm that he might be about to pat her hand as if she was his slightly doolally grandmother.

'Important is *absolutely* the word,' he emphasized. 'It covers both the quality of the building and the scarcity of this type of property. Of course it varies. A century older and we'd use "distinguished" or possibly even "imposing"; two centuries or more comes under "historic".'

'Right. I get it.' Lottie was impressed at his seriousness (she'd bet he earned zillions in sale commission) but couldn't resist a tease, even though Clover, beside her, was now huffing with impatience. 'So where does "stately" come in?'

Harry gave a small, dismissive laugh. 'Actually, it simply doesn't,' he explained patiently. 'That, frankly . . .' and here he twinkled at her in a way that seemed far too avuncular for his early thirties years, '. . . would be considered rather . . . er . . . *coach party*.'

That was it, Lottie thought. She *definitely* didn't like him. She thought tenderly of her mother and her much-loved Friday trips to the great – presumably 'historic' – houses of the nation. She wasn't having her memory put down, albeit unwittingly, by this oily young fool. Now, time-wasting as it may be, she'd have to choose another agent. It would involve going through all this again, through pointing out that the turquoise and green glass tiles in the emerald bathroom might be cracked and dulled but they were original; that all the fireplaces were fully functioning ones (so long as the rooks weren't currently nesting) and that the panelling in the hall was actually fir wood, not the more traditional oak. Mac could take the next turn, Angelina Jolie or not.

Clover spoke at last, challenging Harry. 'But it'll be ages

till the house is actually sold, won't it? Big places like this, well, they don't exactly shift in days, do they? Could be months . . . years even?'

She gazed unblinking at him and he smiled back in a way that made Lottie sure he'd spent his entire career being tactful with the hopelessly ignorant.

'On the contrary,' he said. 'Houses like this don't come up every day of the week. You'll find there are people out there willing to trade their souls for a genuine Lutyens. Even . . .' Lottie, amused, watched him hesitate, daring him to add what he'd so obviously been about to blurt out: 'even one in as dire a condition as this'.

'. . . I mean, *especially*, one with potential for a certain amount of *updating*, if you don't mind me saying, Mrs MacIntyre. Planning consents notwithstanding, of course.'

'No, I don't mind at all,' Lottie reassured him. 'I'm sure anyone would want to tweak a place to make it feel like their own. We did.'

*Notwithstanding?* Whoever, under sixty and not conducting a court case, used terms like that?

The house would take more than a tweak these days, she now considered; more like a huge shove. Why had she never before noticed the way the east-wing chimney leaned? Was it something recent? One good storm and they could all be killed. The chimneys on this house were massive things.

'Yes. Um, exactly,' Harry agreed, shifting slightly and looking across the room to the six-foot-square painting of a naked Lottie dancing in a field of buttercups, beneath an orange and purple sunset. Her body may have been entirely exposed in it, but the patch on the wall where the plaster had fallen off was successfully covered.

Lottie grinned and followed his gaze. 'One of my better efforts, that one. Do you think I should leave it as a moving-in gift for the next people?'

'Oh, you painted it yourself?' Harry's eyes opened wide and his face went a shade more pink. 'Goodness! It's . . . er . . . really—'

'It's really terrible,' Clover snapped. 'You'll have to take it with you, Mum. No one else in their right mind would want to live with it.'

'Don't get in a stress, Clover, I was only joking.' Never mind sending her to sit on the stairs, Lottie's fingers now itched to give her daughter a slap.

'Well, I can't tell, these days. After all, Ilex and I thought you were joking about selling the house.'

Harry stowed his Blackberry in his briefcase and turned to Lottie. 'And have you decided on a property to move to? Perhaps DJH could help you there? What sort of place were you looking for? Something smaller, a whole lot easier to manage, I assume?'

Lottie minded the assumption, but then to be fair she'd mind whatever he said, now she'd taken against him on behalf of her mother. Why smaller? Did he have her and Mac in mind for a snug warden flatlet in a retirement development? Or something with a ready-fitted stairlift and one of those strange, walk-in baths, all prepared for an infirm old age? It would be (please God) a long, long time before they were ready for all that kind of kit. She was tempted to invent an impulsive move to a palatial French chateau complete with fully functioning champagne vineyard, or to a swish New York apartment in the Dakota Building, alongside Yoko Ono and a selection of movie stars who were generally thought to be already dead, but decided the truth would do just as well.

'No. We're not looking for anywhere else to live, not for a while anyway. Mac and I intend to travel a bit. Well, a *lot* actually. We'll simply put everything we want to keep into storage and take a long, long trip around the world's wonders. At any given moment, you'll find that some-where in the world it's party time!'

Harry looked confused, and Lottie could see he was clearly picturing sedate middle-aged drinks gatherings, like golf-club ladies' night functions, events that differed only as to whether the host nation was hot, cold or temperate. She decided to enlighten him a little.

'You see, there's always so much going on, all the time, all over the world. It's just a matter of getting on a plane and going along to join in the fun! You can start in the Philippines in January with the Kalibo Ati-Atihan, party on round the world for the rest of the year then get to Thailand for the Koh Pangan full moon party in December. See? A fabulous year of festivals, carnivals and celebration.' She could see Clover raising her eyes ceiling-ward, but ignored her.

'And then, you see, forget the Olympic Games – too dull and worthy,' she said, leaning forward to hold his attention. 'Have you ever heard of Naadam?'

'I can't say I have. What is it?' Harry looked profession-ally interested, if slightly worried. Clover simply looked, which was, this difficult afternoon, an improvement.

'Well, it's three days of Mongolian traditional sports held in Ulaanbaatar in July: wrestling, archery, horse racing and so on. It's a centuries-old event, and first properly organized by Genghis Khan, can you believe? It's also a time of festival and fireworks, music and food and dancing. Absolutely *not* to be missed! You younger ones, you really should get out more.'

Harry smiled nervously, looking across to Clover for some kind of sign that Lottie wasn't crazy.

'Right, OK.' Clover sighed, closed her notebook and stood up, ready to leave. 'So far with your plans, Mum, that's the Genghis Khan games, the thing where the whole town rolls about in squashed tomatoes in Spain, some Junk-what'sit in the Bahamas—'

'Junkanoo,' Lottie corrected her, then turned to Harry. 'That's another amazing festival, starting on Boxing Day. Fabulous costumes, apparently. And,' she reminded Clover, 'don't forget the Pushkar camel fair in India.'

'Oh how could I have forgotten that one?' Clover groaned. 'I'm sure you'll come home with some lovely new pets.'

'It all sounds . . . er . . . brilliant. Um . . . meanwhile . . .' Harry brought them back to the matter in hand. 'Meanwhile there's the question of what I'm here for. Of, er, a potential value for this house. Obviously I need to write up a proper proposal for the sale, if you're sure you'd like me to go ahead, but . . .' He now looked at Lottie uncertainly, clearly, she could tell, wondering if he'd been entirely wasting his time on a mad, idle dreamer who could at any whimsical moment completely change her mind and instead turn the house into a refuge for abandoned cats. He was probably already mentally concocting an invoice for an afternoon frittered away.

'But I can, I think, assure you that you're going to be looking at a figure well into the top end of the close to three million mark.' He twinkled again, anticipating a joyous reaction.

'Really?' Lottie said, as matter-of-factly as she could. She actually felt almost breathless at the amount but refused to let Harry have the satisfaction of seeing her behave like one of the hopefuls on *The Antiques Roadshow* who has just been told that the battered tin toy they've brought for a valuation will auction for more than enough to put little Hermione through boarding-school.

'Well, that's quite good,' she conceded, starting to gather up the used teacups. 'We should be able to take in the Sossusvlei National Park as well, then.'

Clover and Harry looked blank. 'It's in Namibia,' Lottie explained. 'A beautiful, desolate place with absolutely nothing in it. Nothing but sand and colour and camelthorn trees. Magnificent!'

*Somewhere easier to manage*, Lottie thought, as she slammed the crockery into the rusty dishwasher, she'd give him bloody easier to sodding manage.

Clover had found the grace, at last, to attempt to be pleasant. It had, given the way she'd behaved, been really kind of Harry to offer her a lift back to London and *really* kind to insist on going out of his way, via Richmond, so she would get home in good time to collect the girls from Mary-Jane.

Slowing down to negotiate some roadworks on the A3, Harry asked tentatively, 'Tell me if I'm out of order but do I get the impression you're not terribly keen on the house being sold?'

She smiled, accepting that given her open hostility, it was a pretty brave question.

'Sorry – was it that obvious? I've been a total bitch all afternoon, haven't I? Now I'm out of the house I feel really bad about that.'

Harry's hands gestured on the steering wheel. 'Well, obviously your family politics are nothing to do with me, but to be honest, I don't think it's me you need to apologize to. Still, I expect you had your reasons,' he ventured, shooting her a small and rather sexy grin.

'Clever answer,' she conceded, smiling back. 'You must know that makes a person want to talk about it!'

'Really?' He laughed. 'I had no idea, honestly! And please don't tell me if you'd rather not.'

'Now you're making it worse! OK – all I'll say is that my parents have a bit of a track record in spur-of-the-moment decisions on fairly major issues.' She hesitated. After all, Digby, James and Humphreys knew perfectly well who their client – potential client – was. She also knew that although estate agents claimed they were going to treat you with the utmost discretion, there could always be someone bored with typing up house details in the back office who might want to make a bid for a bit of holiday money from calling up the showbiz gossip pages of the tabloids. She could just see a small derisory piece about her dad, something smirky along the – untrue – lines of him having to sell up to make ends meet. They revelled in that sort of story, anything that smacked of formerly rolling-rich rock stars biting the humble dust of insolvency. It would be graced by an ancient onstage photo of Mac from his bearded and beaded days, probably with Lottie along-side, all pre-Raphaelite hair and skinny in a gold kaftan.

'So . . .' Harry ventured as he approached the Kingston roundabout. 'Does that mean that you think they haven't really thought things through? Are they not really serious about selling?'

'No, no – they're serious all right. They're always serious – till the next project.' Until it all goes horribly wrong, she thought. She wasn't going to say that – her conscience told her that, tabloids or not, it came under 'disloyal'.

'I worry that they might . . . regret it.' Clover fished in her bag for a tissue. She suddenly felt in danger of tears. 'It's been home for so many years – all their grown-up lives, really.'

'And yours too?' Harry said softly.

Why couldn't Sean be all sympathy and understanding like this? Clover thought, feeling fat tears overflowing onto her cheeks. Why did he have to be all insensitive and 'good on 'em' about it? All he saw was the likelihood that Mac and Lottie would spend a few weeks on a beach some-where then come home and settle again, much as before, but with money in the bank instead of in high-maintenance bricks. He should know them better than that by now. Didn't he realize the two of them could actually blow the entire lot, no qualms, no problems? Where, as Ilex worried, would their pension be then? Where (and she hated herself for it, but there it was) would her idea for family gatherings in a pink-walled French farmhouse be? Selfish, selfish, she told herself.

'Holbrook House hasn't been my home for quite a few years now. So really, it absolutely isn't anything to do with me.'

Clover tried laughing about it but only a strangled squawk emerged. It was eight years, two months and a couple of weeks ago to be exact that she'd moved out, though she wasn't going to tell this Harry-person that. It sounded so juvenile. It was simply that she could date it from her wedding day. She'd never minded about not doing the girlie flat-share thing, having had plenty of territory of her own in the house, not to mention parents who were more likely to wonder if there was something wrong with you if you *didn't* bring boys in to sleep with, rather than getting huffy if you did. And she'd so very much enjoyed *not* living with Sean before they got married. Dating, from home, in a rather nineteen-fifties American sort of way had been brilliant fun. Having quasi-illicit sex with him in his office, in hotel rooms, once on a freezing snowy night up on a sports pavilion roof outside Guildford (where the security lights had suddenly come on) somehow had turned out to be more thrillingly delicious than the real-life marital bed sort of stuff. It was probably her fault. Mary-Jane, when Clover had confessed this over sinful afternoon Chablis (and cake, of course – a walnut and coffee one that time) while the children were safely in school, had said she should fantasize more. 'Buy yourself a big fat vibrator down at the Ann Summers shop,' she'd suggested, quite straight-faced. 'Or have a fling with someone else now and then – it sure gives your marriage an edge.' So matter-of-fact, you'd have thought she was suggesting a logical remedy for too-tight shoes or something.

She should have gone to Manchester when Sean had asked her that time. It'd been a sexy, back-to-the-old-days impulse and she'd blown it. He'd been a bit cool with her since then, a bit too hands-off. Mary-Jane would have gone. She wouldn't have let a little thing like what to do with the children get in the way. Now Clover came to think of it, perhaps that answered the question of what Mary-Jane did with all her free time. She'd have to ask her, had she had a thing with the Hugh-Grant-lookalike school dad? Had she whizzed him back to her place after the school drop-off, hurled the piles of paperbacks from her bed and had him before the nanny got back from Waitrose? How did you learn to be that guiltless?

'Home is where the heart is, don't they say?' Harry, now in Roehampton, turned the car down Clarence Lane towards Richmond Park. 'I know it's a cliché but you can't be expected to watch the house you grew up in, particularly a house as special as Holbrook, being sold off without feeling a bit upset. I do understand, you know. I see it a lot. I've had to deal with vendors who need to have their fingernails prised from the front door on moving day.'

'No, no. I should be over it. It's fine. Really, it'll be fine!' Clover blew her nose and tried a smile.

'And,' Harry ventured, 'if you want to talk about it, maybe even meet up, you can always call me?'

Clover took the business card he'd pulled out of the car's dashboard shelf and looked at it.

'My mobile number's on there,' he told her. 'Just call, anytime. And I'll try really hard, I promise, to find your old home a caring new owner.'

'You make it sound like an abandoned puppy.' Clover laughed, stowing the card carefully at the back of her wallet. She felt strangely light and quivery and knew, though as yet for no discernible reason, that she wouldn't be mentioning Harry, or this drive home, to Sean.

Mac crossed Piccadilly quickly, dodging stop-start traffic, and went into the courtyard of the Royal Academy. He just wanted somewhere quiet to sit by himself, to collect his thoughts before he set out for home. If he didn't, he'd be mulling over the lunchtime conversation to the point where he'd probably walk absent-mindedly straight onto the track at Waterloo. He went and sat on the steps, to the side of the entrance, attracting some wary looks from a small group of ladies who'd come to visit the tea room and check out the dates for the Summer Exhibition. He didn't blame them. With his scraggy, thinning hair and in his old jeans, sockless Docksiders and unlined linen jacket (several years old but a classy Victor and Victoria number in its day) they probably had him down as one of London's homeless thousands and about to ask them for cash. The very idea made him smile. If they only knew the kind of money that had been discussed over the Wolseley's finest;

the synchronization fees over the oysters and the performing rights royalty predictions over the shepherd's pie. He
lit a cigarette and tried to calm his heart's busy fluttering.
He really mustn't get carried away – he'd been (almost)
here before. His old compositions had seen some action in
adverts for ketchup, a major used-car dealer, dog food, a
lawnmower and for tampons. Fortunately for Sorrel, as she
had been only twelve at the time and sensitive to playground teasing, that particular one had been rejected after
a regional trial run and no one outside Plymouth had
known about it. His music had never yet, till now, come up
as a contender for a major international film. He tried hard
not to get over-excited, not to think of what happened with
the revived 'Love is All Around' when it went into *Four
Weddings* . . . Knowing his luck, this lunch with Doug and
his music publisher would represent the beginning and
end of the whole deal. Next thing he'd hear was bound to
be that they'd decided to go with an old-but-good number
written by a musician who'd been careless over losing his
copyright. Or somebody long dead. So much cheaper that
way and in spite of mega-million budgets, there was
always some careful money-wallah in a production office
watching the costs.

Mac stubbed his cigarette out on the step beside him and
stood up, stretching his aching legs. Cold stone, even in
late May, wasn't the most sensible thing to sit on. He
actually felt chilled, right through the worn denim.
Perhaps he should take a cab down to Harvey Nicks and
stock up on some new threads. He made his way, rather
stiffly, and feeling mildly dizzy, out into the bustle of

Piccadilly and back towards Green Park station. Possibly he'd had more to drink than he'd thought – though he was sure Doug had drunk the bigger half of the claret, and they'd each only had the one glass of champagne with the oysters. The dizziness receded, now he'd picked up pace towards the station, though his head was starting to throb and he hoped he wasn't going to turn into one of those people who, as they age, start picking up weird sensitivities and allergies to all the things they'd most enjoyed in life. What was that all about? You heard about it happening – Mike on the pub quiz team couldn't eat soft cheese any more – it made him wheezy. Lottie had a friend who'd suddenly gone allergic to her own twelve-year-old cat. Was it some kind of celestial revenge, some paranormal way of telling you that you've drunk/eaten/smoked quite enough of whatever it is for one lifetime?

Mac hesitated outside the station. The dizziness briefly kicked back in and then out again, leaving him feeling nervously certain that if he ventured down the steps he'd be sure to lose his footing and tumble down at least half of them. Instead he walked to the roadside and hailed a cab, giving the driver the address of Holbrook House and feeling relief and gratitude that the driver accepted the thirty-five-mile journey without a quibble. Well, it was worth it, Mac thought. He couldn't wait to see Lottie's face when he told her that this time next year, as the Del-Boy saying went, they could be millionaires. Again.

# ELEVEN

'I hope there won't be fish. I hate fish.' Gaz was sprawled low in the Mini's passenger seat with his feet twitching away on the dashboard more or less in time with Gorillaz. Sorrel hated him doing that. OK, so her car might rattle with empty Diet Coke cans and Pringles tubes and the seats might be mostly hidden under various items of clothing, books and odd pages from magazines but that didn't mean she also wanted the dusty imprint of huge trainers all over the vinyl. She made a conscious, calm decision not to say anything about it, as practice for when they went travelling. If she picked on every little thing he did that just slightly annoyed her while they were away, they wouldn't last three days together, let alone three months. Perhaps it would rack up some good karma, as her mother would put it, if she bit back on negative comments and saved her grumbles only for things that might actually be dangerous. One of these was that Gaz always messed around with door handles. He'd once fallen out of the Mini when she'd first had it. Luckily they'd still been on the Holbrook House driveway at the time, rather than doing seventy on the A3. His excuse had been that he liked to check he could get out in a hurry, in case of a crash or something. If he mucked about with the doors on the plane to Australia she'd definitely have something to say about it. She thought briefly of warning the crew that he'd need watching, in case he started trying to do the Doors To Manual thing thirty thousand feet up, but that would have them on full-scale nutter-alert and the two of them would be sure to get bumped off the plane somewhere in Germany.

'There won't be fish,' Sorrel promised him. 'I told Clover you don't like it so she won't be cooking it. She'll probably play it safe with chicken. Either that or she'll be ordering in a Chinese delivery from The Good Earth.'

'She might do fish. She might do it on purpose. She might hate me.' Gaz was now gripping the sides of the seat. Sorrel smiled to herself, put her foot down and over-took a builder's van, narrowly missing the central reservation, and sending adrenalin lurching. She didn't risk taking her concentration off the road to look at Gaz but she imagined he had his eyes tight shut and his fingers crossed. Sometimes it was quite cute that he was such a wuss, like when he needed her to take spiders out of the bath or opened her bedroom door so warily in case a bat had got in, but in the car it was really infuriating and counted as a definite criticism of her driving.

'Why would Clover hate you? Why would you think that? She invited you tonight, didn't she?' Sorrel wasn't having this. He'd been willing enough to come to her sister's for this loony siblings' dinner where they were apparently (according to Clover) supposed to hold some kind of secret top-level talks about the parents' plans for selling up and running out on them all. He'd said he was really pleased Clover had asked Sorrel to bring him along (Sorrel wasn't going to tell him that it was probably because Clover couldn't face the thought of a dinner that didn't conform to the equal-numbers male and female rule). All Gaz had to do now was try to have a good time. Not a lot to ask.

'Manda will be there,' she continued. 'You like Manda, don't you?'

This was like soothing a three year old. This had so better not be a new role he was thinking of taking on: the whingy, hang-back boyfriend, borderline agoraphobic. Next thing, he'd morph into one of those weird stay-home adults who never went anywhere because they 'wouldn't know anyone'. Lazy, that's all *that* was. That friend of her parents, Kate, the one who was married to junkie George, the guitarist from Charisma who'd died, she'd gone through all that. Sorrel remembered Lottie phoning her every time there was a party on somewhere, or to see if she fancied going to the theatre or out with the women or whatever and Kate always said no, because it might involve new people, new places. Lottie had lost patience eventually. Sorrel had sat on the stairs cuddled up to the dog for comfort (she couldn't have been more than ten, she recalled the soft, shaggy wolfhound had been so huge) and listened in excited alarm to her mother shouting down the phone, something she'd absolutely *not* normally do: 'Kate, stop bloody thinking everyone's going to be looking at *you*! They're *not*, OK?' And then the next thing, Kate suddenly married an earl and moved to a Scottish castle. That probably counted as one top result: living on a remote Highland rock, it was more than likely that finding anyone at all to socialize with (apart from sheep) was pretty much out of the question.

As she parked the Mini, it occurred to Sorrel that Clover's house looked like something made by the My Little Pony people. It had plaster mouldings like icing-sugar flowers and was so birthday-cake pink and white. The top of the wall to the small front garden was planted with a froth of pale blue forget-me-nots and at each side of the front door there was a pink pot painted with white spots and trailing with something that looked to Sorrel like tiny starry daisies. She supposed that was what you did when you were a mother with no job – you spent your time prettifying your surroundings. Would she do that? On balance she rather hoped she'd have a career that left her just that bit short of free time (journalism was the current choice, something comfortable in a magazine office, preferably with lots of clothes and make-up freebies thrown in) so that she wouldn't have to do stuff like gardening. But hey, it worked for Clover. Clover was a born nest-maker.

'Nice gaff,' Gaz commented, looking up at the windows. Sorrel felt more optimistic. Either he meant it (good) or he had decided to make an effort at last (very good).

She slid her arm round him and gave him a soft, slow kiss. 'It'll be all right. You know them all and they won't bite you. I might though . . .' She sank her teeth gently into his bottom lip and he pulled her closer but she opened her car door and backed away from him.

'Later, maybe!' she teased. 'But only if you're good.'

'Aren't I always?' Gaz grinned at her, climbing out of the passenger door.

'Perhaps you are,' she said. 'But I wouldn't tell you, in case you get conceited.'

'It's times like this I really wish we had a nanny,' Clover grumbled to Sean as she ripped up basil leaves to scatter onto six individual tomato tarts. Sophia and Elsa were playing a boisterous game that involved weaving in and out of the chair and table legs, rolling around on the floor and squealing at the tops of their voices. What she'd give right now to have some kind, capable girl take the two of them off her hands, lead them to their rooms to be bathed and put to bed and have a chapter of *Peter Pan* read to them. If she ever *did* get one, the nanny would have to be able to read English really well – a good grounding in classic children's books was something Clover believed in devoutly: these were stories that stayed with you through your whole life, along with cosy memories of who read them to you and where you were. Her earliest story-memories somehow mixed Peter Rabbit with the scent of cannabis, someone playing a guitar and lights flashing by in the Mont Blanc tunnel, but when she thought of Holbrook House, she could conjure up the Bambi figures patterning her white nightdress, the pinkish glow from the toadstool bedside lamp and Lottie, cosy in a purple velour Dance Centre outfit, reading her and Ilex to sleep with *The Wind in the Willows*.

There was another piercing shriek from Elsa and Clover wasn't quite fast enough to stop her landing a hefty punch on her sister's arm. Any minute and it would be all-out battle-stations.

'Could you take them upstairs for me, please, Sean? Settle them on our bed with a DVD or something? They're so hyper, they're driving me mad. There'll be tears.'

Probably mine, she thought to herself. Why couldn't he think of it himself? It was obvious she was up to her eyes in the cooking. He was willing enough to join in and do his bit with the girls whenever Clover asked him but sometimes she really wished he'd see what needed to be done and take the initiative. It was so exhausting, thinking of everything. All Sean's thinking-processes were kept for his work. Ask him to organize a full-scale bells-and-whistles launch for a major new product or a multi-celebrity post-premier party for a West End show and he'd be Mr Organization. But on his way home he pressed a sort of 'delete' button in his brain. Her own fault, she supposed as she drizzled olive oil on the tarts, for making the house so decidedly her own territory. But then could you blame her? She needed a secure comfort zone. It was her citadel against Sean once more pressing that other 'delete' button: the one labelled 'fidelity'. If it happened again, at least she'd have her . . . what? For a moment it crossed her mind that the proper term for what she hid behind was nothing more profound than soft furnishings. She felt all her confidence wavering. It wasn't *just* soft furnishings. No. Her home was a lot more than that. It was about heart and soul – all those things Sean would think soppy. That was what Holbrook House was all about and the reason for this dinner.

'Jeez, Clover, you've gone to town a bit, haven't you?' Sean said as he came back into the kitchen after depositing his daughters in front of *Chicken Little*. 'The table looks like something out of the Harrods fine china department. I didn't know we had that many glasses! It's only your family, isn't it? Looks more like you're expecting Charles and Camilla!'

Clover froze. 'It's not too much, is it? I wanted to do it properly. They won't . . .' She bit her lip. 'They won't laugh at me, will they? I know I wouldn't usually – it's just—'

'Course they won't, princess!' Sean gave her a swift kiss. 'They'll love it! Especially Manda – right up her street. I bet Ilex's idea of a posh home dinner is using a fork for his pizza. Come on, let's you and me have a sneaky glass of fizz before they get here. Just a livener, get us in the mood.' He gave her a fond hug and nuzzled her hair. 'You smell gorgeous,' he murmured. 'And you're doing a great job in here – I'm starving.'

Clover sipped the cold champagne and felt the bubbles sizzle on her tongue. Perhaps she had overdone things. What was she doing, coming over all 1980s corporate wife when it was just a family supper? Maybe the importance of what they were supposed to discuss had got the better of her. Still, it was too late now to change anything: the doorbell was ringing and she could see the spike-haired outline of Gaz's head in the frosted glass of the front door.

'Why do you keep looking round?' Manda asked Ilex as he turned the car into Clover's road. 'You keep peering about all over the place, like you aren't sure where she lives or something, or maybe like you're looking for someone.'

Ilex smiled nervously at her. 'Um, just keeping an eye on the traffic, road conditions, all that.'

'There isn't any traffic down this road,' Manda pointed out.'You've been driving like some nervous learner all the way here, slowing down and staring up side roads and stuff. Are you all right?' Ilex didn't reply, concentrating instead on backing the BMW into a space that might turn out to be a bit too small.

Manda reached her hand across and laid it on his thigh. 'Are you a bit worried about this evening? About whether it might end up in a big family row?' Ilex glanced at her. Manda's eyes were glittering strangely as if a big family row was the one thing she was really, really looking forward to. Perhaps there would be one. It hadn't really occurred to him. Surely they were all there because they had opinions (though possibly not the same ones) about Holbrook House being sold. What was there to argue about unless someone had changed their mind and was all for it? He wasn't actually that much against it – so long as Mac and Lottie did something sensible with the proceeds. Some hope, there.

'I'm fine, honestly,' he insisted, giving up on the space

and aiming instead for one further up the road, past Sorrel's black Mini.

'Honestly' wasn't exactly the most accurate word, he admitted to himself. If he was to use 'honestly' in the sense of 'completely truthful', he'd have to admit that he was only fine while there wasn't a pink, cat-painted Beetle in sight either in front or in his rear-view mirror. It seemed to be everywhere he went and he was wondering if feeling borderline terrified was going to be a permanent emotion. He was *way* over the terrified borderline tonight, that was for sure; Wendy could be out stalking, a few cars behind him. He could picture her with that little gleeful smile and her tongue between her teeth, playing cat and mouse among the traffic while trailing him from Battersea to Richmond. If she had, she could knock on Clover's door at some point during the evening, stride in and claim him as her property. God, he hadn't even slept with her. Not that anyone would believe that, if she told them otherwise. Especially Manda.

'OK, are you ready for this?' Ilex asked, removing the ignition key and tidying a couple of petrol receipts away into the glove compartment.

'Ready for what? It's only dinner at your sister's, not World War Three!' Manda laughed, opening her door.

'Don't leave anything out in the car,' Ilex warned her, glancing across to see if she'd dropped a CD or had been looking in the *A to Z*.

'Ilex, has anyone ever told you you're in danger of turning into an old woman?'

He didn't reply, leaving the accusation hanging in the air

with Manda's scornful laughter. He didn't mind being in danger of turning into an old woman. It sure beat the hell out of simply being a stalker's target.

They'd now eaten all the tomato tarts, followed by the roast chicken, the sweet potato mash, ratatouille and asparagus. They'd also got through a couple of bottles of champagne and a fair bit of both red and white wine and Clover wondered when anyone would mention what they'd all come to the house to talk about. She couldn't believe how very much they were all on Best Behaviour. In a couple of hours of well-mannered, non-challenging conversation they'd covered wood versus vinyl for garden furniture, Elsa's approaching ballet exam (pre-primary level), whether Ilex should trade in the BMW, Manda's work move from North Terminal check-in to Executive Lounge reception and the chances of Jamie Oliver ending up in the House of Lords. Even Sorrel was polite and sociable and answered Manda's questions about her A-level exams without a single don't-care shrug or dismissive comment. Clover was beginning to despair that they'd ever get round to the subject they'd all been assembled here for. She stood up and started clearing plates – Gaz leaped up to help her, collecting a worryingly tall, tottering heap of crockery. She wouldn't point out it was her best – the others had already commented (though nicely, thank goodness) about the effort she'd put in.

'I'll bring the ... um ... pudding,' Clover said as she took the plates to the sink. 'And cheese; would anyone like that first?'

'We could just take both, then they can choose,' Gaz suggested, disentangling forks from knives and stashing them with their handles facing upwards into a bowl of hot soapy water in the sink.

'Thanks, Gaz – expertly done,' Clover commented.

'I worked in a restaurant last summer,' he said. 'They'd kill you if you mixed the cutlery. Yours is smart stuff – I thought it didn't look dishwasher safe.'

She smiled. 'You're right! Sorrel would have just flung it all into the machine. You'll make someone a lovely—' She stopped, confused and embarrassed. Surely she hadn't been about to say 'husband'? Sorrel was a long, long way from thinking about weddings, or even settling for one man, surely. Manda wasn't, though . . . which made her feel that somewhere in the back of her mind an embryonic idea might just be stirring into life.

'Yeah, you're right. I'll make someone a lovely head waiter,' Gaz said with a laugh.

'Mmmmm! Sticky toffee pudding! I haven't had that since . . . well, I can't remember when.' Ilex spooned a dollop of clotted cream over his pudding and sank his spoon into it, his face, Manda thought, as blissed out as if she'd offered him dirty back-seat action in the car. Maybe her darling, late mother had been right about this too – food really was the way to a man's heart, or at least one way. She'd put it on her list, give serious cooking a go, see if that stirred Ilex into a new direction of appreciation, a direction that lead to that emerald ring in Tiffany's.

'Actually, we had it two weeks ago,' she now pointed out, cutting herself a slender piece of Yarg cheese.

'Yes, but that was from Marks and Sparks. Not home-made,' Ilex said. 'You can't compare them.'

Clover rather thought you could but wasn't going to tell Ilex that hers were also from M&S, though slyly decanted onto a pretty serving dish, disguised with a dusting of icing sugar and surrounded by a selection of luscious scarlet berries.

'Er ... look ...' Clover cleared her throat and started again, thrown by the way the rest of them fell suddenly silent as if she'd rapped on the table with a hammer. 'Everybody? I think maybe while we're here without Mum and Dad, there's something we should talk about. No one's mentioned it yet and it's here like some kind of elephant in the room.'

'Possibly a great big white elephant,' Sean chuckled.

Clover glowered at him and continued, 'We really need to talk about what they're doing with Holbrook House.'

'They're selling it, aren't they?' Manda looked puzzled, as if there were new plans no one had told her about, such as turning it into a nursing home or converting it to offices. As ever, she thought what a lovely wedding party venue it would make. Oh well.

'Yes. Well, that's what they say they're doing. They've had an agent round for a preliminary valuation. I was there,' Clover told them. They must know all this – was she the only one who cared?

'I don't know why they didn't ask me,' Ilex grumbled, topping up his glass. 'I could have pointed them in the direction of exactly the right people for the job. I sometimes think they imagine I'm still ten and completely unqualified for anything.'

'If you had, would you have copped for commission?' Sean asked.

'No, of course not!' Ilex looked offended. 'I'd have just been looking out for them, so they could get the best deal.'

'Yes, but ... deal or not, there are other things to think about first, aren't there?' Clover said. 'Things like—'

'Like where am I going to live when I get back? I'll have, like, *nowhere*?' Sorrel said. 'No one's mentioned *that* little problem.'

No one was mentioning it now either. Clover thought about her own immaculate guest room upstairs: soft pinky-lavender walls (Paint Library's 'Subtle Angel' – who gave these colours such delicious names?), antique Amish patchwork on the bed. She couldn't picture careless, chaotic Sorrel making herself at home in there without being close to hyper-ventilating. It was bad enough that she and Gaz would be staying in it tonight. She hoped they'd be ... well, *gentle* with the room. And quiet if they had sex. She didn't want the girls in the morning asking what the squealing was all about. Oh, if only she'd gone to stay with Sean in Manchester – in the fabulous private space of their room in the Lowry Hotel (where she now knew he'd stayed) she could have squealed all she wanted.

'They said they'd buy you a flat, didn't they?' Ilex said to Sorrel. 'And you're going to Exeter University, which is such a good place to buy, right now ...'

'Ilex, are you mad? What if I hate it? What if the course isn't right for me and I want to come home again after a month? Oh, except I haven't *got* a home! Plus I've got a hall of residence place all lined up for the first year so I can meet people – what do I do with the flat then? Rent it out and then have *students* trash my pad? *Derr!'*

'Look, we're getting off the point here,' Clover interrupted.

'Are we? Oh, OK – you're right.' Sorrel put her hands up in surrender. 'Me being homeless doesn't matter at all, obviously. Go on then, Clover, please tell us, what *is* the point?'

'Well . . .' Clover considered. 'Maybe Mum and Dad haven't really thought this through properly. I mean, it's not just any old house they're selling, it's a lot more important than that. It's not a, oh I don't know, like a *used car* or something, is it? It's been our home; it's full of memories.'

'It's full of my *stuff*,' Sorrel growled. 'I haven't got time to go through all of it right now; I've got exams. Not that they've noticed.'

'It's still got a lot of my stuff in it too – a lot of all our stuff. All our artwork from school, things we've made, childhood toys, books and games and things.'

'Yeah, but to be fair, darlin', you can't expect your folks to hang on to all that tat for ever.' Sean took a corkscrew to another bottle of red wine and glanced at Ilex, who nodded. Manda's lips narrowed crossly. He'd said he'd drive, so she could have a drink. Now they were going to have to get a cab home and waste time in the morning coming back for the car. Clover glared at Sean, furious at his disloyalty.

'OK, discount the actual *things*,' she conceded, worried they were all thinking she was on the wrong track here.

'What about the speed of all this? Don't you think they should slow down a little, make plans that are a bit sensible? Especially for Sorrel . . . she shouldn't have to worry about where she's going to be living when she's got the most important exams of her life to think about.'

'It's worth a fair whack too. They should plan something safe for investment for when they come back. They can't surely be planning to blow the lot on this big trip, can they?' Ilex's brow was furrowed with worry. 'You know what they're like, they'll probably come back completely broke and have to camp on the floor of Sorrel's one-bedder.'

'I'd want more than one bedroom. Where would my mates sleep?' she snapped. '*And* I'd want a garden, you know, for parties in summer and that.'

Sean laughed. 'Jeez, girl, do you know how spoilt you sound? But surely even Mac and Lottie would find it hard to get through more than a couple of million trekking round the world? I mean, you'd really have to go some to do that.'

'Don't bet on it, Sean,' Ilex warned. 'The way they're talking they could gamble it away on camel races.'

'You see, I had this lovely idea,' Clover said, looking misty-eyed. 'I sort of thought that if they're really determined that Holbrook House isn't where they want to live any more, then maybe they'd like to think about finding somewhere else, something we could *all* enjoy, either together or separately. Some lovely, warm base where we could get together, as a family.'

'It all sounds a bit *Waltons*, Clover,' Ilex sniggered. 'Where would this magical place be?'

'I was thinking, maybe, somewhere like ... um ... France.' There was a silence while they all considered this.

Manda looked puzzled. 'France? Why *France*? Do Mac and Lottie like France?'

'Oh, it doesn't have to be France ... could be Spain or Portugal. Greece even, though it's tricky, the property-buying thing there. France is ... easiest.' Her voice tailed away. There, she'd said it. She'd put in her bid for what she wanted more than anything. If she couldn't keep her – *their* – comfort base here in England, she'd now let them know she was willing and able to create another one for them all. Obviously she'd have to give them time to think it over, to get a picture of vines and bougainvillea and a terrace of flourishing herbs and creamy lemon-scented pelargoniums that flowered for months and months. And the pool and the tiling, and the mural she'd be so happy to paint on the surrounding wall, possibly depicting them all being happy and leaving space for additions if Manda or Sorrel had children.

'Not that you've been thinking about this for ages or anything, surely, Clover?' Ilex's voice was almost menacing.

'What?' She was startled out of her dreaminess. 'No, no! Of course not, how could I? They've only recently decided to sell!'

Sean, for once loyal, said nothing, but silently offered Gaz a cigarette and lit one for himself. Clover was hardly going to make them smoke in the garden when she so needed him on-side.

'If they're selling up, they should be thinking in terms of pensions and their future, not chucking it away on a holiday house for you and your kids,' Ilex said. 'They don't seem to have a clue what it's going to cost them to make it into their nineties without us lot having to fork out for care homes and so on. I mean, suppose they get Alzheimer's or something? That could take twenty-four-hour nursing care. If they're clever, they'll be able to have top of the range, no question. If they squander, we'll *all* be on in-continence duty. Don't suppose you've thought of that, have you, Clover?'

'But Dad's songs still earn, don't they?' Sorrel suggested. 'They're not completely broke. He could afford my Mini, OK. Or at least, if he couldn't, he didn't say. I told him I'd have been happy with one of the old-style ones.'

'The earnings are bound to go down – they are already. If they weren't, they'd have kept the roof repaired, re-done the electrics. You only have to look at the place to see they can't keep up with it any more – it's not just that they can't be arsed. Sad, that,' Ilex told her. He looked depressed, Manda thought. She'd do her best, later, to cheer him up. If he wasn't too pissed, that was. She moved his glass away a bit, in a small bid to make him forget it was there.

'Maybe if you just slow them down a bit. Till Sorrel gets back from her trip,' Sean suggested. 'That way, they might have made more definite arrangements. You could talk to them. Frankly, none of you three have, really, have you? You've just seethed in silence, hoping they'll snap out of it.'

'How do we slow them down?' Sorrel asked. 'Every day new stuff comes through the post. You should have seen what was on the kitchen table – something about a cruise ship you can buy an apartment on. It travels all over the world, calling in for various events at places. Apparently in June everyone gets to stop off at the Sultan of Brunei's birthday bash.'

Clover laughed. 'I can't see Mum going for that one!' she said. 'Can you see her cooped up on a ship, however big? She'd think it was like being trapped in the *Big Brother* house, except with golfers and industrialists. And she's hardly the cocktail frock and captain's table type either. And Dad – in a dinner jacket!'

'I don't think it's quite like that, but anyway – the point is, they're wading through info on Everest base camps and safaris in Kenya and joining a camel train in the Sahara and all sorts of things. Pretty ace, actually. A bit up on what Gaz and I were planning.'

'I don't want to be funny but . . .' Gaz's voice was tentative. 'But . . . well, is what you're all worried about them spending their own money when you think it should be, like, sort of coming to *you*? Because I don't want to be rude, but it does sound a bit like that.' No one spoke.

'Sorry,' Gaz said. He looked as if he'd wished he'd brought his own car so he could simply get up, pick up his jacket and leave right this minute.

'Gaz, it's not that. It's not that *at all*.' As he spoke, Ilex caught a glimpse of Manda sneaking a smile at Gaz. Did she agree? Is that what they all sounded like?

'We're not a bunch of grasping bastards.' Ilex almost spat the words. 'We don't need to be, do we? Look around you here, Gaz. Sean and Clover are doing fine on their own, don't you think?'

Clover blinked. They *had* been doing fine. Sean was

going to be home, he'd said, for three days next week. It wasn't leave – just, well, not quite enough to do at work. Having him home was better than having to think about what he was up to when she hadn't leaped on that plane to Manchester, but in the long run it could be financial disaster.

'And I'm an independent grown-up who hasn't needed hand-outs from home for a lot of years now.' Even to his own ears, he sounded as if he protested too much.

'Sorry,' Gaz muttered again. Sorrel squeezed his hand, not entirely sure he was all that far out.

'So all you really need is an event – something distracting.' Gaz brightened. 'Why don't you have a massive great party at the house for them? Tell them it was going to be a surprise, like when're their birthdays? What about that?'

Brains ticked over. Sean swigged wine noisily and Clover looked round the table at them all, certain now she'd completely wasted her time, for she was obviously on her own with this. Neither Ilex nor Sorrel were actually that outraged that Holbrook House was to be sold. So long as Mac and Lottie got it all together in a way that suited them, it had turned into something more or less inevitable. Was it that easy to say goodbye to all those years there? Had they no souls at all?

'There's Sorrel's eighteenth in July,' Ilex suggested.

'No *way*.' Sorrel rejected that one immediately. 'I really, *really* don't want a poncy party at home. Me and my mates, we've made plans. We're just going to hang at a festival and see bands. No party. Definitely no party.' No way was she having those wasters from school crashing in – and

Carly would make a point of it – just so they could sneer at the raggy curtains and the tiles missing in the bathrooms, and the weird black walls in the sitting room. They were so stupid, they'd probably draw on the walls or scratch filthy words on the panelling in the hallway. Not a chance.

Clover sighed. 'Well, I don't know what else to suggest. That's it then.'

'What do you mean, "that's it"?' Sorrel snapped. 'Don't even think of making it all my fault!'

'No wait, you need something bigger than that,' Gaz said. 'Something they'll need to make lots of plans for, like, I dunno, does the village have a carnival or fête or . . . ?'

They all considered for a moment. 'It's not really a fête type of village, actually. Mostly commuters and that, now,' Sorrel said. 'Or at least . . .' she giggled, 'Mum and Dad aren't really fête type of people!'

Ilex laughed. 'No, you're right there. Can you imagine Mum in a big flowery hat, drawing the raffle and running the tombola? "Another spliff, Vicar?" '

'She would if it was for a charity. OK, not the hat.' Clover grinned.

'What you really need is a wedding.' Gaz was only just heard over the laughter. 'My sister's took months to organize.'

'It's gone very quiet,' Sean commented, a good minute later. 'Anyone got any more suggestions?'

'Um . . . right,' Clover said. 'Coffee anyone?'

# TWELVE

Ten o'clock in the morning and the sun blazed beyond the curtains. Mac stared at the crackled ochre paint of the ceiling and considered the possibility of Zanzibar. If he was there, right now, in the Peace of Love wing of the Emerson and Green Hotel, Stone Town, he'd be gazing up at a gauzy mosquito net, edged with gold-threaded blue silk. Later, he and Lottie would have breakfast up a flight of steps in a private, open-sided terracotta tower, looking out across the narrow alleyways of the city to the harbour and the sea. July might be better than now, he thought – unless it was just too unbearably hot, then they could take in the Zanzibar Film Festival, which seemed to be as much about art and music as movies. Perhaps that would be a good place to start their travels, and they could go for some lion-watching in Tanzania as well.

Mac rubbed at a nagging ache in his left leg then pushed the duvet back and considered beginning the day. It crossed his mind that if at some future time he was ever institutionalized (and where would that be? Not prison, as he'd been fully legal since he'd quit smoking dope on the day George keeled over, dead from cocaine-induced heart failure. Old folks' home? That was more of an option – so long as involuntary euthanasia for the financially feckless hadn't by then become law), there would be someone else dictating his rising times and he would be forced to give up his habitual late-night/late-morning rock 'n' roll hours. This, he felt, would be a shame, for it suited him to go to bed after the rest of the civilized working world. He saw it as part of the privilege of *not* having a nine-to-five career, a non-job perk. In summer he loved the post-midnight silence out there in the garden's silky darkness, especially the rich grey/blue of a mid-June night sky that never quite went blacker than the richest inky dusk. Even since last November, since there was no longer a wolfhound to usher out for a late-night pee, he always went out in all weathers for a breather before bed and was sure in the still solitude he could feel the earth turning beneath him, that he was at one with the little night creatures that scurried and fed and bred only feet away in the walls and hedges. In winter he loved slobbing out on the tatty purple Knoll sofa with the lunatic-hour trash TV programmes – old films, bizarre reality shows, news from unknown bits of the world. And it very much pleased him that at closing time on quiz nights at the Feathers, when the scores had been totted up, winners announced and Mike the landlord was roaming around collecting glasses and reminding people that they had homes to go to, he felt wide awake and just getting under way. Plenty of energy he had then, more than enough to go back to Al's place, drink some of Al's Scotch and strum half-remembered tunes on Al's guitar (with Al on piano) till Mrs Al came downstairs and complained that some people had work in the morning, even if they didn't. Of course the difference between him and the younger, fitter Al was obvious. Al, come morning, would be up and out early to one of his three garden/handyman jobs, regardless of sleep hours. Mondays, Wednesdays and the sunnier Fridays, by eight he'd be leaning against Lottie's chicken house having his third cigarette of the day and waiting till Charlie the cockerel had wandered down the orchard before venturing into the hen-run to collect any eggs. What would happen to Al when they sold the place? Mac's conscience prodded him uncomfortably about the fact that they hadn't properly talked about it yet. Mrs Howard would be all right: top-rate cleaners were snapped up by an eager queue of neighbours. There'd been many an attempt to poach her in the past. Susie with the gallery had apparently already put in a bid, now she knew they were selling. The Al question was something he and Lottie would obviously need to talk about, and soon. Mac had mentioned the travel plan to him, but somehow the moment where he then said, 'Oh yes, and by the way, once we've flogged the house, you'll be out of one of your cushy, cash-in-hand numbers,' hadn't come up. Perhaps the new people would take Al on, though they'd probably want him to up his hours. Even a total horticultural novice who couldn't tell a rose from a stick of rhubarb could see that Al wasn't entirely keeping on top of the job. Maybe he could make it a condition of the sale that the premises came complete with staff. It would certainly save the incomers the hassle of looking for a gardener and unless they already had their own horticulture company or something or were planning to accommodate students from nearby Wisley, they'd certainly need one.

Mac sat up in bed, swung his legs to the floor and stood up quickly. Too quickly, as it turned out, for the room swam and shimmered. He dropped back safely on to the bed, feeling shaky and breathless and slightly nauseous. He shouldn't do that, he realized. He should take things more slowly – his blood pressure must be low, or was it high? Whichever one it was that made you fall over if you stood up too fast, it seemed he had it.

Something told him that one of these options was better than the other but as it was a few years since he'd had a medical overhaul (partly in case the results sent his health insurance premiums rocketing), he'd lost track of his body's internal vital statistics. The ones on the outside, and here he fondled the spare, squashy flesh of his stomach, were quite enough to take notice of, thank you.

All the same, Mac felt himself notching up another hint of mortality on life's (or, dear God, was it death's?) checklist. First the bus pass thing, now this. Whatever this was, it felt like a spiteful little nudge from the Reaper, a reminder that Mac had been added to the old soul-snatcher's To Do list and he'd be dealt with in due course. He hoped, right now, as he massaged his achy leg, that it wouldn't be before he'd had that breakfast in Zanzibar.

What was Ilex doing in a police car? Clover was sure it was him. She had just come out of Steinberg and Tolkien on the King's Road, having spent a small fortune on a fabulous vintage, pink and orange chiffon Zandra Rhodes dress that would be such a perfect present for Sorrel's eighteenth birthday in July. The police car, heading west at no great speed, had slowed so that a woman, one of those ancient Chelsea eccentrics in balding mink, lime-green tights and a lavishly veiled hat, could cross the road and Clover had caught sight of Ilex through the car's open window as he turned to look in her direction, then had speedily turned back again, his head obscured by his upraised hand. She didn't see the driver as the car suddenly sped away, turned off past Heal's and disappeared out of range, but she pictured for herself a chunky, pleased-with-himself cop, school of *The Bill*. Ilex couldn't have been arrested, she felt sure, as she walked back in the direction of the Bluebird where she was to meet Mary-Jane for lunch, or he'd have been sitting in the back seat and the windows wouldn't have been open.

Outside Designers Guild, Clover stopped for a quick look at a luscious purple and lime devoré velvet sofa, then delved into her bag for her phone. She searched for Ilex's mobile number and called it. It must have been him in that car, she concluded as she was put straight through to voice-mail; it must have been him, he must have seen her and had deliberately switched the phone off. What was he up to? She hadn't heard from him since the night of her dinner. Manda, ever politely proper, had sent a sweet card (featuring line-drawings of classic hangbags), thanking her and Sean and telling them that she and Ilex had had a lovely evening. Nothing else – so presumably Gaz's suggestion of a wedding party at Holbrook House hadn't had a fruitful follow-up. Sometimes, Clover thought exasperatedly, Ilex really wasn't the sharpest pencil in the box.

Mary-Jane was waiting at a sunny table in the Bluebird's courtyard. She wore over-sized sunglasses and was studying a copy of the *A to Z*.

'Hi, sweetie! Isn't this a treat?' She greeted Clover with a hug. 'I got here early and I've been sitting here doing my homework for the tennis job while I waited for you. Go on, you tell me the quickest route from Wimbledon to Buckingham Palace and I'll see if you'd be up to the job.'

'The Palace? Heavens, they are putting the tennis players up in style!' Clover laughed as she draped her jacket over the back of the seat. The day had really warmed up now. She briefly thought of the old lady she'd just seen crossing the road in full-scale mink. Did she wear it whatever the weather? Did it represent the best times she'd had? She felt suddenly sad; were old, treasured, clothes all that was left when you recognized that all the best times were over?

'The players stay all over the city!' Mary-Jane said. 'Go on then, tell me, best route.' She closed the book.

'Well that's easy: Somerset Road, turn right along the Common, Tibbet's corner, down Putney Hill, over the bridge—'

'Completely wrong. And it seems we're not allowed to use the bridge.'

'Ah. How odd. Why's that? OK then, Wandsworth Bridge? Battersea?'

She didn't care, actually, if the tennis stars each took a private helicopter or jet-skied up the Thames: she was still wondering about Ilex and the police car. She half-listened while Mary-Jane gave her a road-by-road account that surely, by Clover's muddled reckoning, would result in a highly nervous potential men's finalist wondering why his chauffeuse had parked outside Battersea Dogs' Home and was now holding a map upside down on the steering wheel.

When Mary-Jane paused for breath, Clover asked, 'Mary-Jane, could I just borrow your mobile for a sec please?'

'Sure, of course you can!' Mary-Jane gave her a swift questioning look as she handed over the phone, then pushed back her chair. 'Tell you what – I'll just go up the stairs for a quick wazz and leave you to it. I'll order a couple of glasses of wine on the way back. Pinot G. OK for you?'

'Oh yes, lovely, thanks,' Clover murmured, dialling Ilex's number. He answered on the second ring, sounding nervous and a bit breathless.

'Hey, brother, how are you? You sound as if you've been running.' Or could it be . . . no, what a horrible thought. You didn't want to picture your own brother having sex with anyone at all, particularly not someone in a cop car. Apart from awful imaginings of flesh and discarded polyester clothing, there might be guns. Or an Alsatian.

'Oh! Clover, it's you! I didn't recognize the number. Where are you?' He sounded relieved. And where was *he*? Was he in a cell, waiting for a pair of detectives to give him the nice and nasty treatment?

'I'm having lunch at the Bluebird with Mary-Jane. I saw you just now, Ilex.'

'No, you didn't. You couldn't have,' Ilex answered too fast and too emphatically. Now she knew it had been him. When he was little he always used to get himself into trouble by leaping in with an answer too quickly. So often he'd blurt out 'It wasn't me' long before Lottie had even known a window was broken or that the dog was covered in paint.

'I did see you. You were in a police car,' Clover told him, watching the stairs for the return of Mary-Jane. Mary-Jane would never believe it wasn't Sean she was interrogating, or that Clover wasn't having an affair and accusing her lover of being unfaithful with his own wife. Ilex now stayed silent.

'And you saw me too and pretended you didn't,' Clover persisted – she knew she'd get there in the end.

There was a sigh from Ilex. Result, thought Clover gleefully, she'd cracked him.

'So what's going on then? Have you been arrested? What have you done?'

'It's nothing,' Ilex told her. 'It's just . . . um . . . someone at work had her bag stolen and they think it was taken by a man I'd seen in reception so the police took me for a quick ride round the area in case I saw him again.'

Clover laughed. 'Are you mad? That's a completely rubbish story, Ilex! Can't you do better than that?'

Mary-Jane was now on her way back, followed by a waiter with a tray of drinks and an order pad.

'You're up to something, aren't you?' she hissed quickly at her brother. 'Who is it?'

'Clover, it's nothing. It nearly was, but it isn't. I've got Manda . . . no intention of being with anyone else. Just *please* don't—'

'It's a *policeman*?' Clover squeaked. 'Have you gone the other—'

'No! A police *woman*. Oooh, Clover the sexist!' he jeered. 'God, if Mum could hear you – she'd be appalled!'

'If Manda could only hear *you*,' Clover retorted, 'how do you think *she'd* feel? Does the word "devastated" mean anything to you?'

'But she won't hear, will she?' Ilex's tone turned almost to pleading. 'Not from you? Think how hurt she'd be. Over nothing, truly. Nothing happened.'

'Hmm. If it was really nothing, then you'd better prove it. Make it up to her.'

'What's to make up for? She doesn't know anything, never needs to,' Ilex reminded her.

'Yes; but *I* know, don't I? Think about it, Ilex, think about our lovely family home being flogged off like some unwanted old toaster on eBay. And in case you're not sure what I'm getting at, think of those eBay toasters,' she said sweetly, 'don't toasters always make you think of wedding presents?'

'That's blackmail.' Ilex sounded defeated.

'Well spotted!' Clover laughed. 'Whoever said it was an ugly word? I think it's rather a pretty one! Just *ask her*, Ilex. Get on with it.'

'Trouble?' Mary-Jane asked as soon as they'd ordered their food and the waiter was out of earshot.

'No! Not any more!' Clover picked up her glass and grinned at Mary-Jane. 'There was a small family tussle but I've dealt with it. I'd definitely say it was game, set and match to me!'

The smooth house agent, Harry, certainly didn't waste any time. Mac and Lottie hadn't yet agreed to take up his Digby, James and Humphreys' offer; hadn't agreed any percentage terms or an advertising budget for the sale of Holbrook House and yet there he was, on the phone and highly persuasive with news of a potential client.

'I wouldn't normally do this, of course,' he told her. 'It's not the usual way we conduct our business, obviously.'

Cynically, Lottie wondered which bits were 'obvious' and 'of course' about it, unless you counted the fact that he would, both obviously and of course, almost kill to get this sale. Before she knew it, and she could almost see his beaming smile, she'd agreed she'd got two days to make the house presentable before a Mr and Mrs Cresswell ('. . . always *dreamed* of a Lutyens property . . .') swished up the weed-strewn drive to give her home a highly critical once-over.

Out on the terrace, Sorrel was supposed to be revising the finer points of Othello's descent into madness for the next day's exam but was instead making a long list of must-haves from the Travel Paraphernalia catalogue. She sat shaded from the sun by a vast green canvas umbrella, which must have been stored over the winter close to a mouse-nest, if the tatty fretwork of holes was anything to go by. What was left of it sheltered the long teak table, an item randomly scarred by years of careless barbecue sparks, its legs chewed – and Lottie never knew why they all did this – by each successive wolfhound. Not, Lottie now thought as she looked at it with the eye of a potential buyer, a scene that spoke of luxury outdoor living. It would take more than a scattering of Cath Kidston floral cushions and a thirty-hole tray of scented tea-lights to turn this terrace into a midsummer feature page from *Living Etc*. And was she supposed to smarten up the people as well as the house? She'd long accepted that Mac hated clothes shopping, but surely, when your elbow had gone through a linen sleeve, it was time to chuck out the shirt?

'So do you think these house buyers are for real?' Sorrel looked up from her list and asked her parents. 'They might just be a plant so that you'll be impressed and sign up with his agency. They could be his mum and dad or something, just posing as buyers.'

'They could be his parents,' Mac agreed, 'or they could be about to hand us a cheque that would have your average Lottery winner popping the champagne and thinking they'd be all right for giving up the day job.'

'Or in your case,' Sorrel sighed, 'abandoning your teenage daughter to a university bedsit and nowhere to go in the holidays.'

'Oh come on now, Sorrel, we did offer to buy you a little

flat in the village. Even Ilex thought that would be a good investment. And there's always Clover. She's got plenty of room for you and she won't mind being a base for when you're not at Exeter.'

'What? You haven't even asked her! The very idea of it made her look scared rigid!' Sorrel bit her lip. She'd been *that* close to letting it out that they'd all been over to Clover's for dinner. If they found out, they'd be so hurt at the thought that all their family had ganged up together behind their backs. And it might make them even more determined to go – sometimes, parents could be more stubborn and silly than small children.

'And we won't be gone for ever. Months rather than years, you know. We'll have to live somewhere when we get back.' Lottie tried to reassure her. 'By then you'll probably think sharing a place with your doddery old folks is a completely horrible idea!'

'You might not be gone for ever but the money will,' Sorrel grumbled. 'You'll blow it all on air fares at silly prices just because you do stuff on impulse. You could do the whole world dead cheap, even first class, if you planned it right. The way you talk, you're just, like, gonna dash from one thing to another all over the place, never mind the cost.' Then she added, with a sly smile, 'Or the jet lag . . . you haven't thought of that, have you? Old people get jet lag much worse than young ones. You'll *really* suffer.'

'Oh we'll be planning it properly, don't you worry. We just haven't quite got round to sorting out an order of play,' Mac said. 'And when we get back, that'll be the time for decisions. We don't know where we want to live. We want open-options on that, probably renting for a bit. It could be a flat in Soho – or it might be something remote on Dartmoor. Who knows?'

'I know it won't be Dartmoor,' Lottie interrupted, shuddering. 'Too cold, too remote, too . . . *sheepy*.'

Sorrel grinned, her face transformed as if all the lights in her head had suddenly come on. 'But Soho – excellent idea! Like, why don't we find somewhere really great there *now*, and then I can move into it and take care of it for you for when you get back? That way, you don't have to worry that I haven't got anywhere to live and you've got some- where with all your stuff in it for coming back to the minute that you get a bit fed up!' She looked appealingly at Lottie. 'I mean, suppose you wanted just to dash back and see us all for a little break, like you felt homesick or something? You'd need a base then.'

'We'd thought of that: we could always stay at a hotel,' Mac said, 'or at a club. We'll join one of those that old fossils who live out in the colonies come to when they need to see their stockbrokers or get their wills looked at by the ancient family solicitor. The sort of place where you'd run into the old Major from across the road, downing a pink gin and reminiscing about tiger-shoots.'

'They'd never let us join,' Lottie said. 'Don't you have to be at least ninety-five and have been big in the Indian Civil Service? And do they let women in?'

'See?' Sorrel was triumphant. 'That's what I mean! You'll need to find somewhere to rent for later on. Great. As soon as the exams are done I'll start. Soho! Fantastic!'

'But you're going to Australia,' Lottie pointed out.

'Oh I know, that's OK. We could get Ilex to sort out a shorthold tenancy for three months and then I can move straight in when I get home. Sorted. See? Now. Mum and Dad, look at this lot: I've made you a list. You're going to need all these.'

Lottie went to take the list from her but Sorrel held on tight and started to read. 'OK, now listen carefully because these things could be life-savers. So. First of all you'll need a strap-on body pocket, for cash and passport and stuff that you absolutely don't need to lose. You wear it under your clothes so it's not nick-able. Because the world isn't really full of sweet old hippies like you two, you know. Or rather you don't.'

'Sounds sensible.' Lottie nodded.

'And a survival whistle. In case you get lost in the out-back or a jungle; then you need a sterile first-aid kit, one that's got all your own syringes and sutures. Oh, and a dental one as well because at your age . . .' Sorrel pulled a face.

'Oh thanks,' Lottie said. 'You think all our teeth are about to fall out.'

'You'll thank me, honestly,' Sorrel said. 'And obviously you'll need a Swiss army knife with just about every attachment that they do, plus an ultralight headlamp in case you're struggling to get out of a ravine in the dark—'

'Hang on a minute, Sorrel,' Mac interrupted. 'When did the "luxury" aspect disappear from our agenda? Because the word "struggling" wasn't actually meant to feature in any of the trips I had in mind.'

'You've got to be prepared,' Sorrel told him sternly. 'And what about a portable smoke alarm? Some of the places you stay in might be death traps in a fire.'

'I don't think the Maharaja's palace in Jaipur is going to be unfamiliar with basic safety issues,' he told her.

'And then there's the Magicool body cooler,' Sorrel continued. 'It says it's great for ladies of a certain age.'

Lottie grimaced. 'That's you, Mum,' Sorrel said, in case Lottie didn't know. 'And Air Flight gel, those flight socks so you won't get an embolism, acupressure jet-lag patches, silk sleeping-bag liners, trek towels, travel soap, plug adaptor, insect repellent—'

'You've forgotten the partridge, and the pear tree,' Mac said. 'And you're certain we need all this stuff?'

'Um . . . well . . . yes. Two lots of everything. Except the dental kit and the body cooler. Just one each of those. I mean, if you're buying it all for your own safety, you'd want to get it all for me too, wouldn't you? Obviously?'

'Obviously,' Lottie agreed, defeated. 'I just wonder about excess baggage, that's all.'

Ilex didn't much mind the idea of marrying Manda. The more he thought about the constantly pursuing terror that was Wendy the more he felt the need to run to Manda for safety. It was such bliss simply to be in his own apartment with someone so easy to live with. He had certain reservations, one of them to do with feeling he was being firmly pushed into it by Clover, but he had to admit that perhaps he needed that push: he'd assumed he'd get round to it some time. Now was as good a time as any. Better, anyway, than waiting for a crisis to be the spur. And that crisis could well be to do with Wendy, if he wasn't careful. There were other reservations he'd simply have to find a way round: for one, that people were definitely going to snigger during the ceremony when it was revealed that his middle name was 'Adonis'. It would ripple all round the church or what-ever venue Manda went for. He'd just have to think about how childish they were being. Maybe he could change it, in the next few months, to Alan or something. Or maybe they wouldn't notice: loads of people had embarrassing middle names. It could be a lot worse – some unlucky sods were named after the England World Cup squad or Ringo or were christened John Elvis-Presley Smith. Parents could be so unthinkingly cruel when their brains were mashed by childbirth.

He looked at Manda now, as she sat looking silky-pretty across from him at their table in Le Caprice and sipping so very neatly at her pre-dinner champagne that her lipstick didn't smudge, and he thought about the many reasons why he should get on with it and simply propose to her. Would she turn him down? He didn't think so. She'd been showing definite signs of nesting: the cookbook collection was growing; she'd taken to buying little things for her sister's twins and pointing out to him how cute they were. New, velvety, jewel-coloured cushions kept appearing on the sofas. As for the positives, at the most superficial level she was a truly stunning woman and was certain to mature, with those super-fine cheekbones, and slender frame, into a very beautiful one. He definitely wouldn't be faced with some lumpy, frizz-haired old boiler in twenty years' time. Also, apart from a perfectly amiable sister, she had no relatives to scrutinize him and find him wanting in any department. From what he'd heard of friends' marriages, in-laws could be a dire interference. Women were fond of their mums. They went out on shopping trips with them where they told them things in a Starbucks break between shoe-purchases. Not good. You wouldn't want every little niggle reported back – suppose they talked about personal stuff? Suppose Manda found his *Fuzz* magazines and had a mum to run to and tell? And look at Clover. She still called Holbrook House 'home' – what must Sean feel about that?

Then there was Manda's tidiness. OK, that was hardly top of the list when you were seeking out a life-long soul-mate but total sloppiness on home premises would be a definite no. If a woman was a dedicated clothes-scatterer and bathroom slob when there were just the two of them in a minimally furnished flat, imagine what she'd be like when there were a couple of children, and all their toy-junk to be dealt with? He'd be forever scooping up Playmobile bits and crunching tiny cars underfoot. Ah but children. That was the big one. She wanted them, he could tell. There was a Mini Boden catalogue in the flat – she claimed her sister Caro had left it there but had she?

Did he want children? He'd probably get used to the idea, eventually, once they turned seven or so. Given the option, it now occurred to Ilex that at the moment he'd really rather have a cat. He liked them but had never owned one – Mac and Lottie had always kept wolfhounds, possibly as many as four or five of them in sequence

196

during his growing up, and each one called Bonzo. Mac had said it was simply what he called his dog and that was that, no choice, no protests allowed. A grey cat would be nice. Simon at work had a cousin who bred British Blue ones – big solid dense-furred creatures with Cheshire-cat grins and fat, cartoon faces. The big question remained to be asked though: what did Manda think? So, he thought, here goes.

'Manda? I just want to ask you something.'

'What is it, Lexy?' Manda purred. Great eyes, he thought. They managed a rare trick of looking soulful and saucy at the same time.

'I just wondered . . .' he asked, hesitating. *Lexy?* God, not her as well. Had she been talking to Wendy?

'Come on . . . you can ask me anything, darling. You know that.' Manda slid her hand across the breadcrumbs he'd nervously scattered on the table.

'It's just . . . Manda, I was wondering, if you'd consider . . .'

'Yes?' She leaned forward and smiled, giving his hand a gentle, encouraging squeeze.

'Would you like to . . . ? Maybe it's time we . . .'

'Mmm . . . go on!' Her eyes were all glittery and excited now. It looked like he was on for a yes.

'I was wondering,' he stroked her fingers, and she curled them round his, caressing, 'do you think,' he continued, 'would you consider the possibility of us maybe . . . getting a cat?'

Only moments later, out on the pavement, Ilex watched in dismay as Manda's taxi sped away. He went back inside to pay the bill for the food they'd ordered but not eaten, but first asked for a restorative brandy and climbed on to the end bar stool, avoiding the eyes of nearby diners who for once weren't being too cool to stare.

'The young lady's had to leave then?' the barman commented sympathetically as he handed Ilex the drink.

'Yeah.' Ilex sighed, wishing he was, at this moment, a smoker. That was one hell of a speedy flurry she'd left in – up from the table, jacket grabbed and out through the revolving door in one fluid movement, leaving it spinning fast and furious, along with the echo of just one heartfelt violently spat-out word: 'Bastard.'

'It seems I said something,' Ilex confided to the barman. 'All I did was ask her one simple question. She didn't even answer.'

'Oh, I think she did, sir,' the barman told him. 'I'd say she definitely did.'

# THIRTEEN

Shifty. That was the word. Clover, driving to collect Elsa from her *Bébé France* class, was quite certain this was precisely the word for the way Sean was behaving at the moment. He had suddenly taken to using his mobile phone for all outgoing calls, and if it rang he'd answer quickly and move swiftly out of the room to talk. He'd developed a peculiar way of speaking into it – as if only half his mouth worked – together with an awkward lopsided stoop when walking, protecting the thing from sight as well as hearing. She no longer dared to check his calls or go through his pockets, not now he really was behaving so strangely. After all, it was one thing to go through life on a level of mild suspicion – that was just sensible self-preservation, wasn't it? Surely safer for the soul than blind trust? But it was quite another to feel thoroughly agonized that you really might have something substantial to be suspicious about. After all, who could blame Sean if he'd found someone more spontaneous and exciting to have sex with? Someone who would be all too willing to cancel everything at a second's notice to go and have sex in a swish hotel? What an idiot she was. If he'd only ask her again, she'd settle for an hour in a Travel Lodge at the back of the nearest Little Chef. She decided, as she drove dangerously subconsciously through the afternoon school-run traffic, that she'd be the one to do the suggesting. What they needed was a couple of nights away somewhere, just the two of them, for some passionate re-bonding. Might as well do these things while they still could, while Mac and Lottie were there at Holbrook House with time and space for their only grandchildren, before they sold up and ran out on them all. Stop it now, Clover told herself, feeling that tension was pushing tears into her eyes again. Stop being such a self-centred baby. Cars behind started beeping and she realized she was sitting staring into space while the traffic lights had turned green. A glossy-looking young woman in a Discovery, presumably also on the school run, put two fingers up at her and shot past her. So rude.

It also crossed Clover's mind, as she pulled into the road by the school, that Sean's new interest might not be a real person at all. He was also, these days, spending hours on the internet in his study upstairs, flicking swiftly to a screen saver whenever Clover tried to slide softly into the room to catch a glimpse at what he was looking at. Oh God, please don't let him develop a porno chat-room habit, she thought as she parked the Touareg behind Mary-Jane's Street Ka. Or even worse, please don't let him have hit on a special new on-line lust-interest. She hoped he hadn't fallen for that old scam – didn't they always turn out to have as much substance as a child's imaginary friend? He could be deluding himself he'd pulled a twenty-two-year-old Russian lovely. She'd read about mid-life men who did that. Men who, driven by a testosterone level that was pumped to a giddy height of over-excitement, would race off to meet their slinky beloved for a session of rampant sex in one of those sleaze-dives that charge for rooms by the hour, only to find instead a couple of burly muggers lying in wait to relieve him of all credit cards, empty his bank account and possibly even subject their gullible victim to a dose of blackmail.

She wished she hadn't been so flippant with that word now, using it the other day on Ilex. There was absolutely nothing funny or pretty about it. And that one had back-fired, hadn't it? Something must have gone horribly wrong there, or Ilex wouldn't now be back in his old bedroom at Holbrook House with no possessions other than what Manda had crammed into a suitcase and hurled down the stairwell of their apartment block. Manda wasn't telling anyone what had happened. Clover and Lottie had both tried but she was keeping both the apartment phone and her mobile switched to voice-mail. And of course it was no good asking Ilex. Lottie said he'd muttered something completely unintelligible about blue cats, then refused point blank to elaborate further. Why didn't men *talk*? Clover was completely convinced that so much that was wrong in the world could be sorted out perfectly easily if men, and, well, everyone really, would just open up to each other a bit more, the way women did. You could get so much straight in your head with a girlfriend, tea and a gooey piece of home-baked chocolate cake.

'Hi, Clover! Everything all right?' Mary-Jane, jaunty and sleek as ever in a new pair of skinny jeans, was already out of the building, firmly stuffing the plump little back end of Jakey through her car door.

Clover looked up, startled out of her dismal thoughts. 'Everything all right?' was that the question?

'Oh . . . hi! Er, yes! Yes everything's fine! Really great!'

Well, there it was. When it came to it, what else could you say?

'So you were growing herbs and salad crops as a commercial enterprise? Won't you miss it?' Mrs Cresswell's delicate high gold sandals were not best suited to the uneven terrain in the orchard. Lottie hoped the poor woman wouldn't turn her ankle. She looked the clued-up, smart sort who might sue. Chickens wandered around, pecking speculatively at her feet in the hope that her painted toenails would turn into sweet berries. Mr Cresswell hung back by the gate, rightly wary of Charlie the cockerel, who was fast approaching and doing his best aggressive sideways strut while trailing one wing stylishly like a bullfighter with his cloak, closing in for the strike.

Commercially? Well, Lottie had to think for a moment before answering that one. 'Commercially' implied there was profit in it, as opposed to loss. Frankly, she and Mac couldn't honestly claim that any of their enterprises had been what a generous-natured person would call 'commercial', not if you wanted to append the word 'success' with any accuracy.

'It was more of an interest that sort of grew,' she explained instead, choosing her words carefully. 'A couple of years ago there was some space that needed filling in the east long border so we decided to mix in some ruby chard and purslane among the flowers, just for family use and it, well . . . sort of took off from there.'

Was Mrs Cresswell really interested? Might she be harbouring thoughts of carrying on the business herself, trusting it could be a convenient, part-time little number that would keep her amused between doing the school run and having lunch with her book club circle? She was probably already certain that she'd make a better go of it than Mac and Lottie, go in for some smart marketing, fancy labels with lots of cute descriptive detail, a pretty little water-colour of the house, all that. Maybe even a couple of goes at a Saturday farmers' market. Perhaps Lottie should warn this so-elegant Mrs Cresswell in her DKNY denims and cream loose-knit Joseph cardi that there was more to supplying your family and a selection of the county's finest restaurants with wholesome home-grown veg than swanning about on sunny mornings in baby-pink Hunter wellies, clutching a hand-crafted Suffolk trug. Really, at the very mention of the garden's earning potential, Lottie should do the woman a huge favour and go, 'Nooooo do not grow herbs! Weed out every floppy snail-magnet lettuce!'

So to the second question it was no, Lottie would have no regrets about giving up this particular enterprise. Whatever had made them start it? They must have been crazy. Lottie was inclined to blame Hugh Fearnley-Whittingstall for making self-sufficiency look such an idyllic option on TV. Did *he* lie awake wondering if the weather forecast would mean drought or drowning for his flourishing veg patch? No, of course not. He had it all much better organized than that. Thinking back, she could date the beginning of this urge to nurture crops from the night she'd watched him (on TV, fortunately, not for close-up real) bedding down naked in his polytunnel to sleep among his seedlings. She must have been feeling a pre-menopausal tweak of earth-mother broodiness at the time, imagining she'd care deeply about whether her radishes were nourished to a plump juicy size and that she'd be lavishing this hand-raised bounty on an eager, benevolent band of grateful consumers. Hugh F-W hadn't said a lot about slugs and snails, other than being shown looking very enthusiastic while he made his nightly torchlight collection of them seem like the second-best fun you could have in the dark. Nor did he seem to suffer the theft of entire beds of crops by rabbits. Maybe after he'd done the slug-round he sat in wait for the bunnies for the rest of the night, leaning against a wall, beneath a perfectly espaliered peach tree with a shotgun, a flask of his own nettle-leaf tea and a substantial slice of home-cooked rook pie.

Annoying as the garden pests were, the customers were possibly the worst of the lot. It would be no loss if she never again had to explain patiently that Good King Henry was a salad ingredient not a forgotten monarch, or that experimental stripy yellow tomatoes deserved better than to be sneered at by people who considered themselves gourmets, and there'd be no more dismay at seeing plump yellow courgettes being poked at suspiciously by idiots who thought they were green ones that had gone off. There would also be no more realizing too late that sorrel and rocket should have been planted in the cooler of the long borders – the one that faced east – rather than in the warmer one where they wilted in the blazing afternoon sun and bolted to seed the moment you took your eyes off them. And, best of all, no more round trips of twenty miles to deliver two boxes of applemint that had been left out of the order for the Pimm's promotion at the sodding Fothering Manor Hotel, only to find that 'someone' had, in the meantime, remembered that the hotel had a rampant patch of the stuff growing wild on the far side of their rose garden. If that was actually true; it could be that 'someone' didn't want to admit they'd actually nipped out to Waitrose and bought up their entire pre-packed supply rather than wait for her to whiz all the way back with the forgotten delivery.

'We still have the plans for the original planting in the long borders,' Lottie told the Cresswells. 'No vegetables there, obviously.' She laughed, slightly nervously. Why were these people making it such hard work? There was an unmistakable air of slightly amazed disapproval about the two of them: a sort of 'goodness, why on earth did you do *that*?' It had started in the house, where the sight of the black-painted sitting room had brought a spluttered 'Well, that's, um ... different!' from Mrs C. Perhaps in future she'd simply go out for a few hours when viewers (if any more turned up) were due and leave the selling-side to the agent. Let Harry – or the next one, she hadn't got round to sounding out another company yet – do his bit to earn his percentage. She'd already had to apologize for the sight of the miserable Ilex, sprawled flat out at midday on a bed wearing a motheaten old tartan dressing gown that he must have dug out from one of the blanket boxes on the middle landing. Not an attractive sight when you were trying to highlight the house's better points.

'It would be lovely to restore all this,' Mrs Cresswell mused tactlessly, 'get it back to how it was originally with banks of lupins and lavender and lots of lovely clematis. And shouldn't there be pergolas?' She looked accusingly at Lottie.

'Well there are, along the other border.' Lottie pointed past the central terrace where the silted-up rill waited its turn to be shown off, if that was the right term.

'The ones on this side had to be removed for safety reasons.' The Cresswells had three young children. They surely wouldn't want them at risk from tumbling, crumbling poles simply for the sake of symmetry.

'I suppose it's all a matter of the right staff.' Mrs Cresswell now addressed her husband, who was looking thoroughly bored and slightly nervous. So far, his wife's comments had added up to a hefty and expensive shopping list. If he mentally added up the cost of several refurbished bathrooms, an entire new kitchen, the mended roof (all authentic hand-cut tiles), plus a renovated garden, Lottie could only be surprised he wasn't already revving up his Mercedes and roaring off in search of a cheaper county. He'd perked up at the sight of Mac's studio though and had looked dangerously close to picking up one of the guitars for a quick strum but had thought better of it. It would serve Mac right if he had messed about with the instruments, Lottie thought, given that Mac's one contribution to this first viewing had been to leave the house for an urgent visit to his drinking friends down at the Feathers – throwing her the not-helpful comment 'Don't let them touch anything' as he left.

After the Cresswells had gone, Lottie walked back down to the orchard. She stopped at the gate to look back at the house and tried to make herself rekindle the deep, loving attachment she'd felt for the place when she and Mac had first lived there. It wasn't at all that she'd developed a dislike for it (who could?), but now that it no longer held a growing family it seemed to have a faintly disappointed air about it, close to accusing its occupants of carelessly underusing its qualifications, like a company MD reduced to doing the filing. If a building could have an expression, it looked as bored as a can-kicking ten year old in mid-August whose playmates have all gone away on holiday. Perhaps Mr and Mrs Cresswell could be the ones to cheer the place up, filling it with children and fresh new furnishings. The garden should have a sand pit again and one of those fantastic swing/slide/activity centres that all three of her own children had so loved. And another tree house. The one that used to be at the far end of the orchard had been Mac's one and only hammer-and-nails enterprise. He, Al and George, equipped with a huge collection of newly bought equipment from B&Q and vague memories of school woodwork classes, had spent an intense weekend building the thing among the low-slung branches of an oak that leaned at a precarious angle from the side bank of the field. The plan had been to make the construction look like a cross between a fort and a fairy castle but it had ended up looking as if someone had carelessly dropped a shed into the tree from a great height and then tried to patch it up. Ilex and Clover had loved it all the same, although Ilex had fought a long and bitter war to fend off Clover's attempts to pretty up the place with cushions and curtains. When the tree, its house and contents had all crashed to the ground on the night of Michael Fish's 'not a hurricane' in 1987, the orchard had been festooned like a field of prayer-flags with her various bits of decorative cloth.

Lottie wandered across the field to look at the tree's replacement – a stout sapling grown from one of the original's acorns. It was doing well – close to twenty years on – but it would be a long time, maybe another century, before it could hold a tree house. Whose children would be here then?

'I don't know what went wrong.' Ilex was well aware that he was bleating his entire tale of woe – even down to the bit where Manda swooshed so dramatically out of the restaurant – to the wrong person, but it was Wendy's own fault if she wouldn't take no for an answer and kept following him around. If she wanted to settle for taking the

'Just Friends' role as she'd now (so contrary this – when would he ever understand women?) told him she'd decided she preferred, then she could bloody well behave like one and deal with the rough bits that came with the deal. He could hardly confide in his male friends, after all. They'd just study the floor in craven embarrassment and mutter about did he fancy another pint and wasn't the Arsenal/Villarreal match a travesty? The metrosexual revolution might be up and running, according to the weekly Man-Style features in the Saturday papers, but he didn't yet know any male who'd a) carry a handbag or b) voluntarily sit around discussing 'feelings' when they could be talking about the next Ashes series.

Wendy was perched opposite him on a bar stool in the King's Head in Putney, dangerously close to Manda-territory. What if she came in *right now*? Ilex wondered, looking at the door in half-hope. That would show her – she'd see he was capable of a life without her. Look at me, he'd be bragging, I'm fine, see? Got your replacement sorted already – it's what happens when you fling your beloved's stuff down the stairs and won't answer the phone. She'd be begging him to come back home, if she could see him now. She'd be desperate to get him away from this scary, bosomy rival. Or maybe she wouldn't. Maybe she'd come in with some big, bronzed pilot she'd pulled at Gatwick, a man who'd say all the right things over a restaurant table and whose pants wouldn't be decoratively dangling from banisters down two flights of stairs, unless they'd been in such a hurry to get them off him . . . Ilex groaned at the thought. The idea of her in bed with someone else, doing all that stuff that was just Manda-and-Ilex, didn't bear thinking about.

'Do you *really* not know what you did wrong, Ilex?' Wendy smirked, taking another sip at her Bacardi and Diet Coke. She'd stopped calling him Lexy, which must mean she was moving herself out of range. She'd also left a vivid lipstick imprint on the glass. He wondered if she'd leave a similar imprint on his dick. A couple of weeks ago and he'd hardly been able to keep her from trying – now she'd gone all hands-off and 'let's just talk'. What was this? A sneaky new tactic? Something she'd read about in one of those 'Bag Your Man' features?

'You asked your long-term girlfriend if she'd like to get a *cat*? Think about it!' He shook his head and sighed dejectedly yet again. The evening wasn't going well. He should have stayed down in Surrey and watched back-to-back repeats of *Dinner Ladies*.

She leaned forward and put her hand on his leg. 'I'll try it out on you,' she murmured. 'I'll start to ask you a question and you see if you can finish the sentence for me . . .'

She leaned closer. Ilex could see the lace edge of a lime-green bra down the front of her black top. And lots of pale, soft flesh. Wendy had the kind of cleavage that you could hatch an orphaned egg in. It crossed his mind that as he was technically a free man, he could, if the mood took him, go back to hers and indulge in an idle night of guilt-free passion. Maybe, feeling sorry for him, she would even be understanding about the uniform thing. Sadly, it was typical of his luck that not only had she suddenly shifted her personal goalposts, the mood, unfortunately, *didn't* take him. A mercy-shag might be just the thing to perk the spirits. Right now though he could barely raise a smile, let alone anything that would impress Wendy in the bedroom department. Even if a whole troop of fully uniformed Policewomen of All Nations came marching through in formation, he'd prefer to look at the bottom of his beer glass and mull over his troubles.

Wendy, strangely, now suddenly seemed to be doing her best to change this. She was whispering close and warm into his ear and her fingers were working their way higher up his leg. Her voice had gone all sultry and she was purring the words: 'You know, Ilex, what I'd really, really like to do to you is . . .' Then she pulled herself and her hand away suddenly, asking, 'OK, now you tell me . . . what is it I'd really, really like to do to you?' She licked her lips, not in an obvious come-and-get-it way, but almost obliviously. So sexy – did they practise that?

Ilex felt very pink and looked around, flustered. The pub was busy for a Tuesday. 'I can't say it here! There's too many people!' He looked at the lipstick mark on her glass and thought again about possibilities. Sadly, even now, after a thigh-mauling, and the view down that cleavage, it barely caused a stirring. If Manda had really gone for good, he hoped this situation, too, wouldn't prove permanent.

'Oh really?' Wendy raised her eyebrows and smirked knowingly. 'So you assume it was *rude* and *suggestive*, do you?'

Ilex smirked.

'Wrong!' She slapped a hand on the bar-top. 'I was going

to say I'd really, really like to tell you to get lost and go and do your oh-poor-me whinging somewhere else!' Ilex shook his head, trying to settle confused thoughts.

'*Now* do you see what I mean?' She sounded triumphant. 'You think I'm on track to say one thing, but really it's something completely different. Think about it from your dippy girlfriend's point of view. I must say,' Wendy sniffed, 'she's a bit of a saddo. Why can't she tell *you* what she wants instead of waiting for you to ask? She'll still be waiting this time next century, dozy cow.'

Ilex sighed. Would he ever understand how women's thought processes worked? No wonder 'what do women want?' was the eternal question. There was just no eternal answer. He'd made Manda think he was going to ask her one question and somehow it was all his fault that he'd asked her the wrong one. OK, he *had* been going to ask her the big one – but she couldn't possibly have known that, could she? No way could she have seen it coming. Not then, not till he'd actually come out with it as a big surprise. So what she'd flounced out of the restaurant over remained a mystery. Only one thing he knew for certain: whatever Manda wanted (a holiday? More bloody shoes? A bigger flat? Eternal love, babies and the whole she-bang?), it definitely wasn't a cat.

Clover took the card out of her bag for possibly the fiftieth time that day and thought about calling Harry. She'd have to come up with a good reason – although he'd seemed to like her, quite a lot, he was probably like that with all his clients and she didn't want to make a total idiot of herself.

Maybe she could ask him about the Cresswells – see if they'd come back to him about buying Holbrook House. But then he'd probably wonder why she didn't simply ask Mac and Lottie. Or he might not. If Harry was anything like Sean he would be a simple soul and not much given to analysis of the emotional stuff. That would be why Sean hadn't really understood why she'd made such a 'song and dance', as he'd called it, years ago when he'd cheated on her. As far as he'd been concerned, it had been a simple episode of out-of-character madness and was all over. Enough said. He didn't get it about the emotional fall-out that she was left with. All the same, she put the card back in her bag and picked up her car keys to go and collect Sophia from school. She didn't really think she had it in her to start an affair. There were too many people who could be hurt.

It was only as she was edging the Touareg out on to the main road that it came to her that Sean had told her he'd pick Sophia up on his way home from the dentist. And he really had gone to the dentist – she'd phoned the surgery on the pretext that he'd forgotten his appointment time and she was just checking for him that it was for 2.30, not 3 p.m.

Clover couldn't see Sean's BMW at first. It was just as well she'd turned up. He must have forgotten. Either that or he'd been persuaded into some must-have dental treatment. He was probably lying back in the chair while some sultry hygienist leaned over him in a short white coat and fluttered her mascara at him, persuading him that for a mere thousand pounds he could have teeth so white he'd need sunglasses just to look in the mirror. Surely someone would have called her? Wouldn't he need her to know, for Sophia's sake, that he'd be late?

The Hugh-Grant-lookalike dad gave her a friendly smile as he walked past her car towards the school gate. Nice man. Had he really fallen prey to Mary-Jane, as she had hinted? She hoped not. She hadn't seen his wife very often (one of the corporate lawyer brigade, rushing late into the carol service with a bulging briefcase and time-management issues) but she seemed a woman who would have no truck with marital silliness in her over-busy life. Lucky her.

And, as Clover climbed out of the Touareg, there was Sean's car after all. It was parked a little way past the school, at the far end of the long line of parent-mobiles and behind a big unfamiliar dark green Ford, covered in bright corporate logos. So, Clover realized, Mary-Jane was using her Wimbledon courtesy car to pick up Polly in her work hours, something Mary-Jane had already mentioned as being strictly forbidden. Nice one – Polly would enjoy that, sitting in the back having people peering in at the traffic lights to see if she was actually Maria Sharapova. Still, at least it was probably a better use for the vehicle's down time than Mary-Jane parking it up by Wimbledon wind-mill so she could have some hot moments down among the ferns on the Common with a third-round drop-out in need of consolation.

Clover hung back for a moment, reaching into the car to collect the bag of Iced Gems she'd brought for Sophia. As she straightened up, her head swam slightly and she wasn't, for a moment, sure of what her eyes were seeing. There, in the middle of the pavement, were Sean and Mary-Jane, arms round each other, hugging and laughing. Just as quickly, they pulled away from each other and crossed the road, separate now but still laughing together. The Hugh-Grant dad, waiting outside the school gate, looked across in Clover's direction and smiled at her again, but this time a little uncertainly. Clover ignored him and his sympathy, her eyes blurry with furious tears. She climbed straight back into the Touareg, started the engine and did a furious three-point turn, not caring that impatient school-run cars were speeding at her from all angles. If she got home in the fastest possible time, she could be packed and have her own, Elsa's and Sophia's bags ready to load into the car by the time he came home. Home! So much for that! Home is where you run to, where you feel safe and secure. She'd be on the A3 down to Holbrook House before Sean could get the first sentence of an excuse out. Bloody Mary-Jane with her perfect bloody idle life and her nanny and her fabulous place in France and her 'Everything all right?'

As if she didn't know. Bitch. Of course it wasn't bloody all right.

# FOURTEEN

'It's a full house down there. You can't move for the kids' toys and bags stuffed with Ilex and Clover's things every-where. Mum's going mad because now she's got a skip on the drive she's trying to get stuff out of the house, not have people bringing more in. Ilex spends all his time lying around watching Sky Sports and Clover's forever bloody crying. Chaos.'

Sorrel turned away from the window, from where she'd been watching Sophia and Elsa racing round the terrace, squealing as they threw handfuls of hedge cuttings about and tried to stuff them down the backs of each other's T-shirts. Al was caught in the middle of their game, trying to clip the hedge but being sent off balance as they crashed around him and into him. The whole scene, Sorrel thought, was a horrible shears-and-arteries accident waiting to happen.

She flopped down on her creaky old brass bed, all her French revision – files, books and notes – squashed beneath her. A copy of Baudelaire's *Les Fleurs du mal*, which lay face down and open, was inch by inch having its spine broken as she wriggled to get comfortable. Gaz was up a stepladder at the end of the bed, carefully adding a pair of Edna Everage-style glasses to his painting of the Queen's head that had so successfully transformed the damp stain on the ceiling. Sorrel was no longer so sure this was a good thing, even though she'd been the one who'd asked him to do it. If she was supposed to side with Clover and help her delay the moment when the house was finally sold then surely it would be better to paint a *trompe-l'oeil* of even more manky and suspicious damp stains to put the punters off rather than disguising the ones that were there. Too late now though, and it did add a certain arty something to the room. Perhaps she'd get him to do the rest of the walls – add the entire royal family, have them doing mad things – a football match would be good. Nothing to do with sex though; this was a room she had to sleep in; for Chrissake, you wouldn't want to open your eyes at three in the morning and see Prince Philip's bits waving at you. Gaz's best subject was art. He was amazing at portraits and could so brilliantly capture the essentials when he painted that made even a rough, quick portrait look just like the person. Perhaps if the two of them ran out of cash when they were away in Australia, he could do sketches of tourists and raise a few dollars that way. It would be like busking, but without the horrible noise. Her contribution could be to fetch the drinks and then lie helpfully on a beach while he worked, keeping nice and still in the sun to conserve energy so they wouldn't need so much expensive food.

'What do you think?' He climbed down and stood back by the door to take a longer view.

'Ace,' Sorrel said, sitting up to appreciate his work. 'Very Rolf Harris. I hope the new people keep it for prosperity and don't just paint over the top. It should stay with the house.'

'Posterity,' Gaz said, giving Sorrel a strange look.

'Posterity. Yeah. Didn't I say that?'

'No. You said "prosperity". You're losing the plot. I thought language was your thing.'

Sorrel slumped back onto the bed. 'It's the pressure. It's getting to me. How am I supposed to concentrate when I don't know if I'll be living on a park bench by September?'

Gaz laughed. 'Come on, Sorrel, don't keep pulling that old one! You know they're gonna be sorting something. And even if they don't, you've always got your sister's place to go to if you need it. It's not like she hasn't got the room.'

'And it's not like she's exactly offered, is it? And anyway, even *she's* not there now, is she? She's here, and howling! "I've leeeeft hiiiim!" ' Sorrel mocked the anguished Clover-wailing that had echoed up the stairs like the keening of a distraught mourner the moment she'd crashed so dramatically into the house the night before, dragging along her two tired and bewildered daughters and a carload of hastily gathered possessions.

'Wha'ever,' Gaz went on. 'We'll be going away ourselves

by then. Your folks will have been away, come back and got themselves a new pad by the time we're home so what does it matter? You're just milking it because of how it's been at school.'

Sorrel threw a pillow at him, which was a mistake as it hit a pot of blue paint which fell off the table and trickled all over the carpet.

'I am so *not* milking it!' she yelled. 'I'm really, *deeply* worried about it!'

No she wasn't. Sorrel knew perfectly well that she had a lucky, lucky life and little to whine about. Even her exams were going well. There'd have to be a massive meltdown for her not to get an A in English and almost certainly in French and history as well, no thanks to parental input and enouragement. Had they once asked how it was going? She'd only had one discussion with her mum, when they'd talked about Jane Austen and the concept of daughters as possessions to be sold off to anyone with a few quid. And even then Lottie hadn't really taken it seriously, saying what a great idea. That Mrs Bennet had had a point: offloading the daughters to the highest bidder was certainly the closest a woman of that era would get to ensuring she'd be properly taken care of in her old age. Sell your daughter: instant pension fund. Sorrel had pointed out that the average female life expectancy in Jane Austen's day had only been about sixty, so then they'd got into a stupid row about whether that was an average brought down by death in childbirth or not. How unhelpful was that? That was the trouble with old parents – it was all about *them*. Millie's mum was much younger and totally busy-busy being a doctor and taking care of her family and wasn't even close to the weirdness Mac and Lottie were going through now they'd decided they had 'Getting Older' and doing things 'While They Could' to deal with.

She slid off the bed and began furiously swabbing at the spilled paint with tissues. There wasn't that much of it but what there was looked as if it meant to leave a dark, fat, oily stain on what used to be quite a good shade of purple. So what? The carpet wasn't going to be staying here for any longer than she was.

Gaz took more tissues from the box and joined in with wiping the paint, spreading the marks even further.

'No, don't, you're making it worse.' Sorrel snatched the tissues from him, rolled them into a knot and hurled them towards the bin. She missed and the knot rolled under the desk.

'You know I'm right,' he said.

'Stop now. You're pushing it, Gaz,' Sorrel warned. She stamped back to the bed and started piling up her books, stacking them on the table beside her computer.

'You know what I mean,' Gaz said, coming to sit beside her. 'You've always hated Carly and that lot, always said they're a bunch of losers. Now they're all being smarmy-nice to you and you're lapping it up. I just don't know how you can even talk to them.'

Sorrel chewed a nail. 'It's only for a bit of peace. And it's not for long, only weeks to go till we're out of that dump for good,' she said, not looking at him. 'You don't know what it's been like, them getting at me for years and years just because I'm some old music legend's baby. Not that he *is* one any more. But the way they've always gone on, you'd think he'd been as famous as Elvis or something. How was I supposed to have known that Carly's dad used to go to every single Charisma gig? I bet he's one of those weirdos who's always sending e-mails to the website and pleading for a come-back concert. And then Dad was so rude to him that time.'

Gaz laughed. 'Yeah, but a) it was years ago and b) it doesn't explain why Carly's always been a cow to you. I mean, people our age, we don't . . . like, no offence to your dad and that but . . . well, all that Charisma stuff isn't exactly our generation's music of choice, is it? I asked my mum once and she said Charisma were somewhere between Fairport Convention and Fleetwood Mac. Like, that gave me a clue what she was talking about?'

'Hey! Bit of respect please!'

'Come on, Soz, what sort of people under forty would have your dad's songs at the top of their i-pod playlists? Only freaks and geeks, man, that's what. So make your mind up, Sorrel. Are Carly's lot evil and jealous like they always have been or are they your new best scummy friends?'

Gaz stood up, looking serious. He was going to leave, she realized, and hate her and never come back. She might not feel a forever kind of love for him – who did at seventeen (apart from that great exception: her mother)? – but it was love of a sort, all the same. Sorrel reached out and took his hand but he pulled it away.

'No, you decide,' he said. 'Those girls at school, they're suddenly being nice to you for a reason. You've just got to think about it. They want something. Work it out for yourself.'

He picked up his bag of books and headed for the door.

'No, Gaz, don't go!' Sorrel shouted. 'Please don't leave me on my own with all these nutters! I'll go insane. You can stay the night?' She stroked her hand across the bed, rearranged the pillows, persuading. 'Mum won't mind. She's too distracted by having Ilex and Clover sulking all over the place. She won't even notice.'

Gaz sighed and leaned on the doorframe. 'Why would I want to stay somewhere where I'm not even *noticed*? Even at home they can offer me a better deal than that.'

'I didn't mean it like that, and you know it!' Sorrel could feel tears threatening. Why did it have to be this stupid way? Gaz doing the 'Me or Them' thing?

'Why are you being like this?' she asked him. 'Why are you suddenly being so critical, just because I've been sitting with some different people during lunch a couple of times? It's no big deal. You and Millie, you're acting like it's some huge betrayal. Isn't it just that they feel sorry for me because I'm moving out with nowhere to go?'

'It's because they've always been so vile to you!' Gaz's eyes blazed furiously. 'And now it's like you're *grateful* they're throwing you scraps of attention! You don't need that, you're *better* than that! Think about what you told me about how Carly was, years ago.'

'Well, she was only a kid. And it was her folks really, not her.'

Sorrel did remember though, remembered how it felt when she'd first gone to that school, eleven years old, and started inviting friends home. At primary school it had been fine, but here at the new, huge school, people were suddenly curious about her. The parents made their daughters invite her home and then when her mum came to collect her they looked a bit cross, disappointed. Something her mother had said – 'They look at me as if I've got horns' – had stuck. And then at last Sorrel was old enough to catch on: people wanted to see her dad, not her mum. They wanted a quick gawp at someone who'd been famous, just so they could drop into a conversation, 'Oh yeah, remember Charisma? Bernie MacIntyre's daughter's in our Nicky's class.'

And then Carly had come to the house for tea one day, and when the doorbell went when it was time for her to go home, there on the doorstep were both Carly's parents, her two brothers, her aunt and uncle and a couple of older cousins, all gathered for a glimpse of The Man. Tradition was that when you came to collect your child, the host parents invited you in for a glass of wine and some social chat about how much maths homework there was and why did they need so much games kit. Mac's reaction had been a grumpy, 'Fuckin' 'ell, bit early for carol singers, isn't it?' before fleeing from the invasion to his studio and leaving Lottie to smooth over the visitors and get them out of the place. Taking her cue from Mac's fury, she hadn't invited them in, but merely fetched and dispatched Carly as swiftly as possible.

How well that had gone down. Not. It had been interpreted as rude, dismissive and snotty and from then on Carly had turned a whole group of that year's girls against

223

Sorrel, picking on her at every opportunity, for every new pair of shoes, for every holiday they'd heard the MacIntyres had taken, for every school ski-trip that Sorrel had paid for in one go rather than in instalments. Most recently it had been for the black Mini, a vehicle of such brand-new, suck-on-that ostentation that Sorrel guiltily wondered if they'd got a point. And now, suddenly, every-one knew the house was being sold, they were all being kind. Or was it kind? Mostly she knew quite well it was just curious. Speculation was that Mac and Lottie were broke. Or was there a divorce coming? Why did things like that make Carly's lot suddenly consider her more human? More one of them? Perhaps Gaz was right – they just wanted the glamour of being the friend in the know. Except there wasn't any glamour. Or anything to know. Just an absorbent audience for Sorrel to pour out the awfulness of stuff and to have sympathy, however insincere.

'Gaz?' He was still loading his brushes into his bag, taking his time. She hoped it was because he wanted to give her a chance to say the right thing.

'What?' He put the bag down and came a bit closer.

'It's just so much easier than always being the outsider. That's all. Because right now I'm even getting the outsider stuff here in my own home.'

There were real tears falling. Sorrel could feel gallons of them welling inside her, all ready for serious flooding. If she really started it could be hours till she stopped.

'Hey. Look, it's going to be all right, just don't cry, OK?'

Gaz squashed her close against him. She could smell fabric conditioner on his T-shirt. He was warm and comforting and solid and real.

'So will you stay? Tonight? Please?' she asked again.

She could feel him shrug and looked up. He was grinning at her, teasing. 'Don't mind. Take it or leave it, me,' he said. 'Depends on what's on offer.'

'House full of crazy hippies, moping, so-called grown-ups, couple of noisy, hyper kids and . . . me?'

'I'll take it,' Gaz said.

'I'm so glad to be out of there,' Lottie said to Mac as they walked across the green to quiz night at the Feathers. 'It's worse than when they were teenagers. Sorrel's the only grown-up one in the house at the moment. You'd think they'd have learned something about relationships by now, wouldn't you? Do you think it was the way we brought them up? We were too young, too irresponsible. I never thought I'd say that.'

She'd failed. It was payback time for making Ilex and Clover spend their earliest summers with a whirl of loved-up music festivals instead of playgroup nursery rhymes; chaotic time zones instead of fixed bedtimes and swirly psychedelic fabrics instead of Pooh Bear brushed cotton. They wore hand-knitted rainbow sweaters and fleece-lined frog wellingtons in winter and on hot summer days frequently nothing but a coating of mud and dust. She'd raised them haphazardly, confusing disorder with freedom, then shooed them out into the world and assumed they could cope, and now they'd come back, licking their wounds and searching out a comfort zone. Oh God, had she really got it so wrong?

'Don't worry so much. It's not our fault,' Mac reassured her. 'They've been grown-up and capable for ages. They're usually pretty well balanced. Stuff happens and these are *their* problems – nothing to do with us. I'm surprised about Sean though, I didn't have him down as the affair type. The odd one-off, maybe, but he got that out of his system years ago and they seemed to survive the fall-out OK. I wonder if Clover's got the right end of the stick there? You know what she's like, always looks on the dark side.'

'And what's Ilex's excuse? I still don't get it. There must be more to it than the cat-thing if Manda's chucked him out. Perhaps neither of them are the sticking types. Perhaps they're the ones who should be going off travelling, not us.'

Mac laughed. 'Manda'll take him back. Give it a few days.'

'God, I hope so. You should tell Ilex about the film music deal – he might cheer up if he thinks we've got some serious funds on the way. You could let him try and talk you into some worthy life insurance plan.'

'Nah – not till it's more definite. Once you start telling people, then it starts going wrong.' He laughed. 'Maybe if we hadn't told the family about the trip till we'd got it all sorted, they might have been OK. We should have just sneaked off, called them from St Petersburg and told them we'd run away from home.'

'We couldn't do that to Sorrel,' Lottie said. 'I'm not sure any more we should be even doing *this* to Sorrel. She needs us to stop being so flippant about not having a place to live. I hate to say it, but maybe we shouldn't rush into going anywhere.'

'If we don't rush we'll never go.' Mac abruptly stopped walking and turned to look at her, surprising her with his expression of total dismay. 'I keep thinking . . . what if it's all going to end soon? I have these thoughts where I wonder things like, is the next passport I get the last one I'm going to need? Or worse, suppose I've already got my last one and its expiry date is way ahead of mine?'

Lottie felt a chill shudder. What he was saying coincided so exactly with what she'd been thinking. Or maybe it was just the effect of the cool night air, she decided; she should have worn a jacket.

'Come on, Mac, we've got years yet, cross fingers. We'll go away, of course we will, but we must do something to make Sorrel feel a bit more secure. I don't think Soho's really a goer, do you? Noise and traffic and bad-tempered media types rushing everywhere swilling lattes on the street and gabbling into phones. We'd hate it after about five minutes.'

The lights were all out in the Major's house. Lottie had seen the removal van outside that morning. By lunchtime it had trundled away, presumably taking the Major's possessions to Eastbourne. She hoped he'd be happy there. She could picture him out for tea at the Grand Hotel, sitting by a well-stoked fire and being offered crustless cucumber sandwiches by an elegant dowager in classic navy and white while the two of them reminisced about long-dead friends and confided that for each of them the war hadn't been altogether a bad time.

'He hasn't sold it yet.' Mac noticed as they passed the gate. 'I'd have thought a pretty Georgian place like that would be snapped up in days.'

'It needs work. Susie told me. Lots and lots of work. And planning permission for just about every roof tile and pane of window.'

'Too much to take on then. You'd need a lot of time, somewhere else to live, all that,' Lottie mused.

'Right. Far too much to take on,' Mac agreed.

Clover felt as nervous as a first-date teenager but she wasn't going to change her mind now. What's sauce for the gander ... she told herself as she drove defiantly out through the Holbrook House electronic gates. And it wasn't as if she was going to do anything really extreme. She was only going for a quiet drink with Harry, not running away for a weekend of porn-passion in a Paris hotel. Whatever. The important thing was Sean would find out and be horribly, stupendously amazed that she could even contemplate going out with someone else. Tough, because it was what he deserved, the lying, cheating bastard. Now he'd know how it felt. She'd told Sorrel and Ilex what to say when he called, and he *would* call because he phoned the house every couple of hours, apologizing to whoever answered (because it sure wasn't going to be her) that he had to keep trying, she was refusing to answer her mobile.

It wasn't far. Just a few miles back towards the M25, through pine woods and down a narrow lane to the sort of not-quite-country pub that people used to drive out of town to for some real ale and a stroll in the resinous air. How lovely this must look when it was covered in snow. That's what pines needed, in her opinion. They somehow weren't at their best in summer; too angular and gawky like a certain type of upright, elderly Englishman she'd see each year holidaying in Cornwall, the sort that walked the cliff-paths in ancient shorts together with long woolly socks and sturdy sandals, trekking dutifully behind determined map-toting wives. God, Cornwall. She hadn't booked anything for the holidays yet. There'd be nothing decent left – and now she'd have to go there without Sean (limited help though he tended to be) and be stuck with the girls in some damp, miserable hovel miles from the sea. The way her luck was going, it would be sure to rain daily. Perhaps she could persuade Sorrel to come, pay her to help take care of her nieces. It would add to her funds for her Australia trip. Or perhaps she would forget about Cornwall, book a last-minute gite in France. But the last-minute ones, weren't they the ones that everyone had tried and no one wanted to go back to, ever again? Where the loo was a hole in the ground at the back of a barn and the owners wouldn't let you run a tap between 9 a.m. and late afternoon?

Clover felt her stomach tighten as she drove into the pub's car park. Harry's car was already there and she parked alongside it. She could actually have done with a longer drive to calm herself; or to have arrived first. Instead, she sat still for a few moments till she could breathe evenly, checking her make-up in the mirror and re-applying some gloss to nerve-dried lips.

She was as ready as she was going to be. It was only a friendly drink after all; nothing to make a song and dance about. All the same, as she climbed out of the car, her instant thought was, Here goes a really, really stupid idea.

'Bloody nerve. They can't change quiz night! It's written in stone!'

'Travesty!'

Mac and Al were taking their outrage out on the bar staff, who carried on obliviously pulling pints and slopping beer across the many customers who jostled at the crowded bar.

'Packed out,' Mac muttered. 'Might as well forget it and go home. Charity bloody Karaoke night! What are they thinking of?'

'Well it says they're thinking of the Shooting Star Hospice, so I'll put some cash in the tin,' Lottie told him. 'Shame about the quiz though – I was looking forward to getting into it, take my mind off the fractured family for a few hours.'

'Hey, you know we might as well stay for a bit and have a laugh,' Al said. 'Pick out the ones we'd go for if we were on the look-out for talent. Music talent I mean,' he said, grinning at Lottie. He looked across to where the sound system was being given a last-minute tweak. Lottie saw a brief wistful look cross his face, as if he'd like to be involved as in his old Charisma roadie days, plugging up the leads and checking the microphones.

'Not what we were expecting though,' Mac said. 'But that's another sign of old age, isn't it, getting set in your ways. You'll stop me if I buy a pewter tankard to keep over the bar, won't you, Al?

'Just one drink then home?' he asked Lottie. 'Unless you want to stay and watch a bunch of golf-club accountants poncing about thinking they're Jagger?'

'No, it's fine by me. Let's just have a look at the song list though.'

'Oh God, tell me you're not joining in?' Mac groaned. 'Sorrel would never live it down.'

'What do you mean? Sorrel's not here to see what we get up to. After all this time are you saying my singing's rubbish?'

'Course I'm not. But you know what she's like. She'd hear about it and she'd say we were making an exhibition of ourselves. Teenagers can't think of anything worse. Look what she was like when the band was on *Top of the Pops* 2 last year. She had to run out of the room shrieking and with her hands over her eyes.'

'Yeah, well, maybe she should remember that the stuff that makes her shriek and hide is what pays her way through life.'

Lottie scanned through the catalogue of songs. 'Look, there's three of Charisma's in here. Maybe we should give it a go. "Target Practice" is in: why don't you do it, Mac? It might bring us luck, with the film and that.'

'Not a chance.' Mac was vehement. 'Not a bloody chance.'

And so it was a good four drinks later that Mac, appalled by an insultingly miserable rendition of his own 'Welcome to the Circus' by the searingly out-of-tune owner of the village Past It (Antiques and Ephemera) shop, found himself on a stage once more, wondering, this time, why he didn't have as much breath as he used to in the days when he'd sung to much vaster audiences. Bloody age, he thought again rather dispiritedly, as he acknowledged polite, but hardly rapturous, applause.

'Well, that went down very averagely,' Mac commented to Al.

'Mmm. Not bad. But a bloke behind me said you were supposed to give your own name, not the name of the original artist.'

Lottie burst out laughing. 'They didn't believe it was you!' she said.

Mac was feeling all wrong. What Lottie had said hadn't really gone in. He also felt as if not enough air had gone in either – he needed to get outside to breathe. And the room wasn't as focused as it should be. He hadn't had that much, enough but not enough to feel this unbalanced. He felt slightly queasy and didn't want the last drops of beer. 'Ready to go, Lottie? I think we've done our bit here. Shall we?'

'Oh come on then, you miserable old git. You're only pissed off because you're not going to win.'

The winner was going to be the man who thought he was Elvis. Al's opinion was that any Karaoke was always going to be won by a person who thought they were Elvis, even when, in this case, they were short, tubby, bald and could make 'Crying in the Chapel' something to laugh long and loud at. Lottie said goodbye to Al and started to make her way to the door. Mac went to follow but his feet didn't seem to want to move. Either he was lurching strangely or the room was tilting. The last thing he heard before his eyes closed against the greasy floral carpet was the voice of Mr Antiques and Ephemera close by his ear saying, 'Not just pissed, is he? What's his name, for the ambulance?'

Then Al: 'Bernie MacIntyre.'

'Yeah, right. I don't think so, mate. Nothing like him. He was rubbish, singing, just now.'

Then nothing.

She'd been right. It was a very, very stupid idea and it had got ludicrously out of hand. Clover now shifted slightly on the bed and wondered where her knickers were. This had been like too-fast teenage sex, though completely lacking the urgent, edgy thrill that she recalled from her own teen years. She was a tangle of clothes and limbs and embarrassment and feeling a deep, deep wish that she was pretty much anywhere else than here in this single man's über-pad, on his low-lit, low-level suede-edged bed. Paddling among sharks would be preferable, or sky-diving into a thick fog. Anything, anywhere. So this was what it was like; this was a no-frills, one-off fling with no emotion and no commitment. Well, you could keep it. Give her Sean's generous sexual warmth and cheerful cowboy whooping any day.

'Oh bay-*beee*,' Harry groaned beside her, a voice that came straight from a cheap porn movie. God. Clover gritted her teeth and hoped he wasn't going to close in for post-coital snuggling. If she could bring herself to speak, she'd love to tell him he could by-pass that pseudo-lovey aftermath bit and go straight to the scene where he went to make her a cup of coffee so she could grab her bag and vanish out of the front door, never to see him again. Whatever she'd hoped to prove, whichever stupid 'what you can do, I can do' trip she was hoping to compete on with Sean, it hadn't worked. This was as dire as it got. Why she hadn't stopped at the point where Harry (while doing the 'how about a tour of the apartment?' bit – to be expected, she supposed, from an estate agent) had first slid her onto the bed and started nuzzling at her neck like a foal after sugarlumps, she'd never know. Sometimes, good manners were such a curse. She would have to make sure her daughters learned there were limits to the concept of being polite.

Clover moved slightly and rubbed the back of her neck. The clasp on her necklace had been digging in painfully, for Harry's idea of a perfect grip was to shove his hands under the pillow and scoop it up around her ears so her head felt squashed to the point of near-suffocation. He'd probably put her wrigglings of protest down to writhings of passion. What had that been about? she wondered, speculating on how close she might have come to being totally smothered. Possibly it was lucky she hadn't been far roused from inert passivity. Maybe distaste had saved her life. Harry, who had blithely floundered on, oblivious to her non-participation, quite possibly wouldn't have noticed if he'd actually killed her; he had surely been absent from the school sex lesson where they did the bit about girls liking to join in too.

'Coffee, sweetie?' Harry murmured in Clover's ear.

'Mm. Please, that'd be great.' Good. At last, a chance to get out.

'Kitchen's through there.' He pointed through the darkness in the general direction of the hallway.

Through there? Clover sat up abruptly and retrieved her watch from the table beside her. Then she scrambled off the bed and picked up her bag and jacket and quickly slid her feet into her shoes. How lucky, as it turned out, that in his school-boyish eagerness Harry hadn't got round to removing more than the absolute minimum of her clothing.

'You want *me* to make it?' she asked.

'Only fair, darling. I did all the work.' Even in the half-dark, she could see the smirk.

'True,' she said, heading for the door, 'all by yourself. But then I expect you're used to that.'

Slam. The front door made a good loud clunk and Clover raced down the stairs to her car.

'Home, home,' she murmured to herself as she leaped into the car, started the engine and hurtled down the road back towards the A3. What a waste of an evening, what a stupid experiment, she thought. And a waste of good knickers too, for they were still in Harry's bedroom, kicked into the dust beneath his bed. No way would she ever want to see them, or him, again.

# FIFTEEN

Considering how much bad news and anxiety hospitals tend to hold, Lottie thought the decor in the waiting area was insultingly upbeat, as if it was trying to convey a jovial 'Cheer up, it might never happen'.

Surely, if you were on the premises either pacing about being a worried relative or flat-out in a cubicle, then 'it' patently already had. What were all these nerve-racked people, fidgeting on the edges of their seats, supposed to make of the candy-pink walls, the bright orange chairs and the floor that was a chequerboard of red (to hide blood-stains?) and sky blue? The place looked like a playgroup's venue of choice and was surely far too hectic for keeping the customers calm and reassured. Were they supposed to think, Ooh that's nice. I feel so relaxed and happy here? Not very likely, was it, if, like Lottie, you were quite possibly about to hear that the person you loved most in the world was ready to be wheeled to the mortuary?

'They don't tell you anything. Why won't they tell me? I'd rather know.' Lottie sat on the tatty orange chair beside Al and put the plastic cup of tea on the floor beside her. She couldn't hold it – her hands were shaking too much.

'I suppose they'll come and tell you when there's something to tell.' Al was looking pale and frightened. He kept gazing longingly at the exit doors, clearly desperate for Ilex or Clover to turn up and take over his stake-out duty. Lottie remembered that when they'd travelled with the band, Al had always been terrified of anything medical, was always the last of the crew to get vital vaccinations done, having to be coaxed to the surgery by the drummer and by George who would haul him, still struggling, into the building, one each side of him like club bouncers in reverse. She hoped he wouldn't faint. He easily might if a patient staggered in, covered in blood. That would make one more to panic about, for *would* it be a faint or another . . . what? Heart attack? Stroke? What was it Mac had had? Either of those options seemed way too grown-up. Surely Mac was still a young, vital man, really? The many years they'd been together seemed compressed, somehow, as if only a few brief months had passed since that Roundhouse night when they'd first met. Vividly, she recalled asking him where he'd got his exquisite flowery shirt. (Granny Takes a Trip, King's Road, hand-made.)

She hoped they'd done the right thing. The barman at the Feathers had pushed through the crush and shoved a tiny aspirin under Mac's tongue, claiming they were kept in the till for exactly this reason; they were probably past their best-before, he'd said, apologetically, but couldn't do any harm and might save his life in the case of heart failure. Or, Lottie now wondered, it might be just one more complication, the one thing he absolutely shouldn't have had. If it was a brain haemorrhage he'd had, wouldn't thinning his blood still further be the worst thing they could have done? The paramedics in the ambulance hadn't seemed too stressed, but as they saw this kind of collapse (presumably) on a daily basis, maybe that didn't mean anything. The fact that Mac had collapsed in a pub though, that wasn't great, Lottie thought. There seemed to be a general bias about that. A presumption that if you were on licensed premises and you fell over, then you must be completely rat-arsed. She hoped the medics (wherever they were) were checking Mac for more than just blood-alcohol levels. Mac hadn't been completely unconscious, which was apparently a good thing, and didn't seem to be in unbearable pain, apart from the terrifying shortness of breath; both he and Lottie becoming more fearful by the second that each of these shallow, painful breaths would be his last.

The accident and emergency department was a busy one, considering it was only a Wednesday night. A girl in a nearby cubical was sobbing constantly, in spite of a kindly nurse's attempts to reassure her. Lottie tried not to speculate that perhaps she'd lost a baby, or been told a lump really was something to worry about. A pair of Goth teenagers clung to each other on chairs beside the reception desk, the expressions of all-out terror on their pale faces contrasting bizarrely with their black, spiked hair, purple lipstick and kohl-eyed make-up. A man with his arm in a sling was wincing every time someone walked past, possibly terrified of drunks carelessly meandering, falling on his shattered limb.

'I couldn't work here,' Al murmured, his knee drumming up and down in agitation. 'How do people stand it, dealing with all this pain every day?'

'I don't have a clue,' Lottie told him. 'But thank God they do.'

At last. Clover. Where the hell had she been? When Lottie and Mac had left Holbrook House that evening it had been full of people. When she'd phoned home from the hospital, there seemed to be only Sorrel and Gaz on the premises, babysitting the two sleeping children and with no idea where either Ilex or Clover had vanished to. She'd always insisted to them, back in the days when they'd lived at home, how important it was to tell someone where they'd be. Just in case. It wasn't enough to have mobile phones – what use was one of those if the battery was down or it had switched itself off in a bag, as Clover's seemed to have done?

Lottie watched her daughter hurtle nervously through the automatic doors as if expecting them to snap shut and cut her in half.

'Mum! What's happened? On my way home I phoned Sorrel to check on the girls and she said Dad was in here, all collapsed! Is he OK?' Clover's face was twisted with anguish, but even so, Lottie couldn't help noticing she was wearing the kind of make-up that was for serious going out. And the shoes ... weren't they her precious last-birthday Jimmy Choos? Lottie pulled Clover down to the chair beside her and hugged her close. She felt shivery and could feel tears on their way.

'I don't know, Clover. He was in the pub, singing ...'

'*Singing?*' Clover pulled back and stared at her mother. 'But he never sings any more! Oh – I get it. He was pissed?'

'No! Look, don't you start. I've had that from everyone else. He wasn't, OK? Well ... hardly at all, nothing serious.' Lottie sniffed. 'And he just, keeled over.'

'I think maybe, if you don't mind, I'll just go and er ...' Al stood up and shuffled his feet around, looking desperate to escape.

'Al, thanks so much for staying,' Lottie said, squeezing his hand. 'I'll be fine now Clover's here. And I promise I'll call if there's anything ...' The tears started to spill over. She could feel them, fat and bead-like, trickling one by one like the first thumping raindrops of a thunderstorm.

'Mum, please don't cry.' Clover squeezed Lottie tight. 'It's scary! It's like you think he's going to—'

'Don't say it!' Lottie snapped. 'Don't even think it!'

Lottie *was* thinking it though. Of course she was. She was thinking, what kind of massive, unfillable trench would the death of Mac leave in her life? Just when they'd decided to take some us-time, to offload all the peripheral ephemera that thirty-something years had accumulated so they could get back to the you-and-me basics. The essentials. Of which, for her, Mac was *the* essential.

\*

Ilex crept round past the garages at the back of the apartments carrying his outrageously pricy hand-tied bunch of deep red roses and loitered by the dustbins, almost colliding with a fat, dirty fox that shot out from behind them and raced past carrying a chicken carcase. He knew, of course, that he could just go into the apartments through the main door, up the stairs and let himself in – he still had his keys. And, he reminded himself, if push came to shove, it was technically his own property. On paper, anyway. Right now, it looked as if Manda had gone for squatters' rights. Which was fine. He didn't want her out, just himself back in, in her life, in her bed and in her good books. Why was it so hard when he'd done nothing wrong? Well, not very wrong anyway.

There was a light on in their bedroom. Or should that be 'her' bedroom now? He imagined her many, many clothes, no longer crushed together now that most of his had been ejected, luxuriating on their padded satin hangers in the space of both sides of the long wardrobe; his sock drawer would have been cleared out to make way for even more froths of her delicious underwear. He shouldn't think along those lines – it would drive him to the kind of crass, clumsy impatience that would have him storming up the stairs and breaking the door down. He didn't think that would impress her – Manda didn't approve of gratuitous breakage. Splintered wood meant finding a carpenter and all the ensuing hassle and expense. Not good.

There was no point phoning Manda's mobile or the flat yet again; she still wasn't answering. Only once had he briefly heard her voice in these last days and that was because he'd used Clover's phone, but after saying hello, and discovering it was him, she'd hung up instantly, not even sparing him a perfunctory 'Sod off'. He'd considered writing a letter but she'd probably put it through a shredder and send it straight back and he couldn't face the angst of opening an envelope of viciously sliced shards that represented his heart and soul. Besides, what did you write without sounding after-the-event soppy? E-mail was definitely out, though he'd considered it. But you couldn't do emotional take-me-back stuff by e-mail, especially not to Manda's work-place. There was too much risk of it getting mixed up in the daily round-the-building joke-swap: one casually miss-pressed key and half Gatwick Airport could know the whole sorry tale in minutes. (If they didn't already. Wasn't that what women did? They told one close friend, in total confidence, over a tears-and-lipgloss moment in the loo, and a mysterious three hours later they were getting God-what-a-bastard sympathy from every female in the building?) And anything electronic for communication was too far along the track of those famous people you heard of who'd so callously dumped their lifetime partners by fax. Not that he was dumping her. He'd turned up tonight, with his rather corny roses, in the hope of entirely the opposite.

First thing was to get Manda's attention. She craved love and romance. Clover said so. Even Sorrel had agreed with that (albeit with a typical teen sneer) so it must be right. Eternal love and a wedding were required apparently, not a cat and a litter tray. Well, fine. If she wanted it, she could have it. Otherwise what would the future be for Ilex? Oh yes, he could see it now and a very gloomy prospect it was. A carpet of empty pizza boxes and beer cans, a Sky Sports habit plus years of pointless and ever more desperate and unsatisfactory skirmishes with scary, predatory women like Wendy. If he ever got access to the flat and to Manda again, his copies of *Fuzz* would be straight out here to these bins. The next person in a uniform he hoped to have dealings with was the vicar who'd conduct the wedding. ('Do you, Ilex *Adonis* MacIntyre . . . ?' Adonis. Aaaagh. The thought of laughter ripples still made him cringe. He'd have to get over it. On the day there'd be so much more to think about. How to pay for it all should keep his mind occupied.)

Ilex, still toting his bouquet and dodging the squares of light cast from windows in the block, crept across the grass and bent to pick up a selection of small stones from the gravel pathway. Then he started gently lobbing them up at the bedroom window. But he was too tentative in his efforts not to have every flat-owner coming out to their balconies to shout at him and managed to miss his target with almost every one. A couple scratched almost noiselessly against the window and fell uselessly onto the bedroom's small outside deck area. Lucky that England weren't depending on him to carry the bowling at the next test, he thought. He had another go, concentrated hard and this time hit the jackpot, centre of the window pane. He hid back in the shadows and waited for a response. If she opened the glass door he'd simply emerge into one of the light-squares and ask her the big question from there, Romeo-style, a full-on balcony-scene. What more could she want? Wouldn't that be something to tell the one ladies'-room confidante at work? By lunchtime there'd be a queue to look at the ring. Ah – that was another thing he hadn't thought of. He'd have to take her out in the morning to choose something and pray his credit limit wouldn't melt under the strain.

But right now, there was no sign of her. What was she doing in there? Maybe she was in the shower, or had music or the television on. He looked at his watch. Nine fifteen. Was it *Celebrity Love Island* that was showing at the moment? Or was it the one in the jungle? Manda liked that sort of faux-reality thing, and became completely engrossed in who was doing what with whom. He found it sweet and appealing that she took it all as gospel, never considering that celebrities might be there to play up to the cameras and the audience and that someone, just off-set, might well be ordering them to gee up the arguments and power-drive the lust interest.

TV or not, a better stone was obviously needed – something that would make more noise but without smashing the glass. Ilex was well aware how much damage could be done with the half-brick that he'd just very nearly trodden on but in the absence of anything better (unless he fought it out with the fox in riffling through the bins) he decided that if he aimed it right, and carefully, it should do the job. To add to the romantic drama, Ilex pulled a couple of the roses from the bouquet (no time for qualms about wrecking the immaculate arrangement), pulled one of the silver raffia strings that held the bunch together from the bottom of the stalks and tied the flowers to the brick. Then, watched by the fat fox that had returned and was now sitting beneath the balcony like a coach-party matinée audience impatient for curtain-up, he hurled the brick at the window. The smash was pretty impressive, Ilex thought. And how amazingly like a cartoon soundtrack was the cascading tinkling of the glass. Stray shards of it rained down from the balcony on to grass and gravel, though most must be on the bedroom floor, which was a bummer. Manda would be seriously unimpressed about that. The fox gave him a look that suggested it was seriously underwhelmed and trotted away at a cool-dude pace towards the front of the building. Lights flicked on all over the block, his neighbours, both curious and furious, appeared at many windows and yet still Manda didn't show her face. Where was she? Why didn't she come to the window and give him hell about the damage? God, please don't say he'd killed her with the brick?

Ilex saw the blue lights whirling long before it occurred to him he might be their target. Why so many? he was vaguely wondering. Had there been a murder nearby while he'd been dallying with his roses and his stones? At least four squad cars were hurtling round the corner of the building towards him, and a police van – the sort they sent to riots – slewed itself at a dramatic angle across the road, blocking his exit. He hadn't seen so much police activity since a new-driver teenager had accidentally run over a swan on the Richmond riverside and half the force had turned up, on account, according to collective wisdom of passers-by, that the birds belonged to the Queen and killing one was tantamount to treason. The poor boy had been in floods: some crazy old biddy had told him it was still a hanging offence.

'Stay right where you are. Don't move.' Light beams were blazing in Ilex's face and the roses were ripped from his hand. It was like being mugged. Something stopped him from blurting out that they'd got the wrong person. Something that told him, rather late, that they hadn't.

He looked up at his former bedroom window: so there was Manda, at last, out on the balcony, watching the action. She had her arms folded across the front of her body, which was wrapped in her pink satin robe. The stance had a look of both the defensive and the vengeful.

'Manda!' Ilex shouted, struggling to haul himself out of the grip of a mountainous police constable who must surely be at least a county prop forward. Handcuffs were jingling and Ilex's arm was so agonizingly twisted by his captor it felt close to snapping as he struggled to get free. 'Manda! I love you!' Ilex yelled up at the silhouetted figure. 'Manda, will you marry me?'

There was an unflattering break-out of tittering from the circle of police. 'Oh dead romantic, mate,' said his burly minder. 'That'll be one for her to remember. Romeo, in handcuffs!'

'I've heard of some bids to get bail . . .' Another one hooted.

'Manda? Will you at least think about it?'

It was too late to hear if she was going to reply. Ilex's head was pushed roughly into the back of a police car and the rest of him followed, hurled onto the back seat and landing smack against a waiting policewoman, where

Ilex grazed his nose on the metal shoulder tag of her hi-vi jacket.

'Oh dear, Mr MacIntyre, you *have* been a naughty vandal, haven't you?' Wendy smirked.

Ilex turned away from her and gazed longingly out of the rear window as the car pulled away. The now-wrecked bouquet lay on the ground beside the dustbins, forlorn and abandoned, like a solitary tribute at the scene of a tragic accident.

'Sean's *what*? Why is he *there*?' Clover studied the sign on the wall across the corridor, the one that ordered her absolutely *not* to use a mobile phone. Surely this was an exception. When your own father might be fighting off all four apocalyptic horsemen, how else were you supposed to let your little sister know what was going on without having to trail down miles of passageway to find an exit door and maybe miss an essential (and she refused to add the word 'last') moment?

'No, we still haven't really been told much. He's seeing someone right now. Mum's in with him, in resuss, like they have on *Casualty*. Sorrel, why did you call Sean? There's nothing he can do about anything.'

A passing nurse gave Clover a glare, presumably relating to the use of the phone. Clover waited till she'd gone past then rudely raised her middle finger at the retreating back. Bloody Sean. What did all this have to do with him? OK, maybe Sorrel had a point – he possibly could be useful, taking care of Sophia and Elsa so that Sorrel could join them at the hospital, but when Clover had left Holbrook

House, Gaz had been lying on the sofa, looking very much as if he wasn't intending to go anywhere. Couldn't he have taken over baby-sitting just for a few hours? If – and horrible what-ifs flickered across her mind – if a few hours was all they needed, to sort out Mac and what was wrong with him and some treatment for fixing it, Gaz could keep an ear open for the girls quite easily. Longer than that . . . and she hardly dared to think what might happen to Mac. It was probably all her fault; rubbish karma or something, for going out and behaving like a slut, just for the sake of simple revenge. It no longer felt even remotely like revenge either. Just a very, very bad and stupid thing to have done.

'And where's Ilex?' Clover demanded to Sorrel. 'Why hasn't he got here yet? I've left messages on his mobile but he hasn't bothered to call. Has he checked in with you? Is he back at the flat with Manda?' Someone else was coming. Clover went and sat on a bench by the window and bent her head so her hair hung over the phone, wishing she could disappear. This person looked more like a visitor than a doctor, but it was hard to tell. No one wore uniform stuff and dangled stethoscopes any more, apart from the nurses and even then it was all a bit basic, dress-code-wise. Wouldn't going back to sterile white coats help with MRSA or something, as well as helping the customers know who they could run to in the event of heart stoppage or blood gushing? She hadn't been inside a hospital since her post-natal check-up after Elsa was born, years ago. Since then, influenced by watching *Holby City* and *Casualty* she'd grown to imagine there'd be an atmosphere of congenial chaos, lots of personal, life-changing input from staff and patients, possibly a heart-warming moment where a para-medic called his mates into the waiting area to announce his engagement to the paediatric registrar and everyone clapped and drank unchilled cheap fizz from plastic mugs. Instead there was cool, distant efficiency and a background of suspicious odours. And the certainty that death had taken up residence and liked to sneak into the action now and then to pick off one of the sick herd's stragglers.

'He's been *what*? *Arrested*? Oh God, whatever for?' Clover pictured Ilex, breaking into Harvey Nichols on a crazy impulse, in search of the perfect take-me-back present for Manda. They'd probably found him riffling through the handbags, wondering if she'd prefer the Prada or the Mulberry. Or had he been caught having a Hugh Grant moment with a hooker in King's Cross, this extra-mural race to have sexual compensation possibly being a previously unsuspected family trait?

Clover, trying to get sense out of Sorrel, caught sight of Lottie at the far end of the corridor, emerging from the resuscitation area, coming towards her. It was hard to read her body language – whether her mother walking normally at a medium pace signified life or death. Feeling a pool of hyper-anxiety flooding in, she stood up to go to her mother, and the cool plastic of the bench peeled itself from her uncomfortably naked flesh beneath her skirt.

'And Sorrel,' Clover hissed into the phone, 'when you come here, please will you bring me some knickers?'

Lottie was getting nearer but it was still hard to tell what her expression was. Clover needed Sorrel *not* to be on the phone if it was bad news. If the worst had happened, it shouldn't be conveyed that way, not with only Sean and Gaz there to comfort her and knowing she'd had no chance to say goodbye.

'No, just bring *knickers*. They're for *me*. Don't ask, Soz, please. Just bring me some, OK?'

# SIXTEEN

'When I mentioned I fancied going to the Burning Man Festival, I didn't have my own cremation in mind,' Mac told Lottie. He seemed to think it was funny and she decided that was a good thing; gallows humour it might be but it was a welcome sign that he was feeling he was likely to survive. Some people go the other way, she'd heard, forever after convinced that the first warning shot would be followed up at any minute by an inescapable, catastrophic fusillade. What a wicked waste of their future that would be.

She and Mac were alone for what felt like the first time in days. Days during which a constant, exhausting stream of hospital staff had come and gone, tweaking drips, taking blood, adjusting monitors and doing that non-committal smile, like waiters who come to your table and ask if you're enjoying the meal, but in a way that makes you suspect they've added a truly foul secret ingredient. And then there were the visitors – was it all down to internet gossip or an elaborate game of Chinese whispers that resulted in just about every person Mac knew turning up with cards and flowers and nervous expressions of barely hidden relief that this wasn't happening to them? Wonderful as it was to have so much attention, it was exhausting. Bizarrely, it reminded Lottie of her wedding; towards the end of that day her entire face had ached from the constant smiling.

Now Lottie and Mac were stretched out together on Mac's bed in his room in the private wing of the hospital with *Deal or No Deal* on the TV. It had been Sean who had organized the transfer from the public ward, where Mac had been distinctly *not* delighted to be opposite a patient who happened to recognize him, claimed he knew every lyric from every record Charisma had ever made, and insisted on proving it over many a long and loud hour. Mac hadn't asked the man what had brought him into the hospital, but told Lottie that if he had to guess he would have said it was something to do with an alcohol-stricken liver. It had also been Sean who had called the health insurance company, sorted the paperwork for the claim and made sure the move was done quickly and efficiently. And then he hadn't hung around to be thanked, which Lottie thought a shame, but had instead taken Sophia and Elsa back to Richmond and to the gentle comfort of home routine so that Clover could stay at Holbrook House within easy visiting distance of her father. Lottie was happy to let Sean take over admin duties, understanding that he felt he had something to prove to Clover about reliability. Ilex seemed to be in a useless dream-world of his own, Clover was concentrating on keeping Holbrook House ticking over and Sorrel was coming to the end of her exams.

Lottie felt pretty comfortable snuggled up to Mac, considering he was still linked to a drip containing an ever-changing dose of warfarin to keep his blood clot-free. She could live with his flippancy about his condition, and although tempted to whack him for it occasionally, this wouldn't be a good idea as any small nudge, while the dose was still being adjusted, could result in a multi-hued bruise the size of a dinner plate.

'Pulmonary embolism' – Lottie turned this seriously grown-up diagnosis over in her mind every now and then, somehow convinced that if she kept the words at the surface of her thoughts they wouldn't get a chance to settle, to do the kind of damage that the arterial clots could have done. Both she and Mac were well aware how lucky an escape this had been. It had been a genuine life-or-death skirmish, over now, but only *for* now. Although this particular problem wasn't likely to recur, given proper treatment and a certain amount of lifestyle care, *something* would obviously get one of them, one day. They were lucky, Lottie thought, that they'd managed to exist this long without any major health teaser jumping out and shouting 'Boo!' at them. Unlike many of her friends, Lottie had so far escaped without so much as a dodgy smear test result or frightening breast lump. You couldn't take it for granted – it all came down to luck, health checks and bless-ings to be counted.

Mac seemed to think his Burning Man quip wasn't tempting fate. So Lottie crossed her fingers again to ward off the possibility that it just might be. If she crossed them much more, they'd weld themselves together. In the last week she'd done all she could, superstition-wise, from ask-ing for help from a God she hadn't believed in since the curate had spent far too long explaining 'fornication' at her teenage confirmation classes to turning her money over on the night of the new moon. She'd even read her horoscopes in all the waiting-room magazines, seeking out significant good-luck clues, greedily soaking up 'happy times for Aquarians just now, health and wealth on the rise . . .' and so on till she'd catch sight of the front cover and find it was all not only months out of date but, in some cases, years.

'Not funny, Mac, joking about the cremation thing,' Lottie told him. 'You had me so scared. I'm far too young to be a widow and I don't look good in black.'

'You're right, don't go for black. Purple is much more you and far grander. You'd look great in full-scale veiled mourning. Quite a sexy look, that.'

'Hmm . . . with an amazing Philip Treacy hat. Just please don't ask me to try it all out while you're still here. That would just be too . . . dangerous.'

'OK I won't. But anyway, more importantly what music did you decide on for my funeral? I was thinking Pink Floyd's "Comfortably Numb" would be pretty good.'

Lottie laughed. 'But you might *not* be comfortable. Or

numb. There might be an afterlife of agonizing hellfire where you're heading.'

'OK then, you'd better go for "Eternal Flame" – The Bangles one, not the Atomic Kitten version. So what *did* you choose?'

'Fairport Convention's "Meet on the Ledge" and that amazing Saint Saëns organ thing, though I wouldn't mind bagging that one for me,' Lottie admitted.

Why are we talking about this? she wondered. Surely it was all wrong, this feeling safe to discuss it now the end wasn't imminent, as far as they could be sure, for either of them? It seemed very much in the spirit of getting the demon out of the box to play with so the terrible mystery and fear went out of it, now that the immediate danger (for now) was past.

'So, go on, what about the rest of it?' Mac nudged her. 'What about the talking bits?'

'Oh, I didn't get as far as any readings, poems and such,' she added. 'But I thought Ilex and Al could maybe say something. I know I just wouldn't be able to, I'd choke; Clover would be a hopeless heap of tears and I couldn't ask Sorrel; she's too young, unless there was a poem she desperately wanted to read. Not something I could really ask her at this stage, is it?'

Definitely not. Lottie instinctively felt you kept that kind of spectral wondering to yourself and well away from the generation below, certainly from Sorrel's age group. They were still at a lucky, almost-oblivious animal stage where the notion of death was mostly something theoretical, out-there, like the concept of light-years. It was something that would keep for an age they couldn't yet imagine themselves being. Even Clover and Ilex had got by more or less unscathed by personal loss, having been merely peripheral congregation at the funerals of a couple of ancient uncles and one of Ilex's work colleagues who had collapsed and died a week after retirement, possibly overwhelmed as to what else to do with too much spare time. No front-row grieving for them, so far.

Mac knew the workings of Lottie's mind so well. He knew she'd try to offset the awfulness of his possible death by imagining her way through the worst of the immediate aftermath. Did everyone do that? Did everyone think, Right, I'll picture the whole worst-case scenario, map out what I'd do, how I'd cope with it and be mentally prepared so the edge is taken off it, in the same way Susie had once said she only went for a bikini wax after the numbing effects of a couple of Nurofen Plus had kicked in? She'd love to ask someone who'd had to deal with the reality if the pre-thinking was any help. Probably not. She could phone Kate in Scotland and run it past her, she supposed, but it would hardly be sensitive, would it, to say, 'So how are you? Oh, and by the way, did you, any time in the months before George dropped dead, think about how you'd feel if it actually happened, and decide which photo of him you'd have on the Order of Service cards, and whether to have flowers or donations to the Musicians' Union Benevolent Fund?'

No of course she couldn't ask her that. For one thing, poor Kate hadn't had so much as an hour's warning (unless you counted George's many years of casual drug abuse). George had been alive and apparently as cheerfully well as a recreational cocaine user could be one minute, playing a sunny afternoon gig with a pick-up band at a festival near Stonehenge. Then, at the very moment Kate was wondering whether it would be a good idea to put a chicken in the oven for a late supper, there was George, stretched out on a trolley, being pronounced dead-on-arrival in a Salisbury hospital.

'And what about hymns?' Mac was, Lottie could see, quite on a roll with this. It was getting morbid and she wished he'd stop, now. But he was the ill one, she'd have to humour him.

'Did you want hymns? I thought you probably wouldn't, seeing as you don't really do God. I was thinking along the lines of a woodland burial site. Do they cater for hymns?'

'You don't have to do God to like hymns. I want the one about the sea, definitely. And please don't put me in a wicker coffin. Cardboard yes, but not wicker. It reminds me of laundry baskets or those Fortnum and Mason hampers that record companies used to send everyone at Christmas.'

'Oh well, I thought I'd get an aluminium flight case made up complete with foam cutout for your body, like for a guitar.'

'And a lining of orange crushed velvet please. You'll have to get Rock-It Cargo to provide a truck for the funeral, instead of a hearse. Pall-bearers could be roadies: all cigarettes, wife-beater vests and tool belts.'

'And access-all-areas passes,' she added, giggling. 'That would scare them.'

No – this was joking too far now, pushing luck. 'Mac, this is making me feel weird. Could we talk about something else? Tell me about the Burning Man thing. Tell me it's not about setting fire to real people.'

'Ah now . . . Burning Man.' Mac's face took on the happy far-away expression she'd come to recognize so well lately when he talked about their travel plans. 'It all goes off at Black Rock City, which isn't a city at all, just a vast space of desert out in the salt-lands of Nevada. It's serious dressing up, the maddest entertainment, craziest art, and at the end there's the burning of a huge effigy, stuffed with pyrotechnics and fireworks to die for.'

'Not the "D" word, please, Mac.' Lottie shuddered. 'So when do they have this Burning Man festival?'

'First week of September.'

'Ah,' Lottie said. 'So not for us this year then.'

Mac hesitated for a moment. He looked, Lottie thought, not so much wistful as defeated.

'No, not this year,' he agreed.

An ASBO? Anti-social behaviour order? Oh great. What a deal to be threatened with. Surely it took more than one broken window (and Ilex's own, at that) and a heartfelt, if chaotic, proposal of marriage to earn one of those? Wasn't it usually people who bugged the neighbours by playing 'Show Me the Way to Amarillo' at full volume thirty-six times in a row who tended to be given ASBOs? He could see that hooded teenagers who picked noisy fights in shopping malls at night and local paper front-page grannies who chucked bricks through the windows of the council tax office were two categories that might consider an ASBO a badge of honour, but for himself, an ambitious and hard-working, law-abiding (till now) property consultant . . . no, he couldn't see it being an item that would do a lot to big up his CV. Let's hope, he touched wood, that it wouldn't come to that. And actually, it was only Wendy who'd told him it could. The rest of the police had seemed happy enough to let him go with a warning and far too much inappropriate hilarity. He seemed to have made their night. Wendy though, she still seemed to have her own axe to grind here.

'And stalking's an offence as well, of course,' Wendy now told him in the pub, adding to the burden of his dread of criminal come-back. 'And I'm only telling you for your own good,' she added, 'in case you were thinking of going back and having another bash at it.' So that's why she was here – for His Own Good; that's why she was out, a mere week later, cavorting with a menace to society.

And why was *he* seeing *her*? he wondered. He must have some sort of mad death-wish. She'd phoned him, texted him, worn him down with a persistent show of sympathy. He only wanted to talk about Manda, to keep dropping her name into their conversation so that she still seemed to be real. Manda hadn't vanished from the MacIntyre circle entirely. She was talking to Clover on a daily basis, no problem. She'd even been to visit Mac in the hospital but only when she was sure Ilex wouldn't also be around. She'd checked on that one with Simon at the office and made sure she picked a time when Ilex was at yet another crucial Pilgrim Prospect meeting, making Simon swear not to say anything. Simon did tell him of course, but too late. She'd probably told Simon to do that, too, now he came to think of it, calculating exactly how to twist that knife.

Wendy sipped her drink tentatively, being so careful not to leave a trace of lipstick on the glass that Ilex could only conclude she was making sure the glossy pink pout stayed firmly in place for him to lust at. This was the first alcoholic drink Ilex had seen her with. A strange and oddly retro choice: Campari and lemonade, as if she'd heard it was a girlie equivalent of James Bond's Martini. Today he felt neither shaken nor stirred by her. What was going on? Last time he'd gone out with her he'd seriously considered doing the dreaded deed at last, if only for the comfort of being wrapped in someone soothing and sympathetic. That time his dishonourable intentions had been scuppered by her unexpectedly coming across with the Just Good Friends card. Now she seemed to have changed her mind yet again. What did she want? And would the two of them ever want whatever it was at the same time? Somehow he doubted it.

'Amazing you happened to be on duty that night,' Ilex commented, seeing if he could dig out of her some big conspiracy, discover that she'd planned his arrest to the last detail, had even been following him to the flat and lying in wait, summoning the over-the-top back-up at the last minute.

'Not really.' She shrugged. 'I'm a cop. It's my job. I must admit though,' and she gave him an under-the-lashes flash of steely eye, 'when I heard the address they were off to I just had to tag along. It shouldn't have really been my call.'

'So you raced through the dark streets, lights and sirens going, just to watch me get dragged away in handcuffs? Thanks.' He drained his drink. Another one? Better not. It was a long drive down to the dark depths of Surrey. If there was ever a time he was likely to lose his licence, this was surely it.

'Of course I did.' Wendy laughed. 'It was irresistible, watching a grown man struggle like that. A real turn-on.' She uncrossed her legs and he heard a slight swoosh of fabric as her silky skirt shifted across her thighs. It wasn't doing anything for him though. Ilex stood up and took their empty glasses back to the bar. He hadn't offered her another drink. Wendy didn't look as if she minded and was busy rearranging her legs, crossing them higher this time, hiking her skirt up, smiling up at him with eyes full of glittery promise.

'Look, I'd better get back,' Ilex said, glancing at his watch. 'I, er, um . . .'

'Oh! Do you have to? But it's still really early! Haven't you got time to . . . ?' Her words faded to an awkward, questioning silence.

To what? She'd left it for Ilex to fill in the blank but she hadn't given him the usual three choices for deletion, only the one. It came down to: hadn't he got time to go back to hers and have a totally dispiriting shag that would leave him feeling wretched, guilt-stricken and worthless? He didn't think so. Ilex looked at her, saw her standing now, too close to him. She was fidgeting nervously with her necklace, stroking it across the soft tender skin of her neck.

It was no good. He just wasn't cut out for anything but the real thing.

'I'm sorry, Wendy,' he said, kissing her gently on the corner of her shiny pink mouth. 'You can do a lot better than me.'

'Yes. I'm beginning to realize I can. At least, I bloody hope so,' she said, swiftly grabbing her handbag from the table. He flinched slightly, for a second convinced she was going to hit him with it. She had that look on her face: fury and danger.

'Go on then, Ilex. Piss off back to your girlfriend, you sad bastard.' And suddenly Wendy was gone, the outside door of the bar swinging like a cowboy movie's bar-room saloon exit. It was close to becoming a pattern, women storming out on him. Ilex trudged out of the door and looked down the street. He could hear the familiar chug-chug sound of the Beetle's engine as it vanished round the corner and just for one frightening moment he felt very close to a flicker of sadness that he'd be seeing no more of that horrible pink and orange cat-daubed vehicle.

For goodness' sake, Ilex, he told himself, get a bloody grip.

Guilt. Clover was so full of it that if she'd been brought up in the Catholic Church (or possibly in any church) she'd have had to go and offload her conscience in a confessional. Oh, did you ever have to be careful what you wished for. Right now, out in the Holbrook House garden picking pretty, stripy courgettes for Al to take to the Farmers' Market, she started wishing again. This time it was that she'd never, in the first place, wished that Mac and Lottie wouldn't sell the house. She'd got what she wanted there, hadn't she? It looked like there was no chance of them doing anything so exhausting and traumatic as moving now. And they sure as hell wouldn't be racing off round the world all carefree and crazy in a loved-up hippie haze now, would they? So that was a result then. *Not* – as Sorrel would say.

'Clover?'

Oh God, Sean. He'd crept up on her at last. She knew he would, knew she couldn't avoid him for ever, though heavens, she'd been trying to. She looked past him, up the garden to where Sophia and Elsa were chasing each other on the terrace. Was it after-school time already? It must be way past that, if Sean had collected them at the usual time then driven them all the way down here. Where did the day go when you worried yourself into the depths of gloom? She'd imagined this moment, the first time she'd face him since she'd . . . since that horrible night full of stupid . . . mistakes. *Mistakes?* Who was she kidding? What kind of a twee euphemism was that for full-on adultery? She should ask Sean maybe . . . he'd certainly be the one to know.

'What do you want, Sean? There's not really anything to say that can't be written down and sent through lawyers.'

Clover put the box of courgettes down on the gravel path and rubbed her earth-smeared hands on a tissue.

'Oh I think there is. I don't know what's the matter with you lot. None of you keep still for long enough to listen to anything or anyone.'

'That's not fair, Sean, or true. Ilex has been trying to sort things out with Manda for ages, Mum's down at the hospital most of the time. Sorrel's up to here with exams. And you want me to be sitting around, available to hear your feeble excuses?'

'I don't need to make excuses.' Well, she'd give him that, a very direct, honest-looking steady gaze. Where did he get the nerve? She wouldn't mind some of that herself.

And wow, he looked so great. Lightly tanned and wearing scuffed old faded jeans with the deep sapphire Paul Smith sweater that made his eyes look even bluer. And his hair had gone lighter in the sun. She guessed he'd been outside more than usual this last hot week, taking the girls into Richmond Park for after-school picnics, letting them race around in the sunshine. She hoped he'd had a good time with them; when it came to sorting out details of parental access she didn't want him to be one of those dads who looked so defeated about spending forced time with their children. You could easily recognize them, slightly at a loss pushing swings in the park or trailing round the zoo for the fifth time in a season while the kids skulked and kicked at litter and were no longer interested in giraffes. The poor girls, they'd be maintenance children, something she'd never anticipated for them.

'I don't need to make excuses because I haven't done anything wrong.'

'Huh. So it was all Mary-Jane, was it? She forced you? I know she's a bit of a slut but couldn't she even try to keep her greedy paws off the husbands of her so-called best friends?' Clover's voice was rising, the fury and hurt coming to the surface at last. 'I mean, hasn't she managed to pull anyone in that Wimbledon job she was so excited about? No number-one seed in her personal centre court? Tell me, Sean, did she drive you down to the Common for a quick one in the woodsy bit by the Windmill, like you and I used to years ago?'

'Now you're just being crude. It doesn't suit you, Clover.' Sean scuffed his shoes on the gravel and looked embarrassed. 'I haven't had any kind of relationship with Mary-Jane.'

'Ha!' Clover laughed. 'And now you sound like Bill Clinton! Please don't tell me any more, I can fill in the rest of the details for myself, thanks.'

'Again, all wrong! If you'd just fucking listen . . . it was all about France.'

'*France?* What about France? Who's going to France?' Clover bent to pick up the courgettes and went to push past Sean but he wasn't moving. She was almost leaning on him, shoving against him with the box. Bloody France, bloody houses. Another dream kiboshed along the way. Your own fault, her conscience mocked at her, your own stupid fault. Sean's hand reached tentatively for her shoulder. She shrugged it off, but without much conviction.

'*We* were going to France, Clover. All of us: you and me and the girls. For six weeks, this summer. And if anyone else in your family wanted to come for part of it, there's room for them too, just the way you always wanted it.'

'Yeah, right. You won't get round me that way, promising something after the event. It'll take more—'

'It was to Mary-Jane's place in Provence, you dim tart.

265

She's lending it to us. Or she was, till you got the wrong idea and suddenly took off.' Sean took the box of courgettes out of her hands and put them back on the ground, then pulled her towards him. He smelled of hot sun and home and safety; everything she missed. No wonder it was called a broken heart – hers really, really hurt.

'But I saw you with her outside the school. Laughing and kissing her and—'

'I didn't kiss her, not even close. If you hadn't been so crazed with suspicion you'd have seen I just hugged her. And I only did that because she'd just said yes, that it was all sorted. Yes, we could borrow the house. She and Lance have got to go to New Zealand this summer for a huge family reunion. They do it every five years, she told me. I thought . . . well, I thought I'd get it fixed up on the quiet and then surprise you. It was so that we could go and try out a whole summer holiday in France and see if we really like it before we commit to buying somewhere. I thought you'd be so happy – just shows how wrong you can be.'

He looked about fifteen, she thought. Anxious and frightened. He wasn't the only one – hell, what had she done? She'd had a stupid, idiotic one-night fling out of petty revenge. A bad enough reason on its own; how much worse was it that it turned out she'd had no reason at all?

'Sean, I . . . I don't know what to say.' She should say a huge, almighty sorry, but then he'd wonder what for. Well OK, he'd understand she was apologizing for not hearing him out, for over-reacting, but how to hide a much bigger 'sorry' in the middle of that? You couldn't. She had to stuff that horrible night, the whole Harry-event, at the back of her conscience and try to forget about it. Clover had made a leap into a more grown-up, more complex world than she'd been used to: perhaps most people carried a dreadful secret something inside them that counter-balanced the good, well-meaning side. It would be her penance, that she'd know what she'd done but could never let it out to be dealt with and forgiven. Well, they were even now – but Sean must never, ever know.

# SEVENTEEN

It was something Susie Granger had said. Susie was Mac's last visitor of the day; last hospital visitor at all, actually, for he'd be on his way home early the next morning. She'd put two ideas into Lottie's head with one short, condemning sentence, unthinkingly uttered as the two women had left the hospital the evening before: 'Of course now you and Mac won't be travelling anywhere, you won't be selling Holbrook House, will you?'

Lottie had replied with no more than a vague murmur, which Susie should feel free to interpret any way she wished, but after they'd parted outside the door to the X-ray department, she had waited for a while in the Audi, thinking. She saw Susie, all elegant straw-coloured linen and a bronze quilted Chanel bag, climb into her sassy little blue Mercedes, watched while the car's roof slid back into the boot space and Susie drove away into the low evening sunlight, her cocoa-coloured hair barely rippling in the light, warm breeze. The scene reminded Lottie of a song, one that Marianne Faithfull used to sing. She delved into her memory for the title and eventually trawled it up: 'The Ballad of Lucy Jordan'. What an annoying song that was – about a young, suburban wife who'd given up on the dream that she'd ever drive through Paris in a sports car on a summer's night. For God's sake, what was with the giving up, at *thirty-seven*? What kind of age was that for whining about things you'd concluded you could never do? Especially simple, easily achievable things like a fun little car trip? What was Lucy's problem – did she think it depended on some man to make it all happen for her? OK, granted, the dream represented a certain romantic euphoria, but what made her so defeatedly decide it was all over? Fictional Lucy, you just wanted to shake her, to tell her life was all still out there for the taking and ask her what she thought age had to do with anything.

Lottie eventually started up the Audi and drove out on to the main road towards home. As she approached the village green, the Major's pretty house with its forlorn For Sale sign caught her attention. The garden was, after a couple of months of being abandoned at the height of the growing season, starting to show signs of serious neglect. The front lawn looked as if someone who'd become obsessed with Monty Don's gardening style was attempting, and failing, at a meadow effect and instead of a delicate sprinkling of poppies, daisies and cornflowers, had found the grass being invaded by fat dandelions, many of whose heads had ripened to bloated, tatty fluff. Bindweed was threaded through the roses that hung over the fence, and the foxgloves and delphiniums had run to tall, rusty seedheads. Just as at Holbrook House, the clematis had triumphantly clambered to the roof and was making its steady way towards the end chimney.

Lottie parked by the bus stop at the side of the green, rummaged among the CDs in the glove compartment and found a pen and an old petrol receipt. She copied down the estate agent's number.

'And those leylandii will definitely have to go,' Lottie startled herself, saying it out loud.

'I'd better do a count-up. How many of us will there be?' Sorrel opened the dresser drawer, took out a heap of cutlery and counted out a handful of forks.

'Ten?' Lottie said, looking up from measuring out olive oil for the marinade. 'Or is your friend Millie staying for lunch too? That'll make it eleven, I think.'

'You, Dad, me and Gaz, Clover and her lot, that's eight, Ilex plus Millie, ten.' Sorrel added them up on her fingers.

Lottie looked round to see if anyone else was in hearing distance. 'And Manda as well. She's coming too but she doesn't want us to let Ilex know, so make sure you don't tell him.'

'Is she? Wow! What, definitely for lunch or just to drop more of Ilex's stuff off?'

'She'll be staying for lunch, she said. Though she did say she was bringing something for Ilex. If she's intending to stay and be sociable then I don't imagine it's a bag of socks. Let's hope it's all back on again.'

'Whatever. Anything that puts Ilex in a better mood. Hey, maybe she's—'

'Sorrel, don't start on that one again!'

'I was only going to say maybe she's missing him! Can't think why, he's a miserable git. And someone really ought to drop him a hint that she might be coming over so that at least he makes an effort. He's starting to look like a crusty. He'll be drifting with the winos down at Guildford station with a dog on a string soon. Can't you do the mumsy thing and tell him to take a shower?'

'He's a grown man, Sorrel.' Even to herself she didn't sound very convinced of that. When was the moment when anyone could be deemed to be grown up? One blip and even the most stable and responsible person could be reduced to childlike insecurity and a juvenile sulk.

'Yeah, right. We're really seeing signs of that lately, aren't we?'

Lottie started on the garlic, crushing it with the back of the knife, chopping it neatly and adding it to the oil, lemon and coriander. She stirred in yoghurt and the cubed lamb went in next.

'And if it *is* all back on, why doesn't Manda just phone and tell him?' Sorrel went on, delving into the drawer again for knives. 'Maybe then he'll stop moping around. Ever since he got here, he's been looking like somebody took all his toys away.'

'Yes, well maybe the only call he needed was a wake-up one. Most people do, now and then.'

'Yeah . . . um, right. Bit deep for me, that. I'll just take this lot out to the garden, do the table,' Sorrel said, heading for the French doors. She didn't want to think about wake-up calls. Hadn't they all had enough of that this last couple of weeks? She'd got through the exams, just, but it hadn't been easy. Gaz had been right about Carly's lot at school – but only partly. When it had been about her folks selling the house, sure – they'd been too interested, too wanting to know stuff. But when they'd heard how her dad had almost died, it had been different. She'd felt that the sympathy was genuine this time. She'd explained to ever-cynical Gaz that it had to be because anyone could relate to something as awful as almost losing a parent, whereas the thing about moving from a multi-million-pound pad was gossip-worthy but hardly a tragedy. There'd been small examples of new kindness, such as when she'd forgotten to take a bottle of water into the second French paper, Carly had been the one who'd immediately given her one from her own supply. Stacey had asked her in the lunch break if she'd like her to pick her up for the next day's exams on the way to school, sensing that Sorrel might not be feeling up to driving herself with so much to think about. School staff, who'd rather tended to leave her to her own devices over the years, had asked every day how Mac was and whether she needed it mentioned to the examination board that she was having to deal with a traumatic family time. It was all a bit late, of course; school was over now, for ever, thank God, but it was a comforting note to go out on.

Lottie went into the garden to sort out the seating. It was the most glorious June day – even given the haphazard standards of Holbrook House's garden maintenance, the place was looking wonderfully full-bloomed. The lupins seemed to have triumphed, this year, over the annual invasion of fat aphids, the self-seeded Cosmos, antirrhinums and ancient clumps of blousy scarlet peonies kept the long borders' vegetables more or less out of sight of the terrace. If Gertrude Jekyll came visiting to check out her original creation, she might, just for today, manage to concede a generous B-plus rather than the usual better deserved D-minus.

The battered old table out on the terrace was plenty big enough for them all but chairs would need to be brought out from the kitchen to supplement the garden benches. Usually it was Clover Lottie could rely on for this kind of help but although Sophia and Elsa had been up and playing in the garden since the early hours, Clover and Sean seemed to be still in bed. Good. Enjoy it while you've got each other, she thought, glancing up at their window in the east wing; you never know when the fates will stop your roundabout and chuck one of you off your painted pony.

Her sister Caro had shrieked when Manda told her that Ilex had proposed and had phoned every day since to demand an update. 'You can't leave it too long,' she'd insisted as the days passed. 'You have to give men an answer pretty soon before they forget they've asked you anything at all.'

Manda had left out the bit about him being in handcuffs at the time and was now wondering two things: first, if he'd only asked her under the duress of the arrest, as a desperate bid to get the police on-side, and, second, that she had actually mistimed her reply after all, leaving it far too late. There was a difference between having a dignified interval between question and answer and leaving it so long that he could only conclude she'd considered him beneath contempt as a marriage prospect. It was possibly her own fault that he was now convinced she'd flounced out of his life for good, but something had had to be done to shake him up. If she'd given in after a couple of days, that would have set a pattern for the rest of their lives together. If they had one. She wasn't going to be a doormat wife, oh no. All the same, if it all worked out, she would keep the half-brick with its now desiccated pair of roses that he'd tied to it as a memento of Ilex's great moment of high romance. If he never gave her another crazy episode to outdo that one, she'd have that brick as a single silly treasure to remind her that when it came to it, Ilex could get her up there with the daftest mushy movie moments that had her damp-eyed and sniffing at the cinema as the credits rolled.

Now – important things: what to wear. The day was a hot one, the lunch was to be a casual garden barbecue to celebrate Mac's return to health and to home. Manda opened the wardrobe and chose her newest dress, a simple sleeveless bluey-grey strappy number she'd bought that week in Whistles. Very demure. And it would so exactly match the present she had for Ilex. Whether he decided he still loved Manda or not, he'd so completely, utterly, adore what she had chosen for him.

*

So easy, a barbecue, Lottie thought as she sat beneath the sunshade, idly stirring the dressing through the salad. Ilex, Mac and Sean were standing around the fire, wielding spatulas like daggers and occasionally poking at the food that was sizzling over the coals. The lamb and chicken kebabs were being turned so competitively often they were practically being spit-roasted. It was such a prehistoric male thing, the fire and the food ritual. Whoever had first confined fire to safe, closed-in quarters had a lot to answer for, in Lottie's opinion, effectively trapping several centuries of women into domestic servitude.

'What do we do about Manda?' Clover whispered to Lottie. 'Is she definitely coming or not? I thought she'd be here by now.'

'She said she was coming. We'll just shove up the bench a bit when she gets here. Unless . . .'

'Oh don't say she won't come . . . I'd so love Ilex to be happy again.'

Like you, Lottie almost said. Clover looked radiant – about five years younger, softer. Lottie recognized that look. She remembered she and Kate used to giggle about it on the road with Charisma, the mornings after they'd stayed in a hotel more lusciously appointed than usual. They'd meet up in the reception area for the check-out and murmur 'POG' at each other – an acronym for post-orgasmic glow. Sorrel had recognized it too, had summed it up with typical conciseness when she'd found Clover and Sean making coffee in the kitchen late that morning and had blurted out, 'Ugh, per-lease! You're all loved-up!'

'I was going to say, unless they just disappear together. They might prefer to go off on their own.'

'But that would . . . No, Manda wouldn't do that. She knows this lunch is all about Dad coming home.'

'*And* it's about Sorrel and Gaz and Millie finishing their exams,' Lottie reminded her. 'Clover . . . Mac's illness . . .'

'Oh Mum, I do know. I know it was such a close call.' Clover reached across and took Lottie's hand. 'But we're all here and we'll all take care of you. Imagine how it would have been if we hadn't all been able to be here with you?' That wasn't what Lottie meant at all; but just now there wasn't time.

'Ah . . . well, OK,' she said instead. 'We'll maybe talk about that later. Food's ready. I'll go and call Sorrel and the others and I'll get the rice and the courgettes while I'm in there.'

Oh lordy, Lottie thought as she picked her way across the uneven terrace, why did Clover have to make things so complicated?

'You'll have to have your blood checked *three* times a *week*? How long for?' Sean asked Mac over lunch.

'God, that's, like, *sooo* rough? You won't have any left,' Gaz said, looking queasy at the thought. 'How much do they take?'

'An armful,' Lottie and Mac said both together, spluttering laughter. All the younger ones looked at them, blankly.

'A line from Tony Hancock? "The Blood Donor"?'

'Oh. I saw that. Once. I think.' Gaz didn't look convinced.

'No, really, it's not that bad,' Mac reassured him. 'They only take a tiny bit to check the clotting levels and make adjustments. And it's just for a few months, till everything's stabilized. Maybe even less.'

Clover looked worried, Lottie thought. She hoped she wasn't going to become ridiculously morbid over Mac's illness. If she started treating her parents as if they'd suddenly morphed into old, frail people, they were all going to come to grief, one way or another. Mac was going to get better and real life would gradually come back. She and Mac had no intention of becoming frozen into a sad still-life of inactivity and over-anxiety. There would be changes – but ones they'd chosen, not, thank the president of the immortals, had forced on them.

Ilex felt a bit like a spare part. Never before had he seen Clover so tactile with Sean. The two of them sat together, hardly able to keep from touching each other. It should have been something he was happy about but instead it made him feel the loss of Manda even more. Sorrel and Gaz were bickering at the table like an old married couple and Millie looked perfectly happy not to be attached to anyone. Not that he'd even consider ... she was only eighteen, for heaven's sake.

He got up from the table and carried plates into the kitchen, simply to escape from the very awful suspicion that, given the horribly lonesome way he was feeling right now, he'd soon have to stop himself asking Millie out to the Feathers that night, simply to have someone to pour his soul out to over a couple of pints. What were you supposed to do with yourself at thirty-seven when your girlfriend hated you, had (justifiably) taken over your flat and you'd slunk home to Mummy and Daddy? He looked in the mirror over the rusty Aga and made an L for loser sign on his head. And in the mirror, he caught sight of a beautiful girl with long sleek hair the colour of cappuccino. Manda was in the room, holding a cardboard box.

'I hope I'm not too late,' she said. She sounded slightly breathless, the way she did – and he so wished he hadn't thought of this – during sex.

'For lunch?' he asked her, thinking at the same time, What a crass response.

She shrugged. 'Lunch, anything really.' Oh Lord, she was as edgy as he was.

'I'm glad I found you in here. I thought this was going to be easy but as I drove in I was a bit . . . worried.' She smiled and chewed at her bottom lip, a sign he recognized as pure nerves.

'Worried? You? What do you have to be worried about? I'm just so . . . happy to see you . . . um . . . if that's all right.' It sounded mad, he knew, but if he said the wrong thing he might frighten her away again. He was barely convinced she was real, that she'd actually turned up in the Holbrook House kitchen and was now alone with him. Manda and this box that had holes in the top.

'Um . . . I got you something. A present.' She held out the box. 'Be careful with it, it's fragile and . . . well, just be gentle. Put it on the table to open it, just in case.'

Oh please, Ilex thought, don't let anyone come in and

break this up. He pulled the top of the box apart and inside was a small chunky grey kitten, looking up at him with huge, round, deep blue eyes. It immediately began both miaowing and purring at the same time, trying to climb out to get to him. It wore a black velvet collar and a chrome name tag.

'Oh, Manda – it's just so . . . cute! I can't believe you'd—'

'Well, I had to give you an answer,' she said, rather rushing her words and looking at him intently. 'And it's yes . . . um . . . I'd like us to have a cat.' There was a silent moment while he relished the 'us', brutally interrupted by a whirl of teen activity as Sorrel came hurtling into the room.

'Mum says where's the cheese. Oh wow! Look at this!' Sorrel went up to Ilex and took the kitten out of his hands.

'Oh Manda, it's so *sweet*! Hello, baby kitty-cat, aren't you just the cutest?' She stroked and patted it, fondling its triangular ears. 'Come on, we must show the others!' And she was gone, clutching the little cat.

'No, wait! Don't go yet! Sorrel, there's something else Ilex needs to see!' Manda chased after her. Ilex followed, and they found Sorrel out by the table, cooing over the kitten and showing it off to the rest of the gathering.

'Oh and look, it's already got a little name tag. Let's see what it's called.'

'No! Sorrel, stop right there!' Manda reached over to grab the kitten but Sorrel was already reading.

'Ooh it's called . . . It's called *Yes*. What kind of a name . . .?' she asked, looking at Manda with a mystified expression. She then turned the name tag over.

'Oh-oh, er, for you, I think,' she said, handing the kitten back to Ilex.

'There wasn't meant to be an audience,' Manda hissed at Ilex, hiding her face in her hands. 'God, I've done this all wrong!'

Ilex, conscious of the gaze of ten silent and tensely wondering people, looked at the kitten's tag: on one side the word 'Yes' was engraved but on the other, and he realized that Manda knew him so well, she understood he might need to be reminded of the question, it said, 'I will marry you.'

'Oh God, another two loved-up ones,' Sorrel groaned as she turned away from the appalling sight of them kissing. 'How can they do that *in front of people*? Can't we, like, go off to Australia tomorrow, Gaz, get away from all this?'

'You don't mean that,' he teased her. Gaz could, she knew, mention – also in front of everyone – that she looked suspiciously tearful, but he wouldn't. She appreciated that.

It was coming to the end of a lazy afternoon. Sophia and Elsa had found a couple of old Badminton racquets and were down on the lawn trying to hit a ping-pong ball to each other while side-stepping a group of hens that had strayed from the orchard. Their shrieks and giggles were the only intrusive sounds. Clover and Manda were quietly discussing tulle and silk and whether veils were un-believably naff or merely ironic, Sean was reading the sports pages and Ilex was dozing on a lounger with his kitten on his lap. Lottie was pretty sure he wasn't actually asleep though – as more and more expensive-sounding wedding items were mentioned, his foot twitched with understandable cash-stress.

'We need to tell them some time soon,' Mac murmured to Lottie.

'I know. Over lunch would have been ideal but it all got a bit hi-jacked, didn't it? Not that I minded, obviously. Shall I send Sorrel in to get some champagne? We should do a proper toast to Ilex and Manda. And Clover made a chocolate cake.'

'Did she?' Mac laughed. 'I'm surprised Sean let her out of bed for long enough! And yes, it'll have to be soon. Isn't the agent phoning at five? We'll have to have told them by then in case we're not the ones who take the call. Then we'll cop it, especially if it's Clover.'

Lottie rounded up Gaz and Sorrel and the three of them went into the kitchen to sort out tea, champagne and cake.

'OK – first of all,' Mac said, when everyone had a glass in their hands, 'huge congratulations to Ilex and Manda. Here's to them having a long and happy life together.'

'Are you supposed to have alcohol, Dad?' Clover looked close to panic-stricken as Mac drank.

'A centimetre of Bolly won't hurt,' he told her. 'I won't have more than that though, I promise. For now anyway. But look, Clover, everyone . . . I really don't want to be treated like a fragile museum specimen from now on just because my blood went a bit iffy. It's being fixed. I'll be back to the real me in a few months.'

'Yes, but . . . I mean it changes things, doesn't it? Like, you won't be able to go off racing round the world now, will you?' Clover went on. 'You'll have to take things more easily.'

Mac laughed. ' "Take things easy"? Clover, sweetheart, that's the sort of thing you say to someone of ninety-six, and even if you say it to me then I'll tell you it's patronizing! Anyway, the thing is . . . I wanted to tell you that a song we did years ago – "Target Practice" – it's got itself a part in a bloody great film. Doug phoned this morning and it's definite. So, we thought we'd go ahead with a few more idle plans, me and Lottie.'

'Wow, a movie! Does that mean we'll all be mega-rich again? Coo-well!' Sorrel leaned across and hugged Mac. 'So does that also mean I can—'

'Hey wait! Don't go giving me a shopping list just yet, please! Just be glad you should be able to get through university without loading yourself up with debts.'

'She probably still will,' Ilex said. 'Students never have enough cash flow. You can't expect her to resist a cheap loan. And they can make sense, in a borrowing—'

'Well actually, I *do* expect her to resist,' Mac interrupted. 'I'm not having her mortgage her soul to some government loan-shark scheme if she doesn't have to.'

'Anyway, the point is, we've sort of decided what we're going to do about the house,' Lottie interrupted.

'The house? What, *this* house?' Sean asked. 'You don't need to sell it now, do you?'

'Well no, but that's not the point. We still intend to get out in the world and do the travelling we'd planned.'

'But how can you? What about Dad? You can't do long-haul flights, *any* flights, with embolisms! It'll kill him!'

Clover looked close to tears. This, Lottie thought, wasn't going as well as it should.

'Well, you're right, Clover, it could have killed me if I'd gone last week. Probably would have. But it didn't, because we didn't. And in a year from now it should be fine. Better, safer even than before because it'll all have been sorted and medicated, do you see?'

'We have to do this,' Lottie insisted quietly, 'while we can. Just as you all must do the things you want to do – don't put them off till it's too late and they're just impossible.'

There was a silence, interrupted by the phone.

'I'll get it!' And Sorrel was out of her seat and racing into the house before Lottie could catch her. In a moment she was back, clutching the phone. 'Mum? It's someone called Harry from the estate agent's for you?'

Lottie took the phone and, before she spoke, caught sight of Clover sitting with her head down, hands over her eyes. She'd looked just like that as a teenager, when Lottie caught her out lying about staying with a girl from school when really she'd stayed at her first boyfriend's flat. So – Harry. That explained the Jimmy Choos and the lack of underwear at the hospital. One for her to forget about, definitely.

'Harry? Hi. Any news?' Mac reached across and took Lottie's hand. 'What, both of them? And they're really prepared to wait that long? Brilliant! Thanks, I'll call you back. Just got to talk about it for another minute.'

'And? What did he want? What's going on?' Ilex demanded.

Lottie took a deep breath. 'The Cresswells – they came round to look at the house a couple of weeks ago. They want to buy it, they've offered just under the asking price but they've got a lot to sort out so they really need to hang on till this time next year, which obviously suits us. So . . . Manda and Ilex, if you like, you'll be able to have your wedding party here.'

'Oh, yes!' Manda squealed. 'We'd love that!' She looked at Ilex, suddenly unsure. 'At least I think we would, wouldn't we?'

'Fine by me.' Ilex grinned. 'I definitely didn't fancy some anonymous hotel.'

'And why have you got to ring . . . him back?' Clover asked. That confirmed it, Lottie thought. She couldn't even use Harry's name.

'Because we still have one more thing to tell him. Mac and I made an offer on the Major's old house on the green and it's been accepted. We just need to tell him for definite about whether to go right ahead with it. What do you all think?'

Much later, when they'd all returned to their various homes and Sorrel and Gaz had gone to the pub to join their friends for yet another evening of post-exam celebrating, Lottie and Mac wandered down past the east long border and into the orchard to lock up the chickens for the night.

'So . . . next year's Burning Man, then?' Lottie suggested as they went through the orchard gate.

'We can start there, make an itinerary . . . be a bit more organized about it than we have been.'

Mac stopped by the pets' graveyard and pulled a piece of ivy off the last wolfhound's gravestone. 'And when we get back ... I was just wondering about getting another dog.'

'Not another wolfhound?'

'No. That would be going backwards. Time to move on, I think.'